MURDER MINDFULLY

Karsten Dusse is a lawyer and has been writing for television formats for a number of years. He has won the German Television Award and the German Comedy Prize several times, with his work also earning him a nomination for the Grimme Award. He spent years working as a radio host in public service broadcasting and has also enjoyed success in front of the camera, appearing on comedy programmes and as a legal expert. He has previously published three non-fiction books and now writes successful crime novels.

MURDER MINDFULLY

KARSTEN DUSSE

translated by Florian Duijsens

faber

First published in this edition in 2025
by Faber & Faber Ltd
The Bindery, 51 Hatton Garden
London ECIN 8HN

First published as *Achtsam Morden* in 2019
by Wilhelm Heyne Verlag, Munich

Typeset by Typo•glyphix, Burton-on-Trent DE14 3HE
Printed and bound in the UK by CPI Group (UK) Ltd, Croydon CRO 4YY

A CIP record for this book
is available from the British Library

ISBN 978–0–571–38404–4

Printed and bound in the UK on FSC® certified paper in line with our continuing
commitment to ethical business practices, sustainability and the environment.
For further information see faber.co.uk/environmental-policy

2 4 6 8 10 9 7 5 3 1

For Lina

1

Mindfulness

When you're waiting outside a door, you're waiting outside a door.

When you're having an argument with your wife, you're having an argument with your wife. That's mindfulness.

When you're waiting outside a door, and you're spending that time having a mental argument with your wife – that's not mindfulness.

That's just plain stupid.

Joschka Breitner, *Slowing Down in the Fast Lane: Mindfulness for Managers*

First off, I'm not a violent man. Quite the opposite. For example, I've never once in my life gotten into a fight. And I didn't even kill anyone until I was forty-two. Which, looking around my current professional environment, seems rather late – though, true, the week after that I *did* bump off almost half a dozen.

That doesn't sound great, I know, but anything I did, I did with the best of intentions. A logical result of my commitment to becoming more mindful. To harmonise my work and my family life.

My first encounter with mindfulness was actually very stressful. My wife, Katharina, tried to force me to relax. To improve my resilience, my unreliability, my twisted values. To give our marriage one more chance.

She said she wanted that well-balanced man back she'd fallen in love with ten years earlier, that young man full of ideals and aspirations. Had I responded I would also like *her* to have the body back that I fell for ten years earlier, our marriage would've been over and done with. And rightly so. Obviously, time should be allowed to leave its marks on a woman's body, but apparently not on a man's soul. And that's why my wife's body was spared a plastic surgeon whereas my soul was sent off to mindfulness training.

Back then, I thought mindfulness was just a different cup of the same esoteric tea that's warmed over and repackaged under a new buzzword every decade or so. Mindfulness was just autogenic training without lying down. Yoga without contorting yourself. Meditation without sitting cross-legged. Or, as the article in *Manager* magazine my wife once demonstratively placed on the breakfast table put it: 'Mindfulness means taking in each moment with love and without judgement.' A definition that made as little sense to me then as those pebbles on the beach pointlessly stacked by people so de-stressed they've become entirely detached from reality.

Would I have even participated in this mindfulness racket if it'd only been about the two of us, my wife and me? Not sure. But we have a little girl, Emily, and for her I would hitchhike from Sodom to Gomorrah if it meant our family would have a future.

She's the real reason why, one Thursday night in January, I had my first appointment with a mindfulness coach. I was already twenty-five minutes late when I rang the bell outside the heavy wooden door of his 'mindfulness studio' to discuss, among other matters, my time-management issues.

The coach rented the ground floor of a lavishly renovated old building in a fancier part of town. I'd spotted his flyer in the wellness area of a five-star hotel and seen his fees online. Someone who charges an arm and a leg to teach people to be more relaxed could probably meditate away any annoyance at a paying client's lack of punctuality – at least, that's what I thought. But when I rang the bell, nothing happened.

Until this relaxation guru refused to open the door, I'd actually been quite relaxed, because my delay was entirely excusable. I was a lawyer – criminal law – and had managed to squeeze in a remand hearing just before. An employee of my main client, Dragan Sergowicz, had found himself in a jewellery shop that afternoon wishing to pick out an engagement ring. Instead of money, however, he only had a loaded pistol on him. And when he didn't like the rings that were presented to him, he smacked the jeweller in the temple with his gun. Since the jeweller had already triggered the silent alarm by then, the police arrived to find the jeweller on the ground, and the armed man offered no resistance when faced with the police's two sub-machine guns. After they took him to the police station, they informed both me and the district judge.

If I'd retained the ideals I had as a law student, I'd have found it completely justified for such an utter lowlife to remain in pretrial detention until the court hearing and then be tossed in the nick for a few years.

With my years of experience as a criminal defence lawyer who specialised in utter lowlifes, however, I managed to free the idiot in under two hours.

So it wasn't like I was running late to my coaching appointment, I'd basically been running a victory lap. And if this relaxation flake didn't waste the remainder of our time being petulant, I could tell him why I'd been so victorious.

The man with a penchant for shopping while carrying was twenty-five and still lived with his parents. His criminal record didn't have any violent offences, only drug-related

5

ones. There was no danger of flight, repeat offence or suppressing evidence. Plus, I'd argued, he shared the common social values of marriage and family – after all, that's why he'd been in the jewellery shop: by purloining an engagement ring, he was expressing his readiness to form a strong marital bond.

Alright, for the jeweller in hospital and the constables on patrol, it must certainly have been difficult to understand that someone who was undoubtedly a violent offender was released to preen and mock the authorities to his friends that same night. When it came to things like this, even my wife occasionally found my work rather questionable. But explaining our legal system to other people wasn't my job. My job was to exploit that system using every trick in the book. I made my money doing good for bad people. That's it. And I'd mastered it perfectly. I was an excellent criminal defence lawyer, employed by one of the most prestigious corporate law firms in the city, ready and available around the clock.

It was stressful, of course it was. And not always compatible with my family responsibilities. That's why I found myself at the door of this mindfulness guy, who wouldn't let me in . . . My neck started to tense up.

But I got a lot in exchange for all that stress: a company car, bespoke suits, expensive watches. I'd never cared much about status symbols before, but once you're a lawyer representing organised crime, status symbols start to matter. If only because, as a lawyer, you become a status symbol for your client.

So I got a large office, a designer desk, and five figures a month to bring home to my family: my delightful daughter, my wonderful wife and me.

Sure – a high four-digit slice of that salary went to paying off our house. A home for my delightful daughter, whom I never saw because I was always working, and for her loving mother, with whom, when I *did* see her, I only ever seemed to argue. Me because I was irritated by my work, which I couldn't tell my wife about because she hated it; and her because she had to take care of our little girl alone all day – and had given up her own serious job as department head at an insurance company to do so. If our love was a delicate plant, we'd obviously been careless when we moved it up into a family-sized pot. In short: we were like so many successful young couples – going to shit.

In order to reconcile work and family, and because I was the only one of us who had *both*, my wife had decided I was the one of us who needed to work on themselves. She'd sent me to this mindfulness coach, a plonker who wouldn't open the door. My neck was really tensing up now, quietly crackling with every shake of my head.

I rang the doorbell next to the heavy wooden door for the second time. The lacquer seemed to be fresh, or at least that's what it smelled like.

It finally opened, revealing a man standing there as though he'd been lurking the whole time, just waiting for that second ring. He was a few years older than me, in his early fifties.

7

'Our appointment was for eight o'clock,' he stated, then he turned and walked down the bare hallway without another word. I followed him into an indirectly lit, sparsely furnished office.

The man looked ascetic, not an ounce of fat on his sinewy body. The type of guy who essentially wouldn't gain a pound even if you subcutaneously injected him with an entire cream cake. He looked well groomed, wearing stonewashed jeans, a chunky wool cardigan over a plain white cotton shirt, and slippers on his otherwise bare feet. No watch. No bling.

The contrast couldn't have been greater. I was wearing my dark-blue bespoke suit, white shirt with cufflinks, a silvery-blue tie with diamond-studded tie pin, Breitling watch, wedding ring, black socks, Budapest brogues. Even just my accessories outnumbered the furniture in his practice. Two armchairs, one table. A bookshelf and a side table for drinks.

'Yes, sorry. Got stuck in traffic.' After his non-greeting, I'd already half a mind to turn around and leave. My wife could complain about me being late free of charge. But if Katharina found out that not only had I been late to my mindfulness course, but I'd also left in a right huff, the resulting argument would cause enough stress to require two additional relaxation coaches.

'I had a sudden remand hearing come up. Aggravated robbery, so I couldn't just . . .' Why did *I* have to be the one talking? He was the host, shouldn't he at least offer me a seat, or say something else? But the guy was just looking at me – almost like my daughter studying a beetle in the forest. Whereas beetles instinctively freeze when they find themselves observed by an unfamiliar species, I reflexively started to chatter.

'Maybe we can just speed things up . . . for the same fee,' I offered, trying to start afresh after our botched beginning.

'A road doesn't get any shorter when you run,' was his response.

I'd read more meaningful slogans on my secretaries' coffee mugs. And this one wasn't even offset by a good cup of coffee. This did not bode well.

'Have a seat, won't you? Can I offer you some tea?'

Finally. I sat down in one of the armchairs. It looked like it had once won a design award back in the antediluvian 1970s and essentially consisted of a single chrome tube, over which was suspended a coarse brown corduroy cushion – astoundingly comfortable, it turned out.

'Do you have espresso as well?'

'Green tea OK?' Ignoring my question, the coach was already pouring me a cup from a glass teapot. Its milky glass showed it had been in daily use for years. 'There you go, room temp.'

I started, 'Well, to be honest, I don't know if this is the right place for me . . .' I clung tightly to my teacup, hoping he would interrupt me, but he didn't. My words stammered to a sudden stop, met with the coach's open expression.

After it became clear I wouldn't finish my sentence, he took a first sip of his tea. 'I've only known you for thirty minutes, but I think you could learn a lot about yourself here.'

'You haven't known me for thirty minutes though,' I remarked astutely. 'I've only been here for three.'

Annoyingly placid, the coach replied: 'You *could* have been here for thirty minutes. Obviously, you spent the first twenty-five or so minutes doing something completely different. Then you stood outside the door for three minutes wondering whether to ring the doorbell a second time. Correct?'

'Uh . . .'

'After you finally decided to ring again, the three minutes you've spent here so far have shown me that you do not consider the rare appointment focusing solely on *you* to be very important, that you exclusively let your priorities be set by external circumstances, that you think you have to justify yourself to a complete stranger, that you cannot stand silence, that you cannot intuitively grasp any situation that deviates from the usual and that you are completely trapped by your habits. How does that make you feel?'

Wow, the bloke was right.

I blurted out, 'If those are also the exact same reasons you don't want to have sex with me, then I'd feel right at home!'

Choking on his green tea, the coach started to cough and then burst into hearty laughter. Once he'd finished, he held out his hand. 'Joschka Breitner, nice to have you here.'

'Björn Diemel, good to meet you.'

The ice was broken.

'So, why are you here?' Breitner asked.

I thought about it. I could think of a thousand reasons, and then not a single one. I felt I should probably display a certain degree of openness towards a mindfulness coach. After his burst of laughter, I also found him quite congenial. But I was far from ready to start sharing intimate details from my private life.

Breitner noticed my hesitation. 'Just tell me five things that are related to you being here.'

I took a deep breath, then launched right in. 'There aren't enough hours in a day, I can't switch off, I'm highly strung, stressed out, my wife annoys me, I never see my daughter and I miss her. When I *can* spend time with her, my mind is always elsewhere. My wife does not appreciate my job, my job does not appreciate me—'

'You've lost count.'

'Excuse me?'

'Nine of these five things are classic symptoms of work-related stress. Can you describe a few situations when you feel this way?'

I didn't need long to remember when I had last felt overwhelmed, so I simply described my fraught experience just outside his door, taking him on my entire mental roller coaster ride.

He nodded. 'As I said earlier, I think learning mindfulness techniques will prove helpful for you.'

'Great, let's go!'

'Do you have any idea what mindfulness might mean?'

'I suppose I'm paying good money to find out over the next few hours.'

'When you were standing outside the door,' he said mildly, 'you actually experienced it for free.'

'I must've been too distracted to notice.'

'That's exactly the point: you stood outside the door for about three minutes, mulling over whether to ring again. For how many of those hundred and eighty seconds was your mind somewhere else?'

'To be honest, maybe a hundred and seventy-six?'

'Where did your mind go?'

'To a jewellery shop, to the police station, to my office, to my clients, to my daughter, to my arguments with my wife.'

'So in just three minutes your mind went to six different places, bringing up all the attendant emotions. Did that help you at all?'

'No, I . . .'

'So why did you do it?' he asked, with real interest.

'It's just how it went.'

If a client of mine had said something like that in court, I would've forbidden him to speak altogether.

'Mindfulness simply and plainly ensures this will not happen to you.'

'OK, but can you explain how exactly?'

'It's really quite simple: when you're waiting outside a door, you're waiting outside a door. When you're having an argument with your wife, you're having an argument with your wife. If you prefer to use your time waiting outside my door to mentally argue with your wife, then you are not being mindful.'

'And how do you *mindfully* stand outside a door?'

'You just stand there and do nothing for three minutes. You note that you are standing there, and that your world will not veer into chaos if you are just standing there, quite the opposite. If you never judge the moment, you also cannot experience it as negative in any way. You simply perceive the natural state of things: your breathing, the smell of freshly lacquered wood, the wind in your hair, you inhabiting your body. And if you take yourself in with love, you will have rid yourself of all stress by the time three minutes are up.'

'I needn't have rung the bell a second time?'

'You never needed to ring the bell at all. Standing outside the door without any intention quite suffices.'

I had the sense I could do something with that basic principle. And funnily enough, I no longer noticed any tension in my neck. It was to be several weeks, however, before I realised that what Breitner revealed next would become the mantra for my first murder.

2

Freedom

Someone who always does whatever they want is not free. The idea of constantly having to do *something* is what holds us captive. Only someone who simply does not do what they do not want to is really free.

Joschka Breitner, *Slowing Down in the Fast Lane: Mindfulness for Managers*

Breitner refilled our teacups.

'Most of our stress is due to a completely distorted idea of what freedom is.'

'Ah.'

'It is a misconception that freedom means being able to do whatever you want.'

'What's so wrong with that?'

'It is based on the assumption that we always have to be doing *something*. That is the main cause of the stress you are experiencing. You are standing outside that door and consider it completely normal to be running through all manner of things in your mind. After all, "thoughts are free", ha! Yet the problem is exactly this: after those free thoughts gallop away from you, it is very hard to corral them again. But you do not have to be thinking at all. Quite the opposite, you can just *not* think if you do not want to. Only then are your thoughts truly free.'

'But I don't just spend my days thinking,' I dared to object. 'What causes me the most bother is what I *do*.'

'The same applies. Only once you internalise that you do not have to do what you do not want to do – only then are you truly free.'

I don't have to do what I don't want to do. I am free.

Less than four months later, I would seize this freedom uncompromisingly. I would seize it to not do something I didn't want to do. Unfortunately, this would mean infringing on someone else's freedom – taking their life. Yet I didn't take this mindfulness course to save the world, I did it to save myself.

Mindfulness does not call for us to live and let live. It calls for us to *live!* And that imperative might affect the less mindful lives of others.

To this day, what still fills me with joy about my first murder is the fact that I was able to take in that moment with love and without judgement. Exactly the way my coach had counselled that very first session. My first murder was spontaneously born out of the moment, out of what I needed. From that perspective, it was a very successful exercise in mindfulness – for me, not for the other guy.

But when I was sitting in that armchair with Breitner and having my second cup of tea, no one was dead yet. I was only there to get a better handle on my professional stress.

'Tell me about your work. You're a lawyer?' Breitner asked.

'Yes, criminal law.'

'So you make sure that every person in this country is ensured a fair trial, no matter what they are accused of. That must be very rewarding.'

'That's exactly why I originally chose to do this – when I was in law school, during my apprenticeship, and also at the beginning of my career. Unfortunately, the reality of a successful criminal defence lawyer is completely different.'

'How so?'

'I mainly make sure that arseholes don't get into the legally appropriate amount of trouble. It might not be as morally worthwhile, but it's extremely lucrative.'

I told him about starting at DED – the law firm of Von Dresen, Erkel and Dannwitz – right after I was admitted to the bar. DED was a medium-sized law firm focusing on businesses, including any criminal elements. A pack of suits who presented themselves as legitimate yet did nothing all day but find new tax loopholes for filthy-rich clients and handle the cases of people who, despite our best efforts, got stuck with criminal proceedings for tax evasion, white-collar crimes, embezzlement or large-scale fraud. Any newcomer wanting to play in this league was expected to graduate with honours as well as complete several unpaid internships. And even out of the applicants who met these requirements, only one in ten was accepted. To get a job here immediately after the second state examination was considered hitting the jackpot in the job lottery. I got lucky, at least that's what I thought at the time.

'You no longer see it that way?' Breitner asked.

'Well, over the years things have just turned out a bit differently than I expected when I was first hired.'

'That sounds like life. What happened?'

In broad strokes, I outlined my career, told him about the shocking starting salary and the shocking working conditions. Six and a half days a week, fourteen hours a day.

Surrounded every minute by cold-blooded donkeys all chasing the same careerist carrot: to make partner.

I know what I'm talking about. I used to be one of them.

My first client was a guy who'd never been represented by the firm before. The new client assigned to the new lawyer. That client was Dragan Sergowicz, but I didn't use his name. I just told Breitner that the client was 'shady'. Though the word 'shady' was rather an understatement when it came to Dragan's lines of business. The red-light district in which he operated, for one, was flashier than a radar trap catching someone doing eighty mph in a thirty zone.

But Dragan's business was financially successful, and he'd been vouched for by some of DED's 'legitimate' clients, who'd owed him a favour.

At our first meeting, Dragan said his case was about tax evasion. That wasn't a complete lie, but it also didn't match the prosecution service's accusations. He had clobbered the tax administrator responsible for his case into hospital after some follow-up questions Dragan considered too critical. After the administrator had recovered to the point where he could eat solid food and make an official statement, he oddly could no longer remember either any suspicion of tax evasion or Dragan's visit. He claimed he'd simply had a bad fall.

In the years that followed, Dragan's two fists were to prove even more effective than my two law degrees.

Dragan was not only a brutal pimp, but also a big drug and arms dealer. When I met him, he did a less than stellar job disguising his lines of work behind a number of semi-legal import–export companies. In short: even for my employer's very broad interpretation of legitimate business, Dragan was a so-called bleurgh-client – one who poured a lot of money into the firm, but one you didn't exactly want to show off.

Of course, this did not prevent the firm's partners from teaching me every financial trick in the book I could bill Dragan for.

Dragan became my first professional challenge. I put all my ambition into bringing his company portfolio up to date and thus keeping his activities under the prosecution service's radar. Like before, his main sources of income were drugs, arms and prostitution, but from then on, I channelled his money through plenty of forwarding companies, franchises or cash-based businesses in which I had acquired a stake for Dragan. In addition, I showed him how to use EU-subsidy fraud to nab money out of non-existent aubergine farms in Bulgaria and how emissions trading allowed for sources of income that were at least as criminal as drug trafficking, but required no one's bones to be broken – plus, both were state-subsidised. With my help, in just a few years, Dragan had transformed his public image from a brutal drug-dealing pimp to a halfway-respectable businessman.

I perfected all the skills I had never learned during my studies: how to 'influence' witnesses, 'pacify' prosecutors, bring employees 'in line'. In short, I got really good at convincing people.

'And you know why?' I asked Breitner.

'Enlighten me.'

'At first, because it was in my employment contract. I'm not a bad person, honestly. I really am rather anxious and boring, dutiful too – my sense of duty is perhaps my worst quality. And I'm fully aware that this system I helped set up is no good at all – neither for others nor for myself. Any system that rewards violence, injustice and deceit, but not love, justice and truth simply cannot be good. But *I* could still be good, at least from inside the system. Out of duty, I've devoted years and years to making this system work. Yet I never noticed how it has slowly but surely changed me from a nerdy honours student into the perfect lawyer for organised crime.'

At some point, I just enjoyed mastering the craft. But perfection isn't everything. Any halfway-decent lawyer can manage saving their client's arse. At heart, nothing really changed. Even wearing the most expensive suit, Dragan never passed for a legitimate businessman. He was and remained a violent lunatic.

As part of lawyer–client privilege, I'd heard him spout more insane atrocities than Charles Manson might've to his confessor. At the same time, I had poured down legal bullshit all over his competitors and any possible witnesses of his crimes, so I really shouldn't have been quite so surprised that I started to reek too. Well, I never noticed it myself; I had to be told by my odour-sensitive wife first. She was the one who finally realised I couldn't keep this up.

3

Breathing

Our breath is what connects our body to our soul.

As long as we are alive, we are breathing. As long as we are breathing, we are alive. We can take refuge in our breathing. When we focus on our breathing, we focus on the connection between body and mind. And through our breath, we can reduce the influence negative emotions have on both.

Joschka Breitner, *Slowing Down in the Fast Lane: Mindfulness for Managers*

I told Breitner I was afraid – almost certain, in fact – that I'd never make partner at my firm precisely *because* of my rather successful handling of a so-called bleurgh-client. I had become a 'bleurgh' lawyer. A successful bleurgh-lawyer, but bleurgh-lawyers don't make partner.

I noticed how, just telling him this, my breathing grew laboured, my stomach started to hurt and my neck tensed up.

'So when was the first time you consciously realised that your values had shifted?'

After I thought for a moment, a key scene very quickly came to mind.

'There was one night when our daughter, Emily, was still very young, maybe two months old. Of course, she didn't sleep through the night yet. Since Emily was bottle-fed from fairly early on, my wife and I could take turns at night. Like always, I'd had a lot on my plate during the day, but I loved those quiet minutes at night. Alone with my little daughter in her room, I felt like I was in a peaceful, self-contained universe . . . In any case, at some point that night I was cradling Emily, who had just done her little burp and was happily gurgling. Completely exhausted and trying to get her to sleep, I was telling her how beautiful the world was. Then suddenly I realised, in horror, that I was talking about the world of my childhood. Not the world I actually lived in.'

Breitner nodded thoughtfully for a while before asking, 'And why are you doing this to yourself? Is it the money?'

I considered his question. No, it would be wrong to say that money was the only part of my job that appealed to me.

'I love what I can do. I just hate the people I do it for.'

'When does this become apparent to you?'

'You mean what I love or what I hate?'

'Which is the reason you are here?'

'The latter.'

'So, how does that affect you physically?'

'My neck feels tense, my stomach hurts, I get short of breath . . .'

'Then it would be best to end today's session with an exercise that should help with your breathing.'

Breitner put down his teacup, gently shook out his hands and stood up in one fluid movement. I got up too, but looked at him sceptically. Was he seriously trying to teach me how to deal with my aggravation over a psychopathic felon and a wife who didn't understand me by simply breathing it all away?

'Please stand up straight. Back straightened, chest slightly forward. Legs shoulder-width apart and knees slightly bent.'

He demonstrated, I emulated.

Nothing happened.

'And now?'

'Are you breathing yet?'

'Have been for forty-two years.'

'Now pay attention to only your breath,' Breitner instructed me. 'Where in your body do you feel it?'

'I can feel it in my . . .'

Breitner interrupted. 'That was a rhetorical question. The beauty of this exercise is that it does not matter *where* you feel your breath. The important thing is that you feel it. So you do not have to answer those questions about your breathing to me, but to yourself. The only thing that matters is that you become aware of the many enjoyable things happening in your body. Your breath is both the reason and the proof that you are alive. Which is a miracle – not just for you specifically, but for all living beings. Our breath is what connects our body to our soul. So, where do you feel your breath when you inhale?'

I didn't say anything and just *felt*.

'Where do you feel your breath when you exhale?'

Again, I didn't say anything.

'And now try to feel your body as a whole.'

I went on breathing and feeling. Boring as fuck.

'So that's mindfulness?' I said, trying to wrap things up.

'Yes, if you're minding your breath, you're being mindful.'

'And that'll somehow change all those idiots around me?' I asked.

'No, it will change your *reaction* to those idiots.'

'So the idiots will still be there?'

'Yes, but their influence on your well-being will not. So now, how are your rapid breathing, your neck tension and your stomach ache?'

27

I tried to simply feel again. Everything was gone. Astounding.

'Gone,' I said.

'So – the next time your wife annoys you or your firm pisses you off, I'd like you to go to the toilet to breathe.'

'To the toilet? But it . . .'

'Then just breathe through your mouth. In any case, it will provide you with a protected space. For three breaths, simply feel your body, then your breathing will be regular again. After that, you will feel better. And you will find it easier to tackle any problem. Enough for today?'

'Sure, same time next week?'

'No, *on* time next week.'

None of what Breitner had told me seemed completely off the mark. And at least all the tension in my neck was gone. From then on, I met with Breitner every Thursday, around eight o'clock. Usually a little later.

4

Time Islands

So as not to drown in the sea of demands that are placed upon you, you need to create your own islands of time. These are protected spaces consciously dedicated to only doing things that are good for you. Here, there is no 'I have to'; there is only 'I am'. A time island is not a place, but a slice of time. It can be a minute or an entire weekend. In any case, it is time that belongs only to you, that only you define and protect. Like a castaway washing up on a desert island, you, too, will find peace, sustenance and energy here. You decide when you enter your time island. You decide when you leave it. You defend it against any intruder. And you know that your time island will always be there for you.

Joschka Breitner, *Slowing Down in the Fast Lane: Mindfulness for Managers*

My breathing exercises didn't magically fix everything. If I had told Dragan about mindfulness training and my first breathing exercise, he would've immediately started calling me his wheezy bum-boy. And with the amount of work Dragan piled on me over the next few weeks, I was wheezing anyway. For example, he had gotten it into his head to convert one of his legal properties into the city's most luxurious brothel. An upmarket temple of lust across all floors of a classic four-storey town house. The itsy-bitsy legal problem I needed to solve first? The upper floors still had tenants, and the ground floor had been taken over by a preschool. Also, the city's current development plan didn't have the building earmarked for use as a brothel. Dozens of officials had to be quietly convinced to play along. Almost every night, I was either out with Dragan or out on his behalf not only to convince, threaten or sweet-talk people, but also to negotiate deals or test people's pain thresholds.

But over each long working day I still managed to incorporate small breathing and mindfulness exercises. I took the time to breathe in the lift of the building control department before determining how much to sweeten the deal for its manager without openly slipping into bribery or intimidation.

I took the time to breathe in the toilets of tenants before informing them that if they didn't move out of the apartment voluntarily, they might suddenly find themselves cut off from water and power.

I took the time to breathe in my office at the firm after a colleague who'd been hired three years after me mentioned that, starting next month, he'd be a partner.

And these small breathing breaks actually did alleviate my tension – the tension anybody with a conscience experiences when they manipulate, threaten or envy other people.

Despite my perpetually high workload, Katharina also noticed that I was willing to work on myself. Despite this willingness, or perhaps because of it, over the next two weeks we ended up making a momentous decision about our relationship.

We decided to separate, at least for the time being – a joint attempt to calm the waters. The magic word in this regard was 'time islands'. It first appeared at my next session with Breitner.

'Tell me about the stress you experience at home,' he had prompted me after he filled both cups of green tea.

'Where to start?' I entreated.

'You two must have first met at some point.'

'Katharina and I met during our legal traineeship. A good ten years ago. She'd hated law school, trudging through it only for the sensible reason of finding a dependable job later on. She really struggled, and I felt sorry for her because I had a very different experience: I found it all fascinating.

I wanted to fight for a better world. One coffee break, we started talking about it – and this contrast turned out to be quite alluring.'

'Surely you didn't end up together because of your differing motivations for law school.'

'No, of course not. We obviously also found each other attractive, and we were both single. We had good banter, and the sex was fun too. So we got together.'

'Ah, a VW Golf relationship.'

'A what?'

'A VW Golf is your generation's go-to compact car for exactly the same reasons. You buy it when you have no other options. It is not all that ugly, it easily gets you from A to B and sometimes it can go pretty fast.'

'What's so wrong with that?'

'Nothing whatsoever. Unless you are really dreaming about an old Ford Mustang and your wife of a Fiat 500.'

'What good is an old Ford Mustang if it only gets me halfway?'

'I do not have the impression that you are here because your Golf took you where you wanted to go.'

'Still, that Golf made us perfectly happy for a very long time.'

'Your wife found that dependable job for which she had tortured herself all those years?'

'She started at an insurance company, because . . . To be honest, I still don't understand why anyone would want to work for an insurance company. Probably because if you start a job without any ideals, you also cannot lose them.

Plus, a job that doesn't offer any illicit kicks can't get you addicted to them.'

'When you're not falling from such a high horse, it probably also hurts less.'

Ouch, that stung all the more. But I continued my story.

'When we both earned our first real payslips, we started spending heaps of it together. Great restaurants, exotic trips, an expensive first apartment of our own – that is, when we had the time.'

'What kind of person is Katharina?'

I started to squirm a little. There were two answers to that question. One I liked and one I didn't like at all. I started with the pleasant answer.

'When we met, she was open, careful, loving, funny. We laughed a lot about other people.'

'And now?'

That was the unpleasant answer.

'Closed off, fearful, loving to Emily, cold to me, and completely humourless. We also don't laugh about other people any more, though Katharina does excel at bitter gossip.'

'When do you think this happened?'

'Somehow, everything that was supposed to be fun became an obligation. "Let's not get out of bed today" became "Let's finally give up our separate places, otherwise we'll never move in together". "I see myself growing old with you" turned into "My mother thinks it's high time we tied the knot". And "I want you to be the father of my children" became "If I don't stop taking the pill, six years from now I'll be too old for a third child".'

'So the dream prince who wanted to rescue the princess from her law-school prison became a biddable Golf driver,' Breitner said, nodding.

'What do you mean, "biddable"? Moving in together, getting married, starting a family – I loved all of it, otherwise I wouldn't have done it. But I would've liked to have had more fun along the way. I would've liked to *experience* it, not just been ticking off a list. The more our relationship followed the typical path, the more trivial it somehow became. We were both working on our careers. And the only thing that mattered to us was that the other person was working on their career too. We both gladly accepted that the other made good money doing *something*. What kind of career didn't particularly interest us that much in the beginning, though over the years it became more and more of a burden. Katharina increasingly hated what I did for a living. What *she* did, meanwhile, I didn't even know.'

'Sounds like a viable foundation, at least financially.'

'When we'd been together for five years, we got married. Emily came two years later.'

'Was having a child always part of your dreams for the future?'

'Absolutely. On top of that, I also dreamed a child would literally bring new life to our relationship. But that was not the case.'

'There's a shocker. If two adults together can't even manage something, why should a child be able to?'

I took a moment to consider that. Somehow, his little interjections all made a shameful sort of sense.

'Katharina focused all her time and energy on Emily. She breastfed according to plan. Weaned according to plan. Took Emily to baby gym according to plan. Baby swimming to plan. Buggyfitness to plan. But each of those plans was exclusively hers. The child of our dreams became the child of her plans. Our relationship was the only thing there wasn't a plan for. At home, I was just a plan-less nobody with a penis. Whenever I was at home, I did everything wrong. But when I came home too late, that was wrong too. I felt like I had no other choice but to plunge even deeper into my much-hated job. At least there I was somebody. There I might not be recognised as a partner either, but at least I have free rein, at least they trust me.'

'And this has been going on since Emily was born?'

'More or less. Since then, I've been working for two. And since then, Katharina has been at home with Emily – at least, when they're not in any mother-and-baby classes. Although Katharina hates other mums, she's so scared of doing anything wrong she still copies every single thing they do. I only get to see my daughter asleep; she hardly gets to see me at all. When I come home irritated and run into my exhausted wife, we argue more and more. Katharina once even asked me why I was bothering to come home at all. I didn't know what to say to that.'

'Do you have a response now?'

'No,' I replied without any hesitation.

My clear 'no' cut the air between us with surgical precision. The break in our conversation that followed was long, but relaxing. Breitner had a surprise waiting for me on the other side.

'Have you heard about the concept of "time islands"?'

'Sorry, what?'

'Time islands. Limited periods of time in which you only do things that feel good to you. And nothing else.'

'You probably mean what my parents' generation used to call "the weekend" and "clocking off".'

'Right, which your generation traded for a smartphone. Instead of weekends, you now have permanent availability and mindfulness consultants.'

'Quite a fucked-up trade.'

'I for one do quite well out of it.'

'And how are these time islands supposed to help me?' I enquired.

'Well, interestingly enough, you have already implemented part of the time island concept. Because you do not feel comfortable at home, you have escaped into work even more. At least there you will not be bothered by your wife. But funnily enough, that psychopath of a client seems to do you no more good than your frustrated wife.'

'And the alternative?'

'Do something for yourself for a change. Create a space for yourself without wives or psychopaths.'

'But I'd like to spend the little time my work does allow me with my family.'

'With your *dream image* of a family that does not actually exist. It obviously does not serve you or your wife, and certainly not your daughter, if at home you are only physically present while mentally you are still grappling with your job and your marriage. Both you and your wife want you to be fully present in your family life. So I would like you to create a fixed time island just for your family. During this time, nothing else matters. This time you can enjoy to the fullest.'

'And on this time island, my wife's in charge again, right?'

'Of course not, it is *your* time island. If you like, you can create a time island just for you and your daughter. When you are there, you are entirely there for your daughter. If you cannot be there for your daughter, you might as well not be there at all. Maybe a spatial separation might even alleviate matters for you and your wife. This way, you – and perhaps your wife too – can allow yourselves to experience the exact things that matter right where you are.'

That same night, I told Katharina about his suggestions, about time islands, about my own dissatisfaction, about separating in order to find ourselves again. To my surprise, Katharina didn't see this suggestion as an ending, but as a glimmer of hope. Instead of accusing me of wanting to end our marriage, she threw her arms around my neck for the first time in months. In tears.

'I'm so grateful you suggested this. I can't take who we are around each other any more.'

'But why didn't you ever suggest I move out for a bit?'

'Because I don't want to kick my daughter's father out, I just want the man I married back.'

She would never get that man back, because the man she thought she married never existed. She had married a blank canvas on which she'd projected her dream husband. But I was willing to pretend to be that projection again – as soon as I recovered the requisite strength.

'So the man you're constantly arguing with moves out, and then the man you married can come for visits?' I asked carefully.

'It would be enough for me if my daughter's father came for visits, just as long as the guy I keep arguing with is gone. For now, I'll just have to do without the man I married.'

We held each other, sobbing.

But this warm moment only lasted until Katharina cooled off again and turned the proposed solution into a condition. She slipped out of my arms and looked into my eyes with a glint of menace.

'If you can't manage to maintain those time islands, we're done. If your job is more important to you than Emily even once, that's it. You'll never see her again. After all, I'm the mother.'

Or, to stick with the metaphor: if the glimmer of hope didn't turn into full daybreak, I would be sunset. It wasn't an empty threat. As a lawyer, it was clear to me that even the most modern woman will gain sole custody as long as she invokes the nineteenth-century ideal of motherhood that still holds sway in the German courts. If the mother does not want him to, the father will never see the child. Full stop. And at her frostiest, Katharina would be able to go through with it too.

Faced with this threat, it was much easier for me to move out. I was glad to climb out of the freezing pond before it froze over me.

I found a furnished apartment in the same neighbourhood. We found islands of time in which I took care of Emily by myself. Initially, this was a few hours in the morning, which I made up for guilt-free by working a few more in the evenings.

After a week or two, those few hours every few days then became Sunday afternoons. Then all of Sunday, every fortnight even the entire weekend.

My job didn't allow for more time islands, or so I thought.

This time with Emily brought me back to life. Spending time alone with this little person made me feel incredibly free. Just playing with her intuitively without having her mum breathing down my neck constantly judging everything I did. Not to have my mind always on the firm, but on my island. And on this island, I was king, wizard, daddy.

In the park, Emily and I could giggle at the waddling ducks without having to listen to Katharina rant about the mums on the other side of the pond. At the playground, we could hop on a swing whenever it was free, not only after Emily had been liberally slathered with sunscreen.

At the ice-cream parlour, it was so much more fun to order whatever tasted good – not pick from the limited selection marked low-sugar and organic.

For Emily and me, there was no longer any right or wrong; there was only beautiful and *very* beautiful. Spending one hour with my daughter on a time island with my head held high was a thousand times more profound than a whole day with the three of us and my head hung low.

And I managed to make that time with my daughter sacrosanct. I communicated it to my firm, and Dragan knew too.

Because when it comes down to it, the leverage a gangster can bring to bear is nothing compared to a mum's. Katharina might've only made her threat once, but now it was out there. If I messed up with the time islands, our relationship would be over. And my time with Emily too.

Katharina and I thus managed to reduce our arguments to zero. We handled each other with kid gloves and were pleased that Emily also obviously enjoyed spending more time with both her parents – albeit separately.

Like many of the tough guys in organised crime, Dragan fancied himself someone who loved children. That is, unless they got in his way. When a man owed him ten euros, Dragan didn't hesitate to have the lug nuts on his car loosened, even if the guy was just about to drive off on a holiday with his family of four. Still, afterwards he'd always make sure the victim's seriously injured kids got season passes to the zoo.

Emily was two-and-a-half when Dragan invaded our time island with all his might.

5

Digital Fasting

Mindfulness means being available to your own needs. Any time you are available to others stands in the way of this mindfulness. Consciously switching off your phone and your computer is a good first step . . . Yet your goal should be to make the decision to switch *on* your phone or your computer a conscious one.

Joschka Breitner, *Slowing Down in the Fast Lane: Mindfulness for Managers*

Over the next weeks and months, my new mindfulness began to have a positive effect on my life. Katharina and I developed a relationship as partners in parenting that seemed more sustainable than the fragile relationship we'd had as a couple. The ice we were skating on grew thicker and thicker. We'd agreed to let my mindfulness course run out its three months and then wait at least another month before making any concrete plans for the future.

I wasn't letting my work get to me that much any more, and my time with Emily worked like an elixir. Breitner taught me not only the importance of breathing and time islands, but also all kinds of exercises I'd be able to use in the future. The principle of 'perception without evaluation' opened my eyes, much as that of 'intentional centring'. Exercises to overcome my internal resistance became just as familiar to me as mindful breathing had.

After twelve weeks, the mindfulness course was over, and I received Breitner's indispensable *Slowing Down in the Fast Lane: Mindfulness for Managers* as a farewell gift – considering the steep course fee, I'd expected his handbook to be bound in leather. I made sure to carry it with me always so I could consult it when needed.

To celebrate my mindful new life, I'd decided to use the

first weekend after the course ended as a time island to take Emily on a mini-break.

Katharina agreed. She also wanted to mark the occasion and enjoy the freedom she'd gained through my increased involvement. She'd booked herself a spa resort for the weekend, something she hadn't done since Emily was born.

As Dragan's lawyer, I had access to many of his properties. I had acquired almost all of them for him and assigned them to his various companies. One of these properties was about eighty kilometres from the city, a fabulous house on a beautiful lake, with a jetty, a sandy beach and a barbecue area. Emily loved water, and we were going to turn the lake house into our time island's own special castle.

I'd bought the house for Dragan out of EU agricultural subsidies he'd received for the Bulgarian aubergine farm. Once you understand that public funding isn't distributed based on the applicants' needs but on their shamelessness, applying for more can become quite addictive. In fact, getting a wheelchair-accessible doorway installed in the guest toilet and providing a five-page proposal to convert the rest of the house into a 'barrier-free training centre for inclusion research' was enough to earn subsidies from the Federal Ministry of Education. These grants in turn financed the luxurious expansion of the house's wellness area.

I knew that Dragan was heading to Bratislava that weekend with a pile of cash to settle some business. Dragan knew that I wanted to spend this time at the lake house with my daughter. Sit on the jetty, eat some nuts, feed the fish.

None of us knew the weekend would unfold very differently.

The week had been stressful. On Friday night, I had been crouched over a brief concerning the upmarket brothel until half past eleven. Unlike all other tenants, who were relatively easy to convince, pay off or intimidate, the preschool on the ground floor stubbornly refused to vacate the premises. So I had to tighten the thumbscrews a little on the co-operative behind it, a parents' initiative made up of uncooperative bleeding hearts – through legal means, of course.

I'd even happened to have met them before. By the summer, Emily would be old enough to attend preschool. But the criteria for getting into a preschool are much more confusing than for liquor licences at brothels. Liquor licences are issued centrally, unlike preschool spots. So Katharina and I had looked at all thirty-one preschools within a ten-minute driving radius together and applied for a place at each. The co-operative ended up twenty-ninth on our wish list. We felt the parents were a bunch of utopian nincompoops, and not entirely without reason. I assumed Emily would get a spot at a place between one and five on our wish list. I mean, I couldn't imagine on what absurd grounds we should be rejected at places one to four. So, I had no problems with the fact that number twenty-nine was about to be turned into a titty temple. I had already offered the co-op a very low severance payment and threatened them with a nasty eviction lawsuit besides. Since the deadline for accepting the severance had expired, I was preparing the eviction proceeding.

I got back to my apartment some time after midnight and, in happy expectation of the weekend, immediately fell asleep.

On Saturday morning, I picked up Emily. It still felt strange to be waiting on my own doorstep like a visitor, but it was a good kind of strange. Only three months earlier, before I moved out, I'd felt so tense when I came home every night, just knowing I would be greeted with accusations or – worse – utter disregard.

Now I rang the doorbell and was greeted by a smiling Katharina: 'Hi, Björn, nice to see you.'

What a difference in such a short time.

'Daddyyyyy!' Emily hurtled towards me from the nursery. After showing me what was new in her world – one doll no longer needed to wear a nappy – she started packing up all her stuffed animals while her mother and I had a coffee.

'Emily is really looking forward to your trip,' Katharina told me.

'I am too . . .'

'But do me a favour and please keep her far away from anything to do with your mafia maniac.'

The mere fact that she formulated this as a request represented a quantum leap in our communication. But Katharina's fears were completely unfounded; there was simply nothing even remotely redolent of criminality in the unused lake house.

'Please don't worry about it. As soon as I notice even a hint of mafioso, I'll immediately break off our trip.'

'And ruin my spa weekend?' Katharina's tone changed abruptly.

'No, I . . .' I stammered.

'Björn, I will assume you can guarantee everything will be fine, without any ifs or buts. This is your first weekend away together. If I can't rely on this to go smoothly, then you'd better not go at all. You know what's on the line here.'

There they were again: the cracks in the ice – and everything underneath. I took a quick breath to myself and then responded lovingly and calmly:

'Katharina, I guarantee you that this weekend will be entirely plain sailing. For Emily, for me and for you too.'

'Thank you,' she said, warmer again.

Katharina gave Emily a fierce hug goodbye and me a friendly kiss on the cheek.

Shortly after, I walked out of the much-too-big apartment hand in hand with Emily, who was skipping for joy. The fact that a single sentence from Katharina could still take the ground out from under me made me shudder. But if I'd learned anything, it was that when I'm standing outside a door, I'm standing outside a door. When I'm having an argument with Katharina, I'm having an argument with Katharina. So I walked outside and let Katharina be Katharina. From now on, we would be on our time island.

It was the perfect day for a father-daughter trip to the lake. The sky was blue, and although it was nine in the morning and only the end of April, it was already a summery 27 degrees.

*

49

A significant issue today is our permanent availability, mainly due to our smartphones. It's an incredible travesty to call any device 'smart' that – through a work call, email, WhatsApp or whatever – can ruthlessly send us to the depths of hell, and from our own pocket! 'Hellphone' would be more apropos. But phones are like weapons: it's not the thing itself that's dangerous, but the person using it. Unlike guns, smartphones only harm their owners. Sure, you can put a gun to your own head. But you usually do it to end a fucked-up life, not to fuck it up some more.

In Breitner's book, I found the following on this issue:

Mindfulness means being available to your own needs. Any time you are available to others stands in the way of this mindfulness. Consciously switching off your phone is a good first step – to the extent that it should make it frighteningly clear that always being available to others has already been completely normalised. Yet your goal should be to make your decision to switch on your phone a conscious one. Until then, at least while on your time island, you should leave your phone and computer switched off.

Pay these sentences heed, they can save lives. In recent weeks, I had kept my phone off while I was on my time islands, and not once had something happened that my voicemail couldn't fill me in on a few hours later. But this had to be the one weekend I forgot about my digital fast. Out of sheer excitement to take a trip with Emily, my mindfulness had slipped. The repercussions were immediate.

I had just strapped Emily in her child seat and left the driveway when my phone rang – I suddenly realised I'd completely failed at mindfulness.

The screen showed an unknown number, which didn't necessarily mean anything. Dragan changed mobile numbers like other people changed lawyers. I could have just declined the call. But if the man who's letting you stay at his lake house calls, it's considered rude to ignore him. After all, he could have just been calling to say: 'Hope you have a great time!' – though that was unlikely. Also not unimportant, he might've been calling to say: 'Hey, Mustafa will also be at the lake this weekend and he's bringing twelve prozzies, doesn't bother you, does it?' I had solemnly promised Katharina that there wouldn't be any such surprises, so I answered.

'Yep,' I said.

'Dude, where are you?'

'A good morning to you too, Dragan. I'm just on my way to the lake house with Emily, you remember . . .'

'I need you here. Now.'

'Dragan, this is my weekend with Emily.'

'We're going for ice cream.' Dragan hung up.

Because we'd known for years that Dragan's phones were being tapped, none of our important talks ever happened over the phone. Instead, we had agreed on a few attorney-client code words. Deciding on code words with a violent psychopath is a delicate matter. If someone already finds it hard to remember whose legs he'd had broken two days earlier, they're usually also not able to retain even just half a dozen designations for specific dangerous situations.

That's why we had *two* code words, no more. One was 'watching *Titanic*', the other 'going for ice cream'.

'Watching *Titanic*' essentially meant 'the ship is going down': throw any incriminating material overboard and get everyone into lifeboats. Dragan had never had to use that one before.

'Going for ice cream' meant 'it's getting hot, we need to meet immediately'. There was an ice-cream parlour on the ground floor of my firm's building. I had rented it for Dragan through one of his own subsidiaries, on the one hand because it was an easy business to launder cash through, on the other because of the place's layout and proximity to my law firm. The staff rooms of the ice-cream parlour were on the floor above and could be reached via the lift from both the underground car park and my office – but only via the lift. The rooms were windowless, and there were exactly two sets of keys: one for Dragan and one for me. 'Going for ice cream' meant meeting there, unnoticed by law enforcement, people from my firm or anyone at all.

So far, Dragan had used the code word twice.

Both times, the reason had been that Dragan was wanted by the police, so before going into hiding he needed to give me instructions in person: which witnesses had to be 'influenced' and how I should instruct his employees until the waters had calmed again. I had a whole stack of powers of attorney and even blank letterhead signed by Dragan. This way, I could easily continue all of his business on his behalf in his absence. This had been tried and tested.

If Dragan wanted to get into the building unnoticed, he'd hide in the back of one of his ice-cream vans, let himself be driven into the underground car park and then disappear into the lift. I'd come down from my office. Nobody saw us.

'Going for ice cream' was not only a code word, but also a conversation killer. It should leave police or prosecutors in the dark, and prevent any discussion between the two of us about why we were meeting. This meant I *had* to meet Dragan. I'd picked up the phone, I'd heard the code word. My time island was moot. But just because my idiot client had once again had someone's bones broken, some smugglers had thundered into a police checkpoint or some drugs shipment had been blown up, did that really mean I should give up my newly acquired principles? Should a single phone call be able to ruin my hard-won father-daughter weekend? Thanks to my job, I didn't have a fucking choice. Ignoring a call would've been forgivable. Ignoring an emergency code word wasn't. With Dragan, doing that could result in repercussions that went beyond employment law straight into the anatomical.

Aggravated, I threw the phone into the passenger foot-well and stepped on the gas. I accelerated to seventy in a thirty zone, took the right of way from a smaller car – accidentally – and, instead of driving towards the motorway, turned onto the main road towards the city centre with deliberately squealing tyres. The little outburst of fury did me good, and Emily was also very impressed. She liked the squealing tyres and shrieked with delight, 'Daddy, what are you doing?'

'I ... I ...'

Yeah, what *was* I doing? I took three deep breaths and made a compromise with myself: I would briefly visit the office, get this unnecessary meeting over with and then officially start on my time island. I was driving to an emergency meeting, nothing more. This wouldn't betray my commitment to time islands; Katharina wouldn't have any grounds for reproach. There was nothing wrong with a father briefly stopping by the office with his daughter on a Saturday morning. Leaving aside the fact that he was doing it completely against his will.

'Daddy is just dropping by the office for a bit,' I said, as if it were the most normal thing in the world. On the car stereo, I selected the kids' music playlist, and we sang 'The Teddy Bears' Picnic' all the way to the city centre.

6

The Other Person's Inner World

Do not focus on what another person says, but on what they *want* to say. What you hear is only an echo of their inner world. If you feel instead of just listen, many insults actually turn out to be cries for help.

Joschka Breitner, *Slowing Down in the Fast Lane: Mindfulness for Managers*

Big law firms don't do weekends, they only loosen their ties a bit. So even on Saturdays, there are countless lawyers, clerks and other bootlickers scurrying around in slightly more casual clothes to book expensive hours onto already inflated client bills. My half-hatched plan was that I would ensnare one of the swotty trainees to play with Emily for half an hour while I 'went for an ice cream'.

Our offices occupied the upper three floors of a five-storey 1970s commercial building in the city centre. Besides the ice-cream parlour, the ground floor also had a clothes shop and a McDonald's.

As we drove up, Emily said, 'I'll have a McFlurry, Chicken McNuggets and chocolate milk', pointing to the apparently familiar golden arches – Katharina no longer seemed to be so strict about healthy nutrition. I was grateful Emily reminded me of our basic human needs.

'Of course, love. We'll just go to the office for a little bit and then to McDonald's.'

'And then to the lake?'

'And then to the lake.'

'Hurray!'

As I approached the driveway to the underground car park, a BMW 5 with two badly dressed constables out of uniform was just backing into the opposite fire lane. One of them was very conspicuously inconspicuously pointing a camera at the entrance to our building. I drove down into the car park, parked, and then, with Emily on my arm, took the lift up to our firm.

My own office was on the fourth floor, but I got off on the third, the reception area. The same dragon had presided over Von Dresen, Erkel and Dannwitz's reception desk for twenty years. Ms Bregenz had wasted her best years as a secretary at the firm, and now she was being saddled with weekend duty more and more. Once she must've been attractive, convinced that she'd be able to capitalise on her looks. Yet she mustn't have realised that looks aren't everything – especially when you lack any charm. Over the years, her looks had levelled down to her charm, and what remained was a disgruntled shrew. As she grew incrementally meaner over the years, it became harder and harder to sympathise with her. All she was now was the dragon at reception.

She looked at me, then at Emily. Emily looked at Ms Bregenz and pointed at her.

'Daddy, does that old lady live here?'

Out of the mouth of a babe – and not entirely off the mark either.

'That's Ms Bregenz,' I tried to state neutrally. 'She makes sure everything's in its place here.'

Ms Bregenz contemptuously eyed the windbreaker and jeans I was wearing instead of my usual tailor-made suits.

'I take it you have no client meetings scheduled today?' she asked.

I took a deep breath, felt my breath, and ignored the crabby remark.

'Good morning, Ms Bregenz. Have you by any chance seen Ms Kerner anywhere?'

'Trainees like her are assigned only to the partners, not the other lawyers. And I don't think *your* clients are the right sort for a young lady like Ms Kerner.'

What was her deal? Was she seriously offended that my daughter had blithely called her old? Did I have to let this dragon talk down to me just because I wasn't a partner? Something, by the way, I also owed to the very client who'd summoned me to the office on a weekend like a lackey. Even if I'd been in a good mood, this kind of rudeness would've been too much for me. And I wasn't in a good mood.

'Save your advice for the coffee break and just tell me where Ms Kerner is,' I barked.

Her eyes widened in shock. Finally, she murmured, 'Ms Kerner is in the trainee room.'

I looked at Emily and said in a much calmer voice, 'You know what, honey, why don't you play in here for a bit, OK?'

Before my daughter could answer, Ms Bregenz had gathered herself again. 'What do you think this office is, a playpen?'

If you practise mindfulness, you'd know, after breathing in and out a couple of times, that deep inside this poor woman was a wounded soul whose needs were crying out to be heard. My mindfulness coach said it very clearly:

*Do not focus on what another person says, but on what
they* want *to say. What you hear is only an echo of their
inner world. If you feel instead of just listen, many insults
actually turn out to be cries for help.*

Inside of Ms Bregenz must be a woman who never had
any children she might've brought to the office. A woman
whose salary was only a fraction of that of the lawyers who
expected her to work weekends because 'she didn't have a
family'. A woman who used the shred of power she'd been
given to take out her life's frustrations on other people.

After twelve weeks of mindfulness classes and one conscious in- and exhale, that much was clear. Though it did
slow my pulse, that didn't quite outweigh the ten years this
bully had already gotten on my wick.

'Well, young lady,' I couldn't help but quip, 'if you went
to law school and had a baby, you might be able to answer
the question yourself.'

With that, I breezed past her to the trainee room, where,
as expected, Emily and I met Clara Kerner, who for the past
three weeks had been assigned to the partner whose department also included me and my bleurgh-client. Clara was the
daft kid of some daft client. That's why she was allowed to
join us as a trainee, to boost a CV this hopeless daughter
of some so-and-so would never really need. In the way of
all trainees who don't have the mental capacity to parse the
prose of jurisprudence, she appeared to be colouring in some
decisions of the Federal Court of Justice. That is, she had
photocopied some decisions and marked up the bits she

considered important with different highlighters. However, since she was overwhelmed by the sheer quantity of potentially important things, she seemed to simply be highlighting *everything*. This was of no more use than her general presence at the firm. There was simply no other reason for her to be there on a Saturday except to be seen – so for me to come in was a win for her. I asked her to stop colouring judgements for half an hour and instead do some proper colouring with Emily. Surely that would be an appropriate amount of stimulus for both girls' mental capacities.

At first, she looked at me helplessly, then the penny dropped. 'I . . . yeah, sure, I . . .'

'Nice of you, thanks,' I said curtly. 'Emily, Daddy has some work to do. I'll be back in a flash, OK?'

Emily looked at Clara sceptically. I followed her gaze: blouse too tight, trousers too tight, scarf too tight. We were hit with a tsunami of Chanel No. 5. Like many trainees, she looked like a fresh bratwurst and smelled like a spinster aunt.

'But where are the crayons?' Emily asked critically.

'Clara has really great markers, they colour even more beautifully than normal crayons, look what Clara has already made!'

I pointed to the colourful court decisions – Clara was glowing with pride over her pink, green and yellow highlights.

'Pink *is* my favourite colour,' Emily said.

'See!' I turned to the newly elected babysitter. 'Clara, by all means take Emily to the big conference room.'

'But there's enough space here . . .'

'Yes, Clara, you're right. But here there aren't any fancy big office chairs you can bounce around on. You can't start practising that early enough. After all, they don't teach you these things at university.'

If my daughter had to spend time at the office, she should enjoy all the perks.

'Ms Bregenz won't like that . . .'

'All the better.' I beamed an enthusiastic smile at her. 'And if there's absolutely anything else, just give me a call.'

As Clara and Emily pottered into the conference room, I hurried to the lift. I pretended to be heading to my office one floor up, while instead I headed down to 'go for ice cream' with Dragan – which I tried but failed to convince myself was just an ordinary meeting.

7

Perception Without Evaluation

What causes us to worry is not whatever may
have happened. It is only after we classify what
happened that it frightens us. No single event is
good or bad in itself.

Joschka Breitner, *Slowing Down in the
Fast Lane: Mindfulness for Managers*

The ice-cream parlour's staff rooms were basically junk closets. Wonky plastic chairs huddled around a few rusty bistro tables, and boxes of ice-cream cups, plastic spoons and uniforms were piled high along the walls. Dragan was already there, nervously smoking. Though his muscular six-foot-four radiated an arrogant brutality, amid this shabby ambience he seemed a little out of place in his designer suit. Like a tiger hiding out in the meerkat enclosure.

'At last,' was his greeting.

'Sorry, there was heavy traffic. I was just on my way to the lake with Emily.' Professional as I was, I'd managed to get my pulse back to nearly normal. This was just an unnecessary meeting, nothing more.

'Who's Emily?'

My pulse quickened. 'My daughter!' A certain indignation started brewing inside me. Dragan obviously didn't have a clue that he was the one blocking me from the time island I had dedicated to my daughter.

'Ah, right. You know I love children, but you shouldn't let your family get in the way of your work.'

There was no point in talking to someone like Dragan about such a thing as 'work–life balance'. But then I wasn't his shrink, just his lawyer. And I just wanted to get back to my daughter.

'So let's talk about work: what happened?'

'They're looking for me.'

'Why?'

'Some drug courier got a few scratches in a motorway lay-by.'

I knew from my first job with Dragan that his precis were always creatively optimistic and usually didn't even reveal the tip of the iceberg he'd rammed into full steam ahead. Obviously, scratches would be the least of it.

'And why are the police looking for you?'

'Because I kind of gave that moron . . . a few knocks.'

'We're sitting here because of a few knocks?'

'Well, no . . . because the bloke is dead.'

When a bank cashier is faced with a robber, most are well trained enough to adopt an admirably professional demeanour. Simply treat the gangster like a highly strung customer and run through the usual routine until they run off with the money. Only then can the cashier let their jelly start to wobble. I still harboured a vague hope that after a professional lawyer's chat Dragan would simply leave, at which point I could mindfully breathe away the stress. So I switched to my professional mode, took a deep breath as I sat down, and felt my pulse going back down to about a hundred.

'What happened exactly?'

'For a few months now, product has been offered in our sales area at half our going rate.'

OK, at first glance, this looked like an economics problem. Nothing special for a lawyer dealing with white-collar crime. Financially, the trade in classic drugs like heroin or cocaine is like a relay race. At each stage, the baton is resold at a profit, and most of the profit is made just before the finish line. Cutting the drugs and portioning it for individual users creates margins that exceed the imaginable. Even at half price, you still stand to earn a lot of money. If a competitor snatches up your territory, however, you lose your chance at *any* profit.

I looked at Dragan questioningly. 'And you know this how?'

'From Toni.'

Toni was the sales manager for Dragan's narcotics division. A hard-hitting wholesale dealer who was in no way Dragan's inferior when it came to brutality. As with many successful felons, the intellectual acquisition of complex constellations of facts wasn't one of his core competences. But he did have an intuitive sense of how to gain an advantage or avert a disadvantage. This intuition enabled him to make the largest turnover in Dragan's operation, and he considered himself number two in the organisation. Not everyone saw it that way, least of all Dragan.

'OK, so why doesn't Toni fix it?' I asked.

If Toni had done his job as described in the organisational chart I created, I wouldn't have to be sitting in this junk room right now.

'Toni thinks Boris's boys are behind it,' Dragan replied.

Boris was Dragan's closest competitor. The two had started out as pimps together. Once best friends, they'd at some point fallen out. After some bloody back-and-forths, both had staked out their territories, and for some years a more or less reliable peace had been established – which was also due to the fact that I'd secretly given Boris a few tips on legalising *his* earnings as well.

'OK, but what does all this have to do with the dead guy in the lay-by?' I asked.

'Sasha and I got a tip that someone would be showing up there to deliver drugs to Igor, who would then distribute them on our turf.'

Igor was Boris's right hand in all his drug dealings, and Sasha was Dragan's driver and personal assistant. A Bulgarian, Sasha had studied environmental engineering back home and come to Germany the day after graduating. Once here, he quickly learned that his diploma wouldn't be recognised, so he didn't become an engineer, but initially applied to work at one of Dragan's bars.

'I see. And the tip came from whom?'

'Murat.'

Murat was Toni's deputy. Dragan stubbed out his cigarette in an ashtray.

So if the whole thing had to be summarised for a prosecutor, it'd sound like this: Dragan, head of a criminal ring, was on his way to Slovakia with his assistant, Sasha. On the way, Dragan got a call, not from the head of his narcotics department, Toni, but from that man's assistant, Murat. Murat told Dragan that Boris, Dragan's nemesis and head of a rival criminal ring, had sent his right hand, Igor, to a motorway lay-by. There, on Dragan's territory, Igor was to conduct a narcotics transaction that was illegal, not just under the Misuse of Drugs Act, but also according to the two syndicates' own code, because it took place in another syndicate's territory.

'And that was reason enough for you to bump off the guy with the drugs?'

Dragan pulled his next cigarette out of the packet – an impressive sight, because the man's giant hands were more like mitts. But as he pulled out the comparatively delicate cigarette, he stuck out his little finger as if he were drinking an espresso. On his right ring finger was a showy signet ring that had marked his flesh over the years.

Unfortunately, this casual act didn't quite match what he casually remarked next:

'I didn't beat the guy with the drugs to death, I beat Igor to death.'

'Well, that might've been a little silly.'

I saw my time island engulfed by ever-higher waves. When the head of one syndicate personally kills the right hand of the head of a competing syndicate, the general mood tends to be negatively affected.

Clearly, immediate action was required.

'Sasha and I just wanted to calmly go over our territorial boundaries, but things somehow got out of hand.'

'Going over territorial boundaries' is based on an old German tradition. In the past, after landowners set the boundaries of a leased patch of land, they'd take the tenant's children out to the boundary marker of the tenancy in question. There, they slapped the children once on their left cheek and once on the right. This ensured the children would never forget the spot and remember exactly where the boundary ran for the rest of their lives.

'Dragan! Why do you still insist on doing these things personally? Why didn't you leave it to Sasha or Toni? I thought you were eager to get to Bratislava?'

'I wanted to go to Bratislava with Sasha. On the way, Sasha got the tip-off. The lay-by was on our way, so I wanted to treat myself to a little bit of fun with the courier. Plus, when it comes to Boris, everything is personal.'

A little bit of fun? And nobody considered what I'd say? My pulse shot up to a hundred and seventy. The fact that my client had interrupted his own weekend trip to 'treat himself' to a murder didn't give him the right to demand I interrupt mine.

There simply wasn't enough space in the small windowless room to breathe away my anger, and seeking out the closest toilet would have taken me past Ms Bregenz. But I couldn't possibly just leave now. Dragan suffering a spontaneous heart attack was the only thing that could've helped me at that moment. I looked at Dragan, but he was far from collapsing. On the contrary, the story seemed to have put him in a chipper mood.

Pretending to think, I closed my eyes for a moment to in- and exhale three times, my pulse going back to one hundred and fifty before I opened my eyes again. 'Are there any witnesses?'

'Well, really there shouldn't have been any. The lay-by is usually deserted that time of night. But then this fucking coach drove up.'

'What kind of coach?'

'One of those intercity ones.'

'Full of myopic pensioners?'

'More like precocious schoolchildren.'

'How many children?'

'No idea. How many fucking twelve-year-olds fit on a coach like that, maybe fifty?'

'"Fucking twelve-year-olds"? I thought you loved children?'

'Children bring sunshine to the world, but not in a lay-by at four in the morning.'

'How many of the children saw the brawl?'

'All of them, I think?'

'How many of them held up mobile phones to film the proceedings?'

'Pfft . . . Kids being kids – probably all of them as well.'

'So there are now fifty different video recordings showing you beating someone to death in front of fifty schoolchildren?'

'Not at all. Forty-nine at most.'

'How do you mean?'

'I jumped in front of the bus, kicked the door in and went inside for a bit. I smashed the first boy's phone out of his hands, stamped on it and told the others to do the same with their phones.'

'And how many twelve-year-olds filmed that part?'

'The other forty-nine. But the sound is guaranteed to be grotty, because all of a sudden they started screaming hysterically.'

Had this madman beaten those children up too?

'And then?'

'Then the police showed up, and we were off.'

'Has the video already been posted online?'

'Yes.'

'On telly?'

'There too.'

'Are you recognisable?'

'Well, it's very shaky. If it'd come from a speed camera, you could certainly dispute it.'

Dragan tapped on his phone and handed over a YouTube video that obviously came from an N24 news report. It was a sensationally high-definition shot of Dragan jumping out of a van with an iron bar and using it to beat a man who was lying on the ground. The brightness of the recording was due not only to the technical specifications of the twelve-year-olds' phones, but also to the fact that the man on the ground was in flames – just like the van, which the man had probably just leapt out of to save himself. Then Dragan had showed up with his iron bar, and soon the man on the ground was no longer moving, just burning.

I paused the video.

I felt sick to my stomach. And I couldn't breathe away the sight of a burning man beaten to death by the man sitting opposite me, as I could hardly stand up now – feet shoulder-width apart, knees slightly bent, chest out – and 'feel my breath'.

This only made me angrier. Dragan couldn't just torpedo twelve weeks of mindfulness training in one morning;

I needed to dig a little deeper into my mindfulness toolbox to find the appropriate strategy to counter my abhorrence, my anger, my fear, disorientation and disgust. I breathed where I sat, going through my memories from the past twelve weeks. Breitner had revealed to me that it wasn't anything that happened that caused us to worry, but our own perspective on what happened. Rephrasing Epictetus, Breitner stated that:

What causes us to worry is not whatever may have happened. It is only after we classify what happened that it frightens us. No single event is good or bad in itself.

I tried to watch the video from this point of view. So there was a man who was on fire. OK. And there was another man who beat the burning man to death. OK. The fact that the beating man must be a psychopath was just my assessment of the situation. Not OK. Had the burning man tried to kidnap my daughter, I'd be much more understanding of the guy who lit him up and then beat him to death. It wasn't the burning and beating to death that was so disgusting; that was just my assessment – or at least that's what the theory suggested.

In fact, the man who'd been beaten to death *hadn't* attempted to kidnap my daughter. He didn't even know my daughter. Unlike Dragan. He knew about Emily, but couldn't remember her name. He knew my situation at home, but he just didn't care. He knew about my plans for the weekend, but fucked them up anyway. In the video, he'd been faced with a living person, but just beaten him to death . . .

At that moment, my phone rang, so I got a brief respite. It was coming from the firm's conference room. Another shock: had something happened to Emily?

'Hello, what is it?'

It was Clara. 'Mr Diemel? Emily just coloured on a leather chair in the conference room.'

'Is she OK?'

'Well, she's having fun, but the chair . . .'

'Then why are you calling me?'

'Because I don't know what to do now. If Ms Bregenz sees . . .'

To hell with Ms Bregenz.

'How many office chairs are there in the conference room?'

'Two, four, six . . . twelve . . . fifteen.'

'Then please tell Emily she's doing a great job, and don't call me again until she's finished all fifteen.'

I ended the call.

Dragan was staring at me.

'Have you gone off your trolley?' he snarled. 'I'm in big trouble and you're talking about office chairs?'

'Look, Emily's up there, and when it comes to her, I always pick up the phone.'

'I don't give a fuck who's up there, mate, this is where the kettle boils. And if that doesn't suit anyone up there, I'll personally go up there to clarify things.'

That would be all I needed. I tried to get Dragan back on topic.

I pointed to the freeze-frame of the man on fire.

'Is that Igor?'

Dragan was briefly irritated. He took a closer look – as if the lay-by had been littered with burning people.

'Yes, that's Igor, the guy on the ground.'

'Why is he on fire?'

'Well, we just lit a little spark under his bum.'

In Dragan's world, that wasn't a metaphor. It meant someone's arse got splashed with lighter fuel and usually only noticed it when it was hit with a lit Zippo. As a rule, however, the fire was usually snuffed out as soon as the first blisters started to appear on their bum cheeks.

'Well, as I said, the situation got a little out of hand. That bender couldn't wait in the van until we'd put his arse out. He just had to rush out.'

'And the guy with the drugs?'

'That's another thing: it turns out he didn't even have any drugs. He only wanted to peddle Igor a crate of hand grenades. But by then, Igor's arse was already on fire.'

'Well, if that's all. Where'd the bloke go?'

'Sasha knocked him out back in the van. He won't be any trouble.'

He won't be any trouble, so he was dead too. I shook my head, grasping for one clear thought: 'Could it be that the tip-off about the drugs was someone taking the piss and subsequently putting you in deep shit, and me right along with you? Is one unverified call from some assistant of Toni's reason enough for you to run entirely amok?'

I'd never spoken to Dragan like this before. But it did

me good. Dragan didn't seem to have noticed my change in tone. He was preoccupied by other issues.

'The fuck was I supposed to know a coach would be stopping there? And with schoolchildren in it!' he ranted. 'Which driver in their right mind would stop a coach full of schoolkids at an unlit lay-by in the middle of the night? Tell me that! You don't do that kind of thing to children. I love kids!'

I turned back to the phone and clicked resume. What Dragan meant by loving kids became clear in the next shot, which showed from inside the coach how Dragan first smashed the windscreen, kicked in the door, then knocked a phone out of the hand of a boy who couldn't be older than ten, threateningly tilting the kid's small, trembling chin with his right mitt as he shouted: 'You haven't seen shite, get that? Or I'll beat you all to death.'

The footage of the forty-nine children's phones obviously provided enough newscast nuggets to splice together a whole story. It cut to a different recording and ended with a close-up of Dragan's Porsche Cayenne, which was apparently lacking number plates. You could see Dragan jumping into the back seat and then speeding out of the lay-by. In the background, the burning van leapt up as the crate of hand grenades exploded, probably tearing the alleged drugs courier unconscious inside into a thousand pieces. A coherently edited piece that would've played to a thrilled audience on the big screen.

So we were not just dealing with some bloke who'd gotten 'a few scratches', there was also a human torch, a witness torn apart by hand grenades, one clear instance of manslaughter and fifty traumatised schoolchildren. For Dragan perhaps incidentals, but for me as a criminal defence lawyer rather essential.

'But where's Sasha?'

'Downstairs in the ice-cream van, he drove me here.'

'No, I mean: where's Sasha in these videos? Is he also recognisable?'

'Nope, he was in the van with me at first, and when the coach showed up, he fetched the Cayenne right away. With a pullover over his face, as a mask like.'

'And the Cayenne's number plates?'

'Sasha tore them off and tossed them in the car.' Sasha did good.

'Where's the Cayenne now?'

'Airport, long-stay parking. Sasha got the ice-cream van and then brought me here.'

'Your phones?'

'In pieces on the motorway. I'm not stupid.' I didn't comment on that.

I looked at Dragan. 'And what am I supposed to do?'

'You're the lawyer, so do something, settle this shit.'

I felt anger catch hold of me again. 'Sure,' I blustered, 'but I'm a lawyer, not a plumber. And when we're treading in turds this massive, I, too, reach my limits.'

'You do your lawyer thing right now, or I'll make you eat shite yourself.'

My carotid artery started throbbing like a maniac. We were silent for a moment. Dragan was right, there was no point fighting it. In any case, he was holding the longer end of the stick.

'OK,' I said, as calmly as I could. 'Option one: you turn yourself in. If you do that, however, I won't be able to get you out so easily. Not with the evidence against you. Even if I give all the children on the bus a puppy and then threaten to kill it, the footage will still be online.'

'Have you gone mental? You want me to turn myself in?'

'Option two: you don't turn yourself in. If you do that, cops aren't your biggest problem. If Boris finds you, you might even wish you were in prison. It won't sit well with him that you set one of his men alight and then beat him to death.'

Dragan slapped both hands on the table.

'Hold up, lawyer man, our roles have been clear for years: I have a problem, you have the solution! So, what do we do?'

He stared at me unblinking, waiting for an answer.

Considering his state of mind, I didn't want to point out the *real* problem: that Dragan had obviously been lured into a trap. In my distress, I tried some black humour: 'Lie low until all this commotion has died down – in like thirty or forty years . . .'

Dragan's eyes narrowed to slits. I suddenly felt hot and cold at the same time, sure he was going to grab me by the throat. But then, very slowly, his mouth relaxed into a wide grin. Dragan reached over the table and patted me on the shoulders.

'That's what we'll do.'

The moron thought keeping a low profile for the next few decades was actually a solution.

'Dragan, you won't even make it out of this building. Coppers in civvies are already waiting for you outside. They'll tear your ice-cream van apart.'

'Then we'll just take your car.'

'Sorry, what?'

'I'll hide in the boot, and you'll drive me out of town. Then we'll figure out what's next.'

I looked at him, stunned. My heartbeat spiked. He couldn't possibly be serious. The fucker didn't just want to dock at my time island for a quick chat; he wanted to take over the whole place. I'd either have to leave Emily at the office or bring her in the car. Both would be difficult to keep from Katharina. Doing either would shatter the promise to save our relationship I'd so solemnly made to Katharina less than an hour earlier. When I'm taking care of Emily, I'm taking care of Emily, no one else. That was the deal. And now that would all be destroyed? By this arsehole, of all fucking people?

'Dragan, please, I've got my little girl here with me! I can't go driving halfway across Europe with you in the boot.'

'You don't need to drive me across Europe, just out of town. Emma will love sitting in front.'

Emma? That was just too much. I yelled at him, 'Emily! The kid whose weekend you're ruining is called *Emily*!'

Luckily, these staff rooms were soundproofed fairly well.

Dragan yelled back, 'Fuck Emilia! This is about *my* life!'

Then he became very still and stated: 'I'm going down to the car park, where Sasha will lock me in your boot. You'll come down with Emilia, and then you'll drive me out of town. When the cops see you with your little brat, they'll never suspect you've got someone hidden in the boot.'

Fuck Emilia? Little brat? Did the guy who was making me break the serious promise I had made my wife to save my family just call my precious angel a brat?

'Her name is Emily, you wanker . . .'

I froze. What had I done? Directly insulted the most brutal gangster in town? That wasn't very mindful of me, a better word would be . . . suicidal.

Dragan stood up, grabbed me by the collar with both hands and got right in my face. I could smell the nicotine on his breath.

'Nobody. Calls. Me. A. Wanker.' He was breathing heavily. 'If I didn't need you for my escape, you'd be dead. If you don't do exactly as I ask, you'll no longer have a child, nor be able to make a new one. Is that clear?'

I nodded. 'Crystal,' I croaked out. I didn't recognise my own voice.

Dragan shoved me back into my chair and sat back down.

'Well then, if you get me to safety, I'm prepared to forget this little incident. But if you screw this up, mister lawyer man, if the escape doesn't work, if for some reason I don't end up safe but with the coppers, you're a dead man. Is that clear?'

I nodded again. My thoughts were racing, but I couldn't think of any way out of this. Alive, that is. I had to bend to Dragan's will, get him out of here. Maybe I could even make sure Emily never had to know about Dragan. Maybe I could still drive Emily to the lake house after. If I was lucky, if I was really fucking lucky . . . Katharina wouldn't even have to find out what happened.

'That'd be obstruction of justice,' I sheepishly wheezed. This put a smile on Dragan's face.

'There he is again, my smart-arse!'

'And where should I take you?'

'Take me to the lake house! That'll give me a bit of a breather.'

I slumped in my chair. This was an utter low point for me as a husband, a father, a lawyer. I was done.

But at that very moment, when even the last spark of hope was about to go out, something fantastic happened. Right then, my entire twelve-week mindfulness training really paid off. Like a celestial glow beaming through the black clouds brewing over my soul, I felt a complete calmness within me. In this sudden moment of clarity, I saw myself standing outside Breitner's door again, too late and wondering whether I should ring a second time. My inner voice said: When I'm waiting outside a door, I'm waiting outside a door.

When I'm 'going for ice cream' with a hardened criminal, I'm 'going for ice cream' with a hardened criminal.

When I'm driving a getaway car, I'm driving a getaway car.

When I'm at the lake, I'm at the lake.

It was so clear. It was so simple.

Thinking through every single scenario, all the possible consequences for my daughter, my marriage, my freedom, none of it would be any help. I might be heading straight for a fall, but that also meant I hadn't yet actually fallen.

I surveyed the situation: one floor above me, at that very moment, was my daughter, my squeakily cheerful daughter, and I would be spending the weekend with her one way or another. I was still alive, I had a wife who didn't know what I was doing, and I wasn't in prison.

Right then, all was true and plumb. There was simply no way to know what might happen at a later date. So there was absolutely no point in being afraid of this later date before it even arrived.

'Fine,' I said. 'Here are the keys. I'll see you in the car park.'

Dragan took the car keys with a look that probably meant 'why not right away?' Then he got up and took the lift down. I waited for it to come back up and headed to the fourth floor.

In my office, I kept several prepaid phones in the bottom drawer of my desk. Although the legal hurdles for a warrant to tap a lawyer's phone were enormous, the technical hurdles were not.

If Dragan really wanted to go into hiding, we needed a secure means of communication.

If I was planning an escape, I was planning an escape.

I hated my job, but I knew how to do it.

8

Relaxation Triangle

When you notice a new tension, you should realise three things:

1. You do not have to change anything.
2. You do not have to explain anything.
3. You do not have to judge anything.

To relax, you do not have to do anything. Even just noticing and accepting the tension often works wonders. You also do not have to root out the cause of the tension. Just allow yourself to be tense. Know that you do not have to judge how the tension affects you. Let the tension be tension – and notice how that makes the tension pass on its own.

Joschka Breitner, *Slowing Down in the Fast Lane: Mindfulness for Managers*

As soon as I got to my office, the phone rang. Ms Bregenz icily informed me that Peter Egmann, Detective Chief Inspector of the Homicide Command, was on the line. I'd known Peter since our student days. We both took an early interest in criminal law. His criminological skills were good enough for the civil service, so he got a homicide squad. My legal skills were too good for the civil service's low salary, so I got a homicidal maniac.

Peter had a functioning marriage and a son Emily's age. We respected each other, even though we were usually on opposite sides of the law.

Though it wasn't easy, I tried my hardest to sound my usual cheerful self.

'Morning, Peter, what can I do for you?'

'Have you seen your favourite client today?'

'You know I won't answer that.'

'You might have already seen him on TV, or online?'

'I'm not answering that either.'

'If you do see him or speak to him in person, can you please pass him a message from me?'

'If you want to talk to him so badly, why don't you look for him yourself? Don't you get paid for that kind of thing?'

'I'm well aware how close you two are. So, if you see him, just tell him thanks: solving a murder has never been easier.'

'I've no idea what you're talking about.'

'Then why are you at the office on a Saturday morning?'

'Because my daughter wanted to play lawyer.'

'How do you play lawyer?'

'By colouring on court decisions in our conference room.'

'My son likes to do that with arrest warrants at police headquarters – but Dragan's arrest warrant already looks quite colourful even without his embellishments.'

'Let's hear it then, Peter. What do you want from me?'

'Tell him to turn himself in. It'd save *all* of us a lot of trouble.'

'Hope you have a great weekend too.'

I hung up. After grabbing two prepaid phones, I turned off my own phone and went down one floor.

Fortunately, I remembered Breitner's three essential rules of mindfulness:

First, take things as they are. When you're tense, you're tense.

Second, accept it. Don't even try to account for the tension. Allow yourself to be tense.

And third, don't judge the situation as either good or bad.

So I accepted that I was violating all points of my agreement with Katharina. I accepted that I would take a psychopath along in my boot as I drove to the lake house where I'd wanted to spend the weekend relaxing with my daughter. And I decided not to judge that situation.

I also tried to see the positive in the here and now: I was picking up my daughter and taking her to the lake!

In the conference room, numerous court decisions, five of the fifteen leather chairs *and* the cherry-wood table had all been successfully used as canvases. When Emily saw me, she ran into my arms, beaming with joy. She was clearly delighted about all the fun things you could do at a law firm.

'Daddy! I drew a really big picture.'

'How wonderful. Let's see . . . But that's marvellous! You know what, it's so nice, we'll leave that up here at the firm.'

'Can't we take it with us?'

'Aren't we going on our mini-break?'

'To the lake?'

'To the lake.'

I thanked Clara for watching Emily and asked her to tell Ms Bregenz to please clean the conference room.

'Don't you want to wish Auntie Bregenz a nice weekend?' I said to Emily as we walked past the reception desk on our way to the lift. To my great delight, Emily said no.

When we got to the underground car park, I could see from afar that Dragan and Sasha were leaning against my Audi A8 company car and smoking. The boot was open. My meticulously packed weekend bags with towels, sunscreen, mixed nuts, Capri-Suns and so on had been carelessly tossed next to the car. The ice-cream van was parked immediately to the right.

I had to think quick: how could I sneak Emily past Dragan?

I picked her up.

'Emily, let's play a game.'

'What kind of game?'

'You'll keep your eyes closed, then I'll say a magic spell. And when I tell you to open your eyes again, you'll be in ice-cream fairyland. OK?'

'OK.'

Emily squished her eyes shut. I ran to the ice-cream van, putting my finger to my lips so Dragan and Sasha wouldn't talk to me. Of course, Dragan did so anyway.

'What's this? Hasn't Evelyn ever seen a murderer?' he roared with a grin.

I glared at him and headed to the ice-cream van, holding my hand in front of Emily's eyes to make sure.

'Daddy, who's there?'

'Oh, no one. Just some people standing by their car and being silly.'

'What is a murderer?'

'That's not important, darling. OK, now get ready for your surprise . . .'

At least the quick-witted Sasha understood what I was doing. He put his hand on Dragan's shoulder and said, 'Boss, don't you want anything to drink for while you're in the boot?'

'For those few miles? Forget about it. It'd only make a mess if I tried to drink anything all scrunched up.'

I was infinitely grateful to Sasha for his distraction.

In the meantime, I had carried Emily into the ice-cream van.

'Alright, open your eyes!'

'First the magic spell!'

'What?'

'You said you would say a magic spell and then we'd get to ice-cream fairyland.'

Emily kept her eyes closed.

'You're right. Ready? Hocus-pocus, one two three . . . Uhm . . . Abracadabra, alakazam, ice-cream fairyland, here we come!'

Emily's eyes were like saucers. She was surrounded by every kind of ice cream. Like an oversized watercolour set, refrigerated containers all around held ice cream in all the colours of the rainbow – in accounting terms, however, this set-up made it possible to turn illegal prostitution revenue into harmless pocket money. And I didn't want Emily to see the man who used this ice-cream van to line his pockets, so she needed to stay inside for a while.

'OK, Emily, try any flavour you like, Daddy will be right back, alright?'

'Ooohhhh.' That meant 'OK'.

I got out, closed the door and went over to Dragan.

He gave me a mocking look. 'Abracadabra? Why are you talking shite?'

'Shite? Didn't you say to separate work and family? Emily doesn't necessarily have to see what we're doing here, right?' I took the daddy-daughter weekend bags and stowed them on the back seat. 'You'll stick to the plan?'

'Duh. And if you want your daughter to have any more ice cream in the future, you better not do anything stupid.'

Turning to Sasha, he said, 'Thanks for your help. You won't see me for a minute.'

And then he uttered the sentence that would irrevocably steer my life onto a new path: 'Björn will help me disappear, and in my absence he'll tell you and the others how to conduct our business. Tell the officers.'

I thought I must've misheard: I was going to do *what*?

Dragan apparently wanted me to be a hand puppet in his underworld Punch and Judy show. And he would be the puppet master. So far, at least in my eyes, it had always been the other way around: I was consulting from backstage, and no one had any idea what I was doing.

The roles were relatively clearly assigned. Organised crime is characterised by the fact that it is, as the name already suggests, organised. And Dragan's organisation was no exception. I had created enough organisational charts for him to know who was operating at which level. At the lowest level, you had the 'groupies' who wanted to join the gang and did little tasks for little money: replenishing drug depots, setting fire to shops, beating people up. They weren't interested in the big picture and had no idea who was running the show. If they were caught, they couldn't give anything away except that someone had given them a hundred euros for putting a package into a locker or smacking someone into intensive care.

Then there were the 'soldiers', whose admission into this level required them to have at least seriously injured several competitors. They did the actual dirty work, transporting drugs and weapons on a large scale and personally inflicting the requisite violence upon bar owners, sex workers and business partners. If they were caught, they kept quiet. Because they'd end up in prison one way or another – and grasses didn't fare well in prison. Usually, it was Sasha who told the soldiers what Dragan wanted them to do.

Then there were 'specialists': weapons experts, laboratory bosses and people like me – the lawyer. My speciality basically was knowing everything Dragan knew. All the names, all the accounts, all the deals. I advised him on strategic decisions and took care of all legal obstacles, but I wasn't part of his organisation. After all these years, my last foothold in the legal world was that I was strictly billing him my employer's hourly fees. Though the bills exceeded my monthly salary many times over, this allowed me to convince myself I was at least financially independent from Dragan.

At the top of the hierarchy, right below Dragan, were the 'officers'. These were people who had become financially and personally intertwined with the gang over the years. These associates enjoyed a certain latitude and, in addition to their salary, also got a cut of the profits. They were managing directors of the front companies that laundered the money. Blokes like Toni, who officially ran a management company for bars and clubs but actually ran the organisation's entire drugs branch. There was also someone like him on weapons and prostitution. Each pillar was headed by an officer who officially was the managing director of a completely legal company.

In my day-to-day business, I kept in touch with the officers, took care of leases and employment contracts, making sure these facades looked clean as a whistle. Aside from Dragan, I was the only one who knew the entire constellation – when it came to the details, probably even better than Dragan himself. And in Dragan's imminent absence, I was supposed to take charge of these officers?

I thought about Emily. I thought about my life. If I wanted to save both, I had to do what Dragan wanted. And if I did what Dragan wanted, nothing would ever be the same again. Cheers, bellend!

Dragan disappeared into the boot without a word. For someone who was six-foot-four and over fifteen and a half stone, he slipped in relatively elegantly. Dragan made himself comfortable on an old down sleeping bag Sasha had found somewhere, or at least he tried. Curled up in a foetal position, he gave us a thumbs-up. He reminded me of a monstrous creature trapped in a much-too-small specimen jar in some dusty anatomical collection. Only that the specimen jar was unfortunately my boot, and the creature very much alive.

Sasha closed the boot and the lock clicked.

'Thanks for distracting him earlier,' I said.

'Of course. Children shouldn't be involved in this kind of stuff.'

'No one should be involved in this kind of stuff.'

'We can't choose our lives. We can only live them.'

Maybe I should quote that to Breitner some time, if I ever saw him again. Before I could say anything more, Sasha disappeared behind the windowless back of the ice-cream van. This way, Emily wouldn't have to see Sasha either, and I wouldn't have to explain anything to her.

I opened the door of the van. Inside stood my little girl, bopping to a cheerful tune she was humming to herself. She was covered all over in different shades of pink and red. I needed to quickly switch: from the torment of my professional life back to the bliss of being with my daughter.

'Well, how'd you like your surprise, love?'

I wiped Emily's mouth with the hem of her dress, the one part that didn't have ice cream on it yet.

'Look, these are my favourite colours. I love them so much!' she exclaimed.

'And I love *you* so much.'

I picked Emily up, kissed her and carried her to her car seat. On the way, my knees nearly buckled. Something in me was vehemently against putting her in the same car that contained a psychopath who'd threatened both our lives. But I didn't have a choice. I forced myself to recite my mindfulness mantra:

When I'm carrying my daughter, I'm carrying my daughter. When I'm getting into a car, I'm getting into a car.

I would take my daughter to the lake house as we had planned. In that moment, nothing else mattered. As for anything else, time would tell.

I clicked Emily into the car seat.

'I want Chicken McNuggets and chocolate milk,' she said.

It had been an eternity since I'd promised her that, and yet only half an hour had passed.

'You just had ice cream.'

'But no Chicken McNuggets.'

'I think McDonald's is already shut for the day. They're not taking any more orders today.'

'You have to ask.'

'OK, I'll ask.'

Another promise I wouldn't be able to keep. While I had a murderer in the boot of my car, I wanted to get out of the city as quickly as possible, not waste any more time at some drive-in counter.

I drove us out of the underground car park. Sasha would stay inside and wait, exiting through the ice-cream shop as a customer some time after they opened.

It was unbearable for me to pretend to my daughter that I was in a good mood and we'd go to McDonald's and then head to the lake to feed the fish as planned. But to my happy surprise, I could soon vent my frustration, as our first, unscheduled stop came quickly. At the ramp's exit stood Klaus Möller, one of the two plain-clothes policemen who'd obviously been watching the firm since this morning. A rather simple soul, he unfortunately looked just like a punching bag.

So, because I'd always wanted to do something like this, because my daughter expected it from me and because my mindful mind could practically no longer give a fuck, I rolled down my window and said to him:

'One order of Chicken McNuggets.'

'And chocolate milk,' Emily added.

'Pardon? I'm not taking orders—'

'See, Emily, McDonald's is already shut.' At least that took McDonald's off the table.

'Boo,' Emily grumbled.

I turned back to Möller. 'So what can I do for you?'

'Routine traffic check. Could you please get out of the vehicle.'

Now this I could manage. I could solve a purely legal problem in my sleep.

'Mr Möller, you can only carry out routine traffic checks in routine traffic. Since you are standing on the ramp of my underground car park, we're on private property. So please save us both all the paperwork of me filing a police complaint against you and just tell me what you want.'

'Have you seen Dragan?'

'Yes, I've got him in my boot.'

I have no idea whether this was when Dragan first wet that sleeping bag.

'Oh really?'

'Sure, there was no more room in the front, as my daughter's sitting there.'

'And why is your daughter sitting in the front?'

'Because here she can be clipped into the car seat, whereas she'd get ice cream all over the boot.'

'I was asking why her seat is not fitted in the back.'

'Because there is no regulation that forces me to secure a child in the back seat. It can be placed in the front just as well, provided that the passenger airbag does not pose a danger to the child, as would be the case with a baby car seat, for example. Do you have children, Mr Möller?'

Möller brushed the question aside with a vague wave of his hand. 'I just wanted to know if you've seen Dragan—'

'As I told your boss on the phone earlier, I neither have to nor will I provide any information about this. You have a nice day now.'

Without any further explanation, I slid the window shut. Möller stepped aside and I accelerated. Emily and I were off to the lake. Dragan was too.

9

Single-tasking

Everyone is ruled by the same clock; we only differ
in how we want to use the time we get. The more
you want to get done in any period of time, the
more stress you feel. This is called multitasking.
Consider what is most important to you and first
do only that. This is called single-tasking. Once
you are done with that first task, move on to the
next-important one. You will find that even before
you finish, you will no longer feel any pressure –
and be left with time to spare.

> Joschka Breitner, *Slowing Down in the
> Fast Lane: Mindfulness for Managers*

Whether the ride was tolerable for Dragan, I do not know. One of the nicest things about an Audi A8 is its sound system. If you turn up the volume in the front even half-way, the criminal in the boot might shout as loud as he can – you won't hear anything but 'The Teddy Bears' Picnic'. On our trip to the lake, I felt myself relax. If I looked at it mindfully, little had actually changed. Sure, we were a good hour late and I had a bad guy in my boot. But otherwise, wasn't this weekend going entirely to plan? Before we even got on the motorway Emily was already asking for nuts to snack on and songs to sing along to, the ultimate signs our mini-break had started. And if my little one was enjoying the ride, so should I. At least I could try. I owed Emily as much. So I tried to see Dragan for what he was: some work I'd brought from the office and tossed in the boot. It was the weekend, work could wait. For the next hour I wasn't supposed to do anything else but drive anyway.

Two rounds of 'The Lion Sleeps Tonight' and one 'Teddy Bears' Picnic' later, the A8 passed through the electric gate, seventy metres later coming to a gritty halt on the gravel in front of the house. The sun was hot and high overhead. Though the house was picturesquely situated on a perfect plot, you could only enjoy it if you had access. Surrounded on three sides by a three-metre-high iron fence completely enclosed by conifers, the property was only open to the lake. Outsiders could just catch a glimpse of the house from the water. From the road, the only access point was the electric gate. Passing the house on the left, you could drive to a boathouse without being seen from the lake. To the right of the boathouse, some reeds rustled on the shore and a wooden jetty extended about fifteen metres into the lake. On the other side of the jetty was a small sandy beach with a barbecue area. The house itself was also fairly well shielded from view by bushes and hedges.

I'd been quietly hoping Emily would fall asleep on the drive; that way, I could let Dragan into the house unnoticed. But she'd been wide awake the whole way. When I turned off the engine and the music, a knocking could be heard from the boot. I walked around the car, but before I could unbuckle Emily from her child seat, she noticed the sound.

'Daddy, what's that sound?' she asked.

'That's . . . work. Daddy left some work in the boot. I should bring it inside right away.'

There are moments when even two-and-a-half-year-olds can suddenly seem very wise and grown-up. This was one of them. Emily raised her index finger and looked at me gravely: 'Daddy, but work is not good. A trip is good. First we do the trip, then you can work.'

Anyone else would probably find it precocious for a thirty-month-old to pronounce life lessons to a forty-two-year-old. But when it's your own daughter, all emotional barriers fall away. 'Out of the mouths of babes' doesn't even begin to reflect the pride a parent feels when they realise that slumbering inside their child might be the next Dalai Lama. My daughter had just independently invented the notion of time islands.

'First our trip, then work,' I repeated. That solved all our problems.

On closer inspection, Emily's approach was a combination of time islands and the philosophy of 'single-tasking'. A time island meant not being disturbed while inside its protected space; single-tasking meant that disturbing things should be processed bit by bit, not all at the same time.

So, according to all the tenets of mindfulness, there was no reason at all to let Dragan out of the boot now. What could he even do, call the police?

My mindfulness guide included page upon page of advice on time islands: you should turn off your phone, ignore the vacuum cleaner and not water any flowers – simply be mindful of yourself and your needs. The time island rules might not explicitly state that you aren't allowed to let mobsters out of your boot, but if you stuck to the single-tasking approach, it was entirely obvious.

After long dehumanising weeks of 'convincing' people, what I needed was to finally enjoy some time with my daughter. Just for a lousy thirty-six hours to sit on the jetty, eat some nuts, feed the fish. I shouldn't deprive myself of that simply because of my exaggerated sense of duty. Usually, I had to force myself to practise mindfulness, but somehow I didn't have to now.

On the contrary, if I let the bloke out of the boot now, it would all be over and done with instantly: Emily's weekend, the fishing, the swimming, the nuts. Plus, Daddy would have lied. Worse, Daddy would suddenly become this criminal's finger puppet. And of course Emily would tell Katharina about it. Then our mindfully reconstructed relationship would collapse, and I'd no longer be allowed to spend any real time with Emily at all.

In that moment, I could imagine no sequence of events I could live with that would involve opening the boot. If I simply left the boot closed, on the other hand, everything would remain as it was.

With the car key in my hand, I looked back and forth between my daughter and the boot.

In my head, I heard the voices of Breitner, Katharina and Dragan:

'You don't have to do what you don't want to.'

'If you screw this up, you won't see Emily again.'

'If I didn't need you for my escape, you'd be dead.'

The solution was so simple. It was that advice that had touched me so deeply back in Breitner's first mindfulness lesson: *I don't have to do what I don't want to do. I am free.*

Dragan was work. Work could wait. I put the car key in my pocket and helped Emily out of her seat.

'You know what? How about we go and sit on the jetty, eat some nuts and feed the fish?'

'Yay!'

*

For the rest of the day, Dragan didn't even enter my mind. Though just a hundred metres away in the car, my work felt light years away.

I sat on the jetty with Emily and nibbled some nuts. While sailboats went by, far from shore, we spat bits of nut into the water to feed the fish. We jumped into the lake. We built sandcastles on the beach.

And while I sprayed Emily with factor-50 sunscreen every thirty minutes, out in the blazing sun in front of the house Dragan's boot steadily heated up to 59.7 degrees.

I'm not a doctor, but lawyers need to be skilled at reading up on new topics. Thanks to the internet, I was later able to compare Dragan's day to ours. While we were sitting on the jetty, the boot was already an estimated 23 degrees warmer than Dragan's body, which would've initially tried to keep its temperature at the usual 36.7 degrees by producing as much sweat as possible in order to cool down. The blood vessels in his skin would've widened to give off heat through increased blood circulation. Perhaps Dragan tried to free himself from the boot – which is difficult when you're a colossus caught in a cramped space and cannot exercise your full strength. In any case, any experiments along those lines did not achieve a positive result, only a further increase in temperature. By the time Emily and I first jumped into the cool water of the lake, Dragan's pulse must have noticeably sped up. He probably felt dizzy and nauseated. Since he had nothing to drink, his sweat production eventually ceased, perhaps around when Emily and I stuck the straws from our empty Capri-Suns into our sandcastle like flagpoles. When we jumped into the lake for the second time after a short nap in the shade of the boathouse, Dragan's body could've no longer fought off the heat due to an inability to produce more sweat. His body temperature would have already topped 40 degrees Celsius. A classic matter of heat accumulation. At some point, his entire cardiovascular system collapsed, his organs no longer adequately supplied with oxygen. His brain would've started experiencing outages, his consciousness increasingly impaired.

I think by the time we were toasting our first marsh-mallows on the beach, Dragan was probably dead. For Emily and me, it was a great day. For Dragan, his last. As fate ironically had it, I enjoyed a day of mindful relaxation while Dragan died of burnout.

10

Happiness

Happiness is not some award that is bestowed upon you. The source of happiness is within us. This is why we should not try to seek happiness outside of ourselves. We can only find it inside of us.

Joschka Breitner, *Slowing Down in the Fast Lane: Mindfulness for Managers*

After toasting the marshmallows, we sat on the beach for a while longer. Emily snuggled up on my lap as I told her the story of 'Hans in Luck', her favourite of the Grimms' fairy tales. And before Hans had even exchanged his piece of silver for a horse, she'd fallen asleep in my arms. I carried her into the house, tucked her in, and turned on the baby monitor. Once I'd got a bottle of wine, a corkscrew and a glass from the kitchen, I sat down on the jetty with the baby monitor.

Back in the kitchen was the first time I'd considered going to check on Dragan, see whether he was angry – I stopped short: or whether he was still alive at all. I considered the summer heat and the fact that Dragan hadn't brought anything to drink in the boot, the idiot. That's when I was struck with a sudden panic. If I opened the boot, there were only two possible outcomes: either I'd killed my client or my client would kill me. But as long as the boot remained closed, I was spared both. So why should I open it now? Out of curiosity? To ruin a perfectly lovely day? How stupid would I have to be to do that? A pile of work doesn't get any smaller the more you look at it. And at that moment, I just didn't want to deal with the fact that whatever happened would be unpleasant. Later, yes, but not just yet.

So instead I stood up, legs shoulder-width apart, knees slightly bent, chest out. I breathed, I felt. For about a minute, but that was enough. I was substantially calmer, and I remembered that Breitner had impressed upon me that happiness requires discipline: *It's not always simple to simply be happy.* I couldn't help but smile as I repeated the mantra my daughter had gifted me today: *First our trip, then work.* Create a time island for yourself, stick to single-tasking. I would table the Dragan issue for the rest of the weekend.

I sat back down on the jetty and let my gaze drift over the water. For the first time in a long time, I felt enjoyably carefree, somehow . . . lighter. I didn't know if that was the right word. I just felt . . . happy? Yes, that was it. I was happy to sit on the warm wood of the jetty with a glass of wine and listen to my daughter's peaceful breathing on the baby monitor. The sailboats were all gone. All except for one that'd apparently dropped anchor out on the lake. As the water lapped against the jetty's pilings, I thought about 'Hans in Luck'. What a numpty that Hans was. After serving his master well for seven years, he's given his freedom and a piece of silver as big as his head. He sets off for home and trades his silver for a horse, only to find it goes too fast. He trades the horse for a cow that's too old to produce any milk. He trades the cow for a pig that turns out to be stolen. The pig he trades for a goose, the goose for a grindstone, which rolls into a pond. Arriving back at his mum's empty-handed, Hans cannot believe his luck: he's finally free of everything!

Emily loved changing up the story. In her latest version, Hans traded the cow for a suitcase full of caramels and four horses. Hans ate it all and got to his mum's with four horses in his tummy and unable to believe his luck. First and foremost because having four horses in your belly must feel funny, but the moral of the fairy tale was still the same: a bad barterer gleefully skips home with nothing but his freedom.

For some reason, my daughter loved this foolish loser who lets himself be bamboozled by everyone he meets and ends up with nothing – nothing, that is, but his freedom.

What was that freedom thing again? *Freedom means not having to do what you do not want to do.* That was the day it must have really sunk in.

Basically, I was the total opposite of Hans. When I finished law school, I hadn't received a piece of silver but a diploma and my freedom. The freedom to no longer have to study, but to do what I wanted with my life. And not to do what I didn't want to do. Unlike Hans, I wasn't heading back to some ominous place called home. I didn't have one yet, so I set out into the world. And I didn't start trading in my wages but my freedom. And what did I get in return?

I traded my freedom for financial obligations to live with a woman I essentially had little in common with. I traded all the lives I could have in this world for a narrow career ladder that was going nowhere. I traded my abstract idea of success for a concrete company car. I traded my sense of justice for vast amounts of money from a hardened criminal. And each trade got me more and more entangled, more dependent on his crime syndicate. Everything I'd received in turn for my freedom now lay in the boot of my Audi A8, and none of it meant anything to me.

So who was I, of all people, to call this Hans an idiot?

On the other hand, if I hadn't made those trades, I'd never in my wildest dreams have found a home like the one I shared with Emily. That precious creature sleeping behind me in the house, she meant everything to me.

It was becoming high time I tossed my grindstone into the pond – but not today.

First our trip, then work.

The bottle of wine was empty and I went back into the house. The solitary boat on the lake stayed where it was. Yes, I was happy.

II

Awakening

Mindfulness means focusing your gaze.
Mindfulness does not mean closing your eyes.
After spending time recharging your batteries, you
have to put them to use. The transition between
these phases is like waking up. Don't fight it.
Allow your breath to flow freely. Let it happen.
Mindfully commit to the task that awaits you.

Joschka Breitner, *Slowing Down in the*
Fast Lane: Mindfulness for Managers

I slept dreamlessly, deeply, happily. I only woke up once, when a little person toddled up and said, 'Daddy, I want to sleep in the big bed,' and I let her climb into bed to cuddle up. As a reward, I was awakened on Sunday morning with a barefoot kick to the face, shoe-size five. It woke Emily up too, and she looked sleepily round the room. When her gaze fell on the balcony door and she saw the lake beyond, she opened her eyes wide, took a deep breath and shouted: 'Daddy, look, the lake's still there!'

It's amazing when children make you realise that the beauty of the world around us is not a matter of course, but a cause for joy.

How fleeting adults' worries were in comparison. Having trouble with something at work? New trouble will surely follow tomorrow. The lake's still there. The lake will even be there when the job's long over. So why wake up and immediately worry about some godforsaken trouble at work when you could look at a lake instead? So I took a deep breath too and looked at the lake. Another one of those exercises from the mindfulness book that worked. It successfully suppressed the realisation that someone from my work setting who'd come to the lake alive would, for the first time in his life, not be waking up at all.

But today was still our mini-break. First our trip, then work.

A magpie flew onto the balcony ledge and gave us a look.

'The bird wants us to have breakfast outside,' Emily helpfully translated.

So we had breakfast on the terrace. The magpie kept us company to the extent that, by the time we were done, it had stolen two teaspoons and almost one salt shaker. Afterwards, I got the wooden motorboat out of the boathouse and we took it out onto the lake. When we came back, I cooked us some spaghetti – which we ate on the jetty so we could also use it to fish with. When it comes to fishing, spaghetti is simply an unbeatable triple threat: fishing rod, line *and* bait.

Our visit was already coming to an end. Since a cleaning lady would be tidying the guest rooms and the kitchen, all I had to do was put our bags in the car and take Emily back to her mother. As I collected our things in the kitchen, I spotted a high-tech infrared thermometer on a shelf. I took it to the front door and aimed it at my boot: it registered a temperature of 59.7 degrees.

I stowed our bags on the back seat. When I strapped Emily into her car seat, she wrinkled her nose. 'It smells funny in here, Daddy.'

I took a sniff myself and noticed a slightly sweetish sour smell. A mixture of sweat, urine and . . . decomposition. It was almost entirely subliminal, like when you're fresh out of the shower and put on a jumper that's been in your gym bag for a week. Still, a significant irritant in the new car, which otherwise smelled only of leather and high-quality plastics.

'That's . . . the work I put in the boot.'

'Can you throw it away?'

'I'll get rid of it later, sweetheart. Until then we can open the window instead, alright?'

'Do you have any gummy bears?'

I gave Emily a small bag of gummy bears and rolled down the windows. After ten minutes, Emily was happily asleep, all worn out from our day on the water.

I don't know if it was because of the open windows or because a sleeping Emily could no longer distract my slowly reappearing negative thoughts – but a slight shiver came over me. In the very near future, I'd have to face the problem in my boot. Given the subliminal smell plus the temperature I'd measured earlier, I surmised that Dragan wouldn't be of any help in this.

I'd never had to rack my brain over how to dispose of a corpse before. Toni and Sasha had done it plenty of times – dispose of corpses, that is, not necessarily rack their brains. But I wanted to involve neither Toni nor Sasha in this new sphere of my legal work, not to mention the staff of the waste-to-energy facility they used for this.

But when we'd taken the motorboat out that morning, I had noticed that the front of the boathouse had a very professionally furnished workshop. It had axes and chainsaws, even a professional wood chipper – nineteen horsepower, eighteen-centimetre log diameter, four-stroke petrol engine and a 360-degree rotating discharge. It also had tarpaulins, spades and a wheelbarrow. Probably everything necessary to dispose of a man built like a tree. In the laundry room back at the house, I'd also spotted several bottles of bleach.

I looked over at my sleeping angel. The warm, low sunlight on Emily's face flickered rhythmically in the shade of the trees lining the road: light, shadow, light, shadow. Like a film being played in slow motion so you could see every frame – and each one showed my daughter. I liked the film I was in just then, and part of this film involved me having to take care of the contents of my boot later. That was OK.

We had reached the motorway and I swiftly drove us back to town. Emily only woke up when we were almost there.

'Are we still at the lake?'

'No, honey, we're almost back at Mum's.'

'That was lovely at the lake. Can we go there again some time?'

Another mantra for me: *'That was lovely at the lake.'*

'All the time, sweetheart.'

Katharina was happy to see Emily again. Emily was happy to tell her mum all about the fish, the boat and the marshmallows. And I was happy Emily didn't have anything to tell her about gangsters or abruptly altered plans.

Katharina also seemed very relaxed. Whereas just three months ago, when I was still living at home, she could no longer even manage small talk, she was now brightly telling me about her spa weekend and the fabulous hotel. The same hotel, funnily enough, where I'd originally found Breitner's flyer.

The three of us tried to outdo each other in who'd had the nicest water, the softest bed, the sunniest sun.

At some point, Katharina broke off her laughter and with surprising seriousness said: 'It's nice to have a laugh about things we did while we weren't together.'

I couldn't disagree.

We had a coffee, and Katharina asked if I had an hour to spare for her in the next few days. She wanted to sort out a few things with me about the kindergarten registrations. It apparently was anything but a smooth ride, but nothing that should spoil the end of this great weekend.

I promised to call in the next week, said goodbye to Emily and Katharina – and drove back to the lake.

That was lovely at the lake, I said to myself. And no small part of that lovely experience was due to the fact that I'd left Dragan in the boot. So now when I would concentrate on my client, I'd be concentrating on a part of this lovely weekend. That thought already took some of the dramatics out of the work that was ahead of me. The time had come to use the energy I had gathered over the weekend.

First, however, I should say that, for me, this weekend's mindful murder had indeed been the solution to all my problems: I had defended my time island, kept my promise to Katharina, and it certainly looked like Dragan would no longer disturb any of my time islands ever again.

From a strictly rational perspective, the weekend had also been a complete success for Dragan. Only one day earlier we both assumed he would end up either in jail or in Boris's clutches. Today, both options were off the table once and for all. The police could no longer arrest him because he was dead; Boris could no longer kill him because I'd already done so.

The downside of my ingenious solution was that, although I may have been rid of all my existential problems from the previous day, now I was stuck with a few not insignificant new ones.

First of all, I was now apparently a murderer, albeit by omission. I took a moment to hear what my conscience had to say about this. I listened for quite a long time. But concerning this matter, I didn't think it presented much of an issue. To put it in more mindful words: I had done nothing wrong. Quite the opposite, my omission had achieved something good. I had prevented something much worse from happening to my daughter and me. So morally, what I'd done was really quite commendable.

Considering my professional dealings with the police, however, I knew they didn't operate according to such strictly mindful standards. And they had very different ideas about what might constitute commendable behaviour. If the police learned Dragan was dead, they'd start looking for his killer, regardless of whether Dragan was a bad person or not. I didn't have the slightest interest in becoming a murder suspect just because I was the lawyer who'd successfully taken him out of the firing line.

Which immediately led to the next two problems: I couldn't even bill him for my brilliant lawyerly performance. Were the firm to learn that Dragan was dead, I would've lost my only client, at which point they could also immediately dispose of me, his bleurgh-lawyer. So Dragan's demise might've saved my life, but if anyone found out, it could still cost me my job.

Boris, the head of the rival gang, posed a completely different problem. As long as he assumed Dragan was alive, he'd be out for blood. Yet if he were to learn that Dragan was dead, he'd no longer be looking for Dragan but looking to become his successor instead – which would lead to turf battles and any amount of bother. And if there was any doubt about his condition, a lot of people whose lives I'd turned upside down for Dragan would want to turn their lives right-side-up again. And though I now had plenty of time due to my lack of a client, I somehow didn't feel like dealing with all that in the slightest.

It was still completely unclear to me who had lured Dragan into that lay-by or why. I really had to discuss that with Sasha, as this unknown was the biggest in my calculations.

And above all: Dragan's gang would not think very well of me if they learned that their boss had joined the choir invisible beneath my Audi's power-operated boot lid.

It was therefore best for everyone involved if no one found out that Dragan was lacking a pulse and therefore no longer my client.

It had to look like Dragan had just disappeared from the scene, as he had many times before. At some point, he'd always shown up again. And hadn't he explicitly told Sasha that I was to represent him during his absence? There you go. All I had to do was to keep passing Sasha idiotic pseudo-instructions and no one would miss the boss much. I didn't even need Dragan's entire body as a proof of life, just his thumb.

The reason for that was simple. Dragan and his officers had built a communication system that was as old-school as it was effective. He'd take a random page from that day's newspaper, circle words, letters, numbers, and connect them into sentences. He'd then initial the page with his scarred thumb, into which he'd had branded an unmistakable 'D'. He'd send the newspaper page to his officer, who could then, based on the date of the newspaper and the thumbprint, determine the timeliness and authenticity of the instructions, and burn the page after reading. This way, they didn't produce any evidence that could be presented at trial.

So all I needed to keep Dragan alive indefinitely was his right thumb. The rest of him could disappear. In general, it shouldn't be too difficult to sell Dragan's death as merely a deliberate disappearance. After all, that kind of death really only differs from a rather long absence in that the person fails to eventually come back.

Sure, at some point there would certainly be questions, uncomfortable questions even – but not just yet. I decided to continue living mindfully in the here and now, and not be distracted by any questions I might be asked in the distant future. One step at a time. Dragan's death was a result of my mindful new approach to lawyering. And I wanted to take my next steps mindfully and full of love for myself. And the very first step was to get that massive bastard and his probably piss-soaked sleeping bag out of my boot.

12

Intentional Centring

Even the longest journey starts with one small step. If you take each step mindfully, you will not be exhausted at the end of your journey, but alleviated. Therefore, as you take each step, focus on what *constitutes* that step:

1. Take in the purpose of what you are about to do.
2. In- and exhale once.
3. Perform the task in a calm and centred manner.

Joschka Breitner, *Slowing Down in the Fast Lane: Mindfulness for Managers*

Around six o'clock I got back to the lake house, made sure the gate closed behind me, drove past the house and backed the car up to the boathouse. After I got out, I checked to make sure I couldn't be seen from either the road or the lake.

The boathouse had the dimensions of a long double garage. The front section had a concrete floor, shelves with tools and boating equipment on either wall – a small but more than lavishly equipped DIY workshop.

In back was the berth of the motorboat I'd taken onto the lake with Emily just that morning. On either side of the slip, a wooden dock extended to the waterfront gate.

I opened the gate, jumped into the motorboat and went to moor it on the other side of the jetty.

Back at the boathouse, I closed the gate again. My workspace thus decently prepared, I needed to turn to my primary subject matter: Dragan.

When I opened the boot for the first time in thirty-six hours, I was hit with a disgusting stench. The esteemed gangster had sweated through his clothes and the whole sleeping bag, wet himself, vomited, and voided his bowels, biological decay now radiating outward from his digest-ive tract. It was so horrible I was barely able to keep from vomiting myself.

As I stepped back from the car to let the worst fumes subside, I tried to focus on the pleasant smells of the garden: the resin of the pine trees next to the boathouse. The breeze from the lake was pleasantly cool and redolent of moss. From the boathouse, I could smell a melange of rubber, oil and petrol.

The clearer my head and nose, the clearer it became to me that I'd have to make this corpse disappear completely. I had killed a human being. The result was sickening, but there was no way to reverse it. I wanted to put this murder behind me as soon as possible. This meant I couldn't dig a grave on the property; there could be no bones that detection dogs might sniff out months or even years hence. Even as a corpse, Dragan should no longer exist at all. This was the problem at hand and I would have the strength to deal with it. I had to dissolve the body somehow, burn it or . . . something.

I went back into the boathouse and looked at the array of available tools. Saw, spade, axe – these were all well and good, but still quite old-fashioned. The machine that might mince up Dragan most effectively was probably the professional wood chipper. It would be a bloody fucking mess to get him into manageable enough pieces that he'd even fit into it. But if I pointed the chip chute at the lake, the fish would take care of the rest. From the roof of the boathouse, the thieving magpie looked me over. Since she was a lawbreaker too, she probably wouldn't be too upset over what I was about to do.

I ambled back to the workshop to look for tools that

could help get my former client out of the boot. On the shelves I found rubber gloves and a complete set of fishing gear, including wellies, trousers, jacket and hat. Because it was still a good 25 degrees outside, I took all my clothes off before dressing in this fisherman's garb. In one corner I found a spade, with which I wanted to prise Dragan out.

When I finally braved the boot again, however, a half-hearted first attempt very quickly showed that neither gloves nor spades would get him out of my car. I might as well have tried to move a massive glacial boulder.

I looked around. The boathouse was fitted with ceiling-mounted tracks and a crane for smaller boats. You could back a boat trailer into the boathouse, hoist the boat with the crane to trolley it over and launch it into the water. Similarly, though, the crane could be used to lift a rigid corpse out of the boot of an A8 and deposit it on the floor of the boathouse.

So I got into the car and reversed into the boathouse. There, I lowered the crane and with some effort managed to slip its two straps under Dragan's knees and neck. I hoisted him up with the crane and let him dangle as I took the car out again.

Back in the boathouse, I put a tarp on the floor, then the soaked sleeping bag and finally Dragan himself.

I searched his clothes, taking his wallet, gold watch and keys. In addition, I took anything that might obstruct the chipper or would not decompose: belt buckle, shoes, cufflinks . . .

Neck pouches or money belts are for backpackers and anxious tourists; Dragan wore jackets that had a few extra inside pockets sewn in. He'd been well prepared for his trip to Bratislava: 110,000 euros in cash divided into eleven packets, each containing twenty 500-euro notes.

The phrase 'money doesn't make you happy' is a lie. Money is a physical manifestation of freedom. Since a lot of people had given up their freedom and hard work for this money – drug dealers, sex workers, weapons smugglers – I felt that simply tossing this money in the chipper along with Dragan would be disrespectful.

I would relinquish the rest of Dragan to the chipper. Though I've never been a shining star when it comes to craftsmanship, disposing of a corpse is fortunately not about aesthetic quality, but about simple efficacy – that is, leaving as little trace as possible. Since it was rather obvious I couldn't put Dragan through the chipper in his entirety, I had to disassemble him first. I spotted a chainsaw. So as not to splatter his bloody DNA all over the boathouse, I used the crane to pitch a kind of tent over Dragan. I laid out a second tarp over the corpse, attached its centre to the crane and lifted it like a tent. The ends I weighed down with heavy things: a jerry can, a coiled rope, a toolbox, a cooler, a fire extinguisher. This improvised sawmill quickly developed the air of a camping tent on the third day of a festival: the light was dim, the stench beastly and the occupant unresponsive.

A pretty stressful work environment, to be honest. To make sure I did everything right, I went back to the car and pulled the mindfulness book out of my briefcase. I remembered a set of rules I'd considered rather silly on paper, but that might actually serve me quite well in the practical dismemberment of a corpse. I found the corresponding section under the heading 'Intentional Centring':

> *Even the longest journey starts with one small step. If you take each step mindfully, you will not be exhausted at the end of your journey, but alleviated. Therefore, as you take each step, focus on what* constitutes *that step:*
> *1. Take in the purpose of what you are about to do.*
> *2. In- and exhale once.*
> *3. Perform the task in a calm and centred manner.*

So when I got back into the tent, I very consciously took in the purpose of my first task: sawing Dragan's head off. I took a deep breath . . . which was a mistake. I immediately choked, involuntarily inhaling even more of the foul air, and launched into a coughing fit. Taking any deep breaths in the tent was impossible. I lifted the top tarp a little, inhaled the fresh, humid air of the boathouse, and gave my nose and lungs a bit of a break. And then, calm and centred, I sawed off Dragan's head. It worked!

I disassembled Dragan into twenty-four handy pieces, each of which would fit the chipper nicely. Once you're determined to no longer consider a human being as a human being but as a piece of work, once you take note of which body part you want to saw off next, inhale a deep breath of fresh outside air and then calmly start the chain-saw, the dismembering basically does itself.

It's still a gory fucking mess, though. When I was finished, my fishing outfit and both tarps were completely covered in crimson. I am an orderly person and I value clean clothes. So I walked to the dock, taking care to only step on the tarp, and jumped into the water fully dressed. The slip was five feet deep at most, but this way I could at least roughly rinse off my clothes and face.

Refreshed and somewhat cleaner, I climbed the step-ladder out again and began to take down the top tarp. After that, I stacked the twenty-four pieces of Dragan in the middle of the bottom tarp. I put the sleeping bag in a wheelbarrow and generously doused it with the bleach from the laundry room. Then I pushed the chipper to the lake end of the boathouse's dock, dragged over the tarp, and brought the sleeping bag in the wheelbarrow. After opening the gate, I took in the placid panorama. The weekend was over, there wasn't a boat on the lake.

It pained me to break this picturesque silence by starting up the chipper. Piece by piece, I tossed my most annoying client into the chipper. Every single piece spurted out a purplish fountain of shredded client over the blue-green lake. Across the water, the late-spring sky turned orange. It was an amazing sight; Dragan had never looked more colourful.

All of a sudden, a dreadful terror swept through me. I'd just sent the first hand and forearm through the chipper when it occurred to me that I hadn't yet severed Dragan's right thumb – the one he should continue to sign his news-paper missives with.

Out of sheer mindfulness, I hadn't paid attention to which hand the chipper had just scattered into the lake.

Panicked, I searched the noticeably smaller anatomical heap on the tarpaulin. One forearm remained. Was it his right or his left? Once a forearm is no longer attached to an arm that's connected to a torso, it's harder to tell than one might imagine. What was it again? When the palm is facing up, a right thumb points right and a left thumb left. So I turned the remaining hand palm up. The thumb pointed to the right – and was also branded with a 'D'. You only ever think of the simplest solutions once you're over the first fright.

I sadly lacked the kind of experience that might have taught me where to trim off a finger and still be able to use it as a stamp. Behind the first knuckle, the second or the third? Fortunately, the hand had four other fingers to prac-tise on. So I pruned off the four fingers in different places. Behind the middle knuckle, the little finger was as easy to cut off as a chicken bone, but the resulting digit felt a little short. I cut off the ring finger with the signet ring behind the distal knuckle, but that seemed too long and wonky. After two further attempts on the middle and index fingers, I decided to snip off the thumb behind the second knuckle.

Having set the severed thumb aside, I was about to toss the remaining four digits into the chipper when I noticed there were only three left: the ring finger was miss-ing. I looked all around and spotted the magpie – with the ring finger in her beak. She must have been attracted to the sparkling signet ring and flown into the boathouse through the open gate. Now she was about to fly off again, along with both signet ring and finger.

Dragan had had this signet ring made years earlier, along with an exact duplicate for Boris. It was chunky, made of solid silver, and studded with a fairly pricy diamond. The ring bore the design of a stylised poppy, an automatic pistol and a naked pole dancer. The set of rings was meant to seal their eternal friendship, but Boris hadn't worn his ring in years. The only reason Dragan still wore it after his rift with Boris was the fact that his fingers had grown too fat to pull the ring off his finger unscathed.

The ring wasn't really to my taste, but of course I couldn't leave it to the bird.

That was all I needed: a sticky-fingered magpie going after Dragan's paws and disrupting my carefully thought-out disposal. I grabbed the first thing I could get my hands on and threw it at the magpie. Stupidly enough, the item happened to be Dragan's thumb. It shot right past as the magpie took to the air in a flutter. That was . . . daft, more than daft. Flapping her powerful wings and carrying the ring finger in her beak, the magpie soared out of the gate towards the neighbouring property. I ran after her for a bit, but I hadn't a single hope of catching her. This was exactly what I'd been trying to avoid at all costs: for there to be even a single piece of Dragan left.

I tried to calm down: I didn't know where the magpie was taking this ring finger and its affixed ring, but no one else did either. The magpie would probably simply bring the ring back to her nest, where the finger would likely be devoured by some cat. If you ever find yourself having been unmindful in your mindfulness practice, you'll have to hope for a lucky break.

So I hoped.

I picked up the thumb I'd thrown in vain and continued my work.

When the last piece of Dragan was gone, I stuffed the sleeping bag through the chipper. The fabric and feathers would break down in the water, and the bleach I soaked it in would destroy any of Dragan's DNA inside the chipper.

Then I straightened my back and focused on Dragan's right thumb.

When it's not attached to a human being, a thumb looks really silly, like a legless shrimp without any eyes. Before this shrimp completely putrefied on me, I had to preserve it somehow, maybe not for eternity, but pretty much.

I looked around the boathouse. There was a tube of silicone sealant on a shelf, the kind used to seal boat joints. That gave me an idea. I went and found some lubricant and rubbed it all over the thumb. Then I sliced open the side of the silicone tube and squished the thumb into the treacly sealant. Once the silicone dried, I'd be left with a nice negative mould of the thumb. At home, I could then cast a positive out of it. Another problem solved.

It was time to clean up. I got a garden hose and hosed off the tarps, the chainsaw and my fishing outfit on the jetty. A reddish broth ran into the lake through the cracks between the planks. Next, I rinsed with stain remover. Then I undressed, put the clothes into the now empty wheelbarrow, poured in the rest of the bleach and stain remover, and let the whole mess soak.

Finally, I spread out one of the cleaned and bleached tarps on the ground once more, put the chipper and wheelbarrow on top, attached the ends of the tear-resistant tarp to the crane, and hoisted up the whole bundle to submerge it in the water for one last proper rinse.

With my own clothes under my arm, I walked back into the house naked. After all, if anyone had been watching me, my nakedness would be the least of it. As someone who put on a tie for years just to go down to my mailbox, I greatly enjoyed this newfound informality.

After indulging in a hot shower, I got dressed and headed back to the boathouse. I hoisted the equipment back out of the water and put the fishing gear, tarps, wheelbarrow, chainsaw and chipper back in their designated places. I didn't give a toss whether the chipper and chainsaw would still work after having a bath in the lake. If not, all the better. Should anyone ever come up with the esoteric idea that I'd sawed and chopped up Dragan, then a wood chipper that wasn't only DNA-free but also defective would not be able to convince a court. Next to the chipper was a pressure sprayer for pesticides. I dumped its contents into the slip, filled it with more bleach, and sprayed my car boot with it. Though Dragan had been lying on the sleeping bag, which by now had been destroyed, I liked to be thorough.

Last but not least, I collected the items I had taken from Dragan and placed them in the fire pit on the beach. I poured over gasoline and burned it all, tossing the gold watch and belt buckle far out into the lake. The ashes went into the water as well.

So that was it for Dragan, nothing left.

I went into the house, grabbed a beer from the fridge and sat down on the dock where I'd eaten spaghetti with Emily less than eight hours earlier – and where, twenty-four hours earlier, I had felt so very free again for the first time in years. I cracked open the beer, listened to the smacking of the fish, drank a big swig, and felt happy.

13

Benevolence

If we observe things without judgement, we can strip them of anything negative. And if we assume a certain benevolence about what we observe, we can even turn them into something positive.

Joschka Breitner, *Slowing Down in the Fast Lane: Mindfulness for Managers*

As a rule, I advised clients who'd been charged with a crime to simply continue their lives as before: avoid drawing attention, don't change any habits, maintain the daily routine. So on Monday morning I decided to start my week as usual. After getting up, I took three deep breaths and imagined there was a lake right outside the window of my apartment. That did wonders.

Until I turned my phone back on, that is. My voicemail was flooded with messages and people wanting me to call them back: Mr Von Dresen, my boss and a founding partner of the firm, urgently wanted to speak to me; Detective Chief Inspector Egmann urgently wanted to speak to me; and a major tabloid newspaper would appreciate a call back. Even Boris, the head of the rival gang, had called. Only two calls stood out.

I was pleased to hear Sasha's message. He hoped the rest of my weekend with my daughter had been nice and asked if we could talk some time in the coming days.

And then there was a very mysterious call from Murat, Toni's right-hand man, the guy who'd passed Sasha and Dragan that disastrous tip about the lay-by. Murat was the bloke Toni used for the rougher stuff. Though he probably wouldn't know how to spell either 'testosterone' or 'dyslexia', he certainly possessed a surfeit of both. On my voicemail, however, he sounded rather doleful: 'Hello Mr Diemel? Uhm, Murat here. I need to talk to Dragan . . . so . . . I'm sorry . . . I didn't mean to . . . It's life or . . . Can you meet me at the deer park tomorrow morning? At the feed dispenser?'

Since the call was from Sunday afternoon, tomorrow morning was actually now. I had no intention of meeting up with a teary-eyed violent offender to hand-feed some deer. All of a sudden I felt fed up with all these calls, all these people wanting something from me. Falling back into old habits, my stomach was already cramping up again, my shoulders tightened and my teeth began to grind.

Surely I hadn't just diced up my most annoying client only to be immediately overrun by a whole new set of idiots! I couldn't allow that to happen. Breitner had advised me to deal with stressful situations by simply leaving them for a bit. Step out of the room, breathe, maybe take a little walk . . .

So no, I wouldn't just pick up my bad old habits. The first thing I did was take some soothing breaths in and out. After that, I decided not to drive to work but to walk at least part of the way. So what if I'd be late, better relaxed and a bit late than tense and on time. Although my apartment was located at the other end of the city centre, the office was just three U-Bahn stops away. And even just the walk to the subway would give my thoughts some breathing room.

During the walk to the station, this was certainly the case, but the subway itself was jam-packed with grumpy people. The air was all but breathed up, and here, too, everyone seemed to want something from me: my air, my seat, my view.

I managed to find an empty spot in a four-seater. So as not to let the miserable faces of my fellow travellers get to me, I pulled out my mindfulness guide and came across a paragraph about the importance of assuming benevolence:

If we observe things without judgement, we can strip them of anything negative. And if we assume a certain benevolence about what we observe, we can even turn them into something positive.

It also suggested a quick mindfulness experiment:

Imagine that everyone has the best intentions: your colleagues, your superiors, your family – everyone around you. Even fate wants to assist you as best it can. Now look within and see what changes as you align your mindfulness with the benevolence of those around you.

Thinking back on my voicemails, I imagined that all these people weren't up to any harm but simply reaching out with the best intentions. My firm, the police, the press, Boris – everyone was just checking in to see if I needed anything. This was a touching thought. Completely absurd, of course, but still reassuring. I wanted to see if I could sense this benevolence in a more concrete manner, so I tried this experiment on my ill-tempered fellow passengers. And funnily enough, my perception changed abruptly.

Just as I could convince myself these people I didn't know must all be in a bad mood, I could also convince myself these strangers were well disposed towards me. This new attitude alone altered my mood completely.

When I got out after three stops, I felt so relaxed I was about to ask my lovely fellow travellers for their numbers so we could have a catch-up some time, talk about that great trip we took together. I just felt a little bad because they all seemed to want to support me, while I just wanted to be supported and had no interest in supporting anyone myself. Otherwise, I was doing really well. What's more, I realised that I would actually arrive at the firm ten minutes earlier than usual; no car meant no rush hour meant no traffic to get stuck in.

To make sure my new habit wouldn't attract any attention, I wasted the ten minutes I gained at the local McDonald's. As I ordered a black coffee, my eyes fell on the front page of a tabloid: the already familiar image of Dragan thrashing a burning Igor. For legal reasons, Dragan's face was pixelated – not Igor's. After all, dead people can no longer assert their right to control their image. The fact that Dragan's face was pixelated was simply because the newspaper didn't want to be sued by a lawyer like myself on behalf of a still-living bastard like Dragan. Newspapers are scared of living perpetrators, not of dead victims. I benevolently noted that, according to the newspaper, Dragan was still alive – how nice for all of us.

When I was handed my coffee, I saw the sign for the gift that came with that week's Happy Meal: a parrot toy.

The small stuffed animal was kitted out with a simple audio recorder that could record ten seconds of whatever you said and then repeat it in an absurdly high voice. I got one in pink; Emily would get a kick out of that. I added a copy of the tabloid; the office would get a kick out of that.

Upstairs at the office, a secretary informed me I was wanted in Mr Von Dresen's office immediately. And you know what? It didn't bother me one bit. In my relaxed state, I had completely brushed off all those urgent requests to call people back.

Hats off to me: how mindful could I get?

With the newspaper under my arm, the McDonald's coffee in my hand and the parrot toy in my jacket pocket, I headed to my boss's office. The interior was impressive in the stark way executive offices usually are: expensive desk, expensive view, expensive abstract art on the wall, an expensive sitting area underneath – perfectly suited for showing off, perfectly unsuited for feeling at all comfortable. Although smoking was prohibited throughout the building, there was an unpleasant smell of stale cigars.

In the sitting area, Von Dresen and the other founding partners, Mr Erkel and Mr Dannwitz, were having their morning meeting. The three gentlemen were all in their early seventies, faces tan from the golf course and with wives at home pouring the first glass of the day. Von Dresen had managed to age in a dignified fashion and looked in shape. Erkel also had a healthy complexion, but that was the only thing that looked healthy about him. He suffered from obesity, shortness of breath and high blood pressure.

Dannwitz was the least remarkable of the three, a small, emaciated gnome of sorts, albeit one with a great deal of money and power.

The three gentlemen may have been partners, but they weren't friends. The only thing that connected them was the money they drew from the law firm they had founded decades earlier. And to protect this money, they joined forces against anyone who would dare disturb their peace. The morning meeting mainly revolved around strategically planning this joint defence project.

On the coffee table in front of them was a copy of the tabloid with Dragan's picture. My friendly greeting was not returned. Von Dresen got straight to the point.

'Is it true what you did over the weekend?' he asked.

I briefly considered which of my weekend activities he might mean: that I'd taken the weekend off? That I'd helped a wanted client escape? Or that I had shoved said client through a wood chipper?

'Could you perhaps be more specific?' I responded politely. 'It was a long weekend.'

'You maligned Ms Bregenz for not having a law degree and for having reached an age at which she is no longer capable of conceiving children,' Erkel fumed.

Dear God, I mince up the biggest criminal client in the history of our firm only to get in trouble for talking back to the receptionist? I couldn't suppress a giggle.

'What's so funny about that?' Dannwitz blurted out.

'I don't think that's funny at all.'

'Ms Bregenz has been employed at this firm for twenty

years. You are not better than her just because you went to law school. We do not condone any such snobbery here.'

'Thank you for that observation.'

'Thank you for that observation, *Mr Erkel*,' Erkel immediately countered.

In my relaxed state, I didn't feel like escalating the situation, so I tried to settle matters diplomatically.

'Please note that it was far from my intention to insult Ms Bregenz. But when my daughter and I come to the office on a free Saturday – a day I'm supposed to spend with my daughter – and I am immediately told off for it at reception, that doesn't exactly make for an inspiring work environment. She barked at me, I barked back. I'm perfectly happy for us to resolve this by apologising to each other.'

I felt very mindful in that moment. My words were confident, diplomatic and aware of my counterparts' perspectives, or so I thought.

'Ms Bregenz has nothing to apologise for,' Erkel volleyed back. 'This office is not a playground. Your daughter defaced the entire conference room!'

I took a deep breath, envisaged a lake outside the office window and felt the ground beneath my feet.

'At home, I usually manage with some window cleaner and a piece of kitchen roll.'

I didn't recognise myself: had I just calmly given my bosses cleaning tips instead of trembling in fear?

'You have insulted Ms Bregenz in a way that borders on sexual discrimination,' Dannwitz said. 'We cannot tolerate such things. This firm believes in equal rights.'

My mindfulness experiment about assuming benevolence was obviously reaching its limits. I switched to lawyer mode and started making my case.

'And how many of the female partners in this firm would agree with that statement about equal rights?' I wondered out loud.

Von Dresen corrected me: 'The firm has no female partners.'

'So much for equality.'

'What are you trying to say?' Erkel huffed.

'I'm just hinting at the fact that even women who do have the required degrees obviously can't move up the career ladder here precisely because of their capacity to conceive children. Without a law degree and without children, even twenty years at this firm apparently only lands a woman at the reception desk to moan about other people's children. So spare me your whingeing about equal rights.'

Somehow, I'd really found my argumentative groove. I wasn't quite sure whether I'd gained this new self-confidence through my mindful breathing, however, or by hacking up Dragan. Or was it because my daughter had been accused of artistic misconduct? Perhaps a mix of all three.

But what was this really about? I couldn't have been summoned here to see all three founding partners only because Ms Bregenz had been offended by my comment about her age-related infertility. And in any case, I'd had enough. I had already breathed an entirely unrealistic amount of benevolence into the world today. Soon I would no longer be able to pretend to unjudgementally accept my bosses' gaffes, or at least not without abandoning my love for myself. Mindfulness also requires truthfulness. Fortunately, Breitner's guide also included tips on how to deal with difficult interlocutors:

Also focus your mindfulness on people who do not seem to be doing you any good. Let the other person finish. Try to take the time to understand their feelings, values and ideas.

So I tried to let the three toffs finish.

Von Dresen was just saying, 'I forbid you to speak about—' when I interrupted, 'You will forbid me absolutely nothing!'

I felt I'd let them finish quite enough. At that moment, I realised this wasn't about Ms Bregenz at all. It was about Dragan, their lucrative bleurgh-client. They had no idea what he'd actually done, nor where he was now. And both scared these gentlemen to their core. They were afraid a whole avalanche of gangster shit was about to inundate the firm. And to motivate me to divert it safely away from them, they were giving my head a wobble. Dutiful as I usually was, playing on my conscience would not only get me back in line, but even allow me to iron out my 'misconduct' in the process.

Wow, after just three seconds of mindful listening, I knew what these men actually wanted from me. They wanted me to get the coals out of this fire Dragan had started. Ha! I'd make sure they'd get what they want, but they wouldn't get it how they thought they would. With unprecedented frankness, I confronted my terrified bosses with everything they didn't know about the situation:

'You have a problem with my daughter "defacing" the conference room? Let me tell you something.' I pointed at the front page on the coffee table. 'Two nights ago, this client of your law firm defaced an entire lay-by with blood, ashes, shrapnel, and children's tears. Is that really less important to you than the emotional state of some ageing disgrace of a secretary? The crap gangsters like that pull is what makes us our money – you significantly more than me, I should add. And you seriously want to accuse me with this politically correct piffle?'

Now that's how you mindfully turn a game around.

'If you take issue with anything we said, you're free to leave the firm.'

'Mr Sergowicz might take issue with me leaving.'

And that's how you ramp up the game.

'We will get to your client in a moment . . .'

'*My* client? I'm not even a partner here, I'm just looking after this gentleman for you. Your names are on every piece of letterhead and every bill. Every invoice is paid to your accounts. You make your money by laundering money for this sadistic mobster, and it's your law firm to which any number of questionable tax-avoidance schemes for drugs and prostitution revenue can be traced back. You want to lecture me about proper manners and decorum? If the newspapers knew how much money you made off this psychopath, sexually discriminating against some dusty old office hag would be the least of your problems.'

'Kindly leave the press out of this,' Dannwitz drily stated. 'I'll remind you that you are bound by confidentiality.'

'I am, yes, but your client is not.'

Erkel widened his eyes in indignation. 'Are you threatening us?'

'Not me, but your client might.'

'What do you mean?'

'Well, if at some point in the distant future Mr Sergowicz should find himself in prison and feel that the partners were preventing his lawyer of record from planning his perfect defence because they preferred nattering on about frustrated secretaries and children's drawings, then I could well imagine he'd take it very badly and start to be more communicative to the press – which would still be the least of your problems.'

I was really leaving behind the stable ground of well-founded criticism and venturing onto the very thin ice of open intimidation. Yet my interlocutors seemed to be much more afraid of falling in than I was. They were all very successful businessmen. They mainly cared about what they had earned in the past and whether they would retain it in the future. For them, the present was always mainly a cause for concern.

Dannwitz cleared his throat. 'And how . . . would that be expressed?'

'Well, I'll put it this way: Mr Sergowicz knows exactly where your wives shop for sherry. And it'd be such a shame if they suffered some drink-driving accident on their way back home, wouldn't it?'

As these three gentlemen probably worried more about their cars than their wives, however, I had to get a little more personal.

'And you know that Dragan likes to express criticism unconventionally.' I casually pointed to the front-page image of a burning Igor.

I was starting to enjoy this conversation.

'If Dragan Sergowicz goes down, you'll all go down with him. So to prevent that from happening, I expect all three of you to fight like hell in his defence.'

And that is how turn you turn their game against them.

It is easy to invoke a psychopath's willingness to resort to violence if you know he's already dead. The venerable partners were momentarily speechless. Von Dresen was the first to break the silence.

'What do you suggest?'

I hesitated, then spotted a chance to make this work for me. I smiled at all three of them in turn. 'Let's dispense with the nonsense. You don't want anything to do with me. I don't want anything to do with you. Why should we cling to each other any longer?' Von Dresen was about to respond, but I raised my index finger. 'I also have no interest in representing Mr Sergowicz, but he trusts me and I can handle him. So here's my proposal: at the end of the month, my employment contract will be terminated. I will start my own firm and take Mr Sergowicz with me.'

'And what guarantee do we have that Mr Sergowicz will not . . . resent us?'

'He will gladly provide you with that in writing, along with a legally binding confidentiality agreement.'

'He would agree to that?'

'I'd ensure he would.'

'Just like that?'

'Well, after my ten years of reliable work here at the firm you would also be moved to generosity. Let's say with a severance payment of ten months' salary.'

I spread my arms towards my bosses in a gesture of reconciliation and then casually dropped them to my sides. It certainly looked confident, but it also activated the on-switch of my newly purchased parrot toy.

'For shame!' thundered Erkel.

The parrot's recording then echoed, five tones higher, but still very understandable: 'For shame!'

The three looked aghast. I took the pink stuffed animal out of my pocket and turned it off.

'Sorry, that's for my daughter. When she's not colouring, she likes to play with stuffed animals. I'll give you some time to think all this over. I'll get on the phone to Mr Sergowicz in about an hour.'

I walked out of the office with the parrot in my hand.

14

Fear

Fear is a natural protective mechanism. It can spark our body to peak performance, but it can also paralyse us. There is no point in judging fear. Even afraid, you can reduce tension through mindfulness.

> Joschka Breitner, *Slowing Down in the Fast Lane: Mindfulness for Managers*

The lawyer in me would've recommended I stick to my old habits and go on exactly as before. Yet thanks to my mindfulness coach, in the very first hour of my very first day back at work after my very first murder I'd already thrown a lot of habits overboard: I'd left my company car at home, gotten a coffee at McDonald's – oh yes, and I had threatened the three founding partners of my firm instead of letting them threaten me. A satisfying experience.

I had once again taken the liberty of not doing what I didn't want to do, which in this case would've been to grovel.

I took stock of what I felt: miraculously, I neither had a stomach ache nor felt any insecurity. Quite the opposite, in fact: my stomach felt great – maybe I should get McDonald's coffee more often.

I had no doubt that my bosses would agree to my proposal. So I confidently started packing up the personal things in my office. It wasn't that much: a few photos of Emily, an external hard drive with copies of documents and work emails, as well as various keys for bank lockers where I had stored countless documents for Dragan. Strictly speaking, the hard drive and lockers didn't fall under the category of personal belongings. But it was now in everyone's interest that I would no longer burden the firm with these matters.

Last but not least, I got all the blank letterhead and powers of attorney signed by Dragan out of my office safe. Ten years of work – and it all fitted in one briefcase.

With the briefcase under my arm, I next did something I hadn't done in years: I went to a home improvement store. I needed plaster to turn the mould of Dragan's thumb into a cast. I also liked its symbolic meaning: turning Dragan's negative into a positive.

My visit to the home improvement store did me good. This place was designed to meet the needs of people who wanted to create something with their own two hands. Any spanners for sale here weren't going to be thrown into anyone's works, but used on something that would be a part of someone's home. Anyone going to a home improvement store is a person of action – they live in the present and have a firm grip on their future – and now I was one of them! I bought a small bag of modelling plaster to give Dragan's quietly decaying thumb a bright new future. After paying at the register, I put the bag in my briefcase.

At that moment, my phone rang. It was the office.

'Hello?'

'I'm connecting you with Mr Von Dresen,' Ms Bregenz said in her automaton voice.

I waited for my usual impulse to remark on the woman's affected mannerisms, but it never came. I just waited mindfully for the line to click and the voice of my soon-to-be-former boss to come on.

'Von Dresen speaking. We accept your offer.'

There we go. 'What does that mean in concrete terms?'

'Your employment will be terminated as of the first of May, and you will receive ten months' salary severance pay. You will take with you Mr Sergowicz and any associated clients. Mr Sergowicz will confirm in writing that he has been looked after exclusively by you and will continue to be looked after exclusively by you in the future. This covers any claims against our firm.'

'Sounds good. Please send it to my personal email address.'

'It'll be on your desk shortly.'

'I won't be coming back to the office today.'

'Now listen here, it is still up to us to determine when you are expected to be in the office!'

'Well, you can always fire me if that's more convenient. After all, you're still my boss. Speaking of which, as long as my termination agreement is not in effect, let alone signed, Mr Sergowicz remains an official client of your firm. So I assume you will take over liaising with the press until then.'

'The press? What are we supposed to tell them?'

'The same thing I am now telling you on Mr Sergowicz's behalf: "No comment."'

Yes! Ten months of severance pay would soon be in my account, and I already had a hundred thousand euros from Dragan in cash. No more obligations to that shitty firm, and my annoying client could no longer annoy anyone either. And on top of that, my current employer would keep the press off me in the name of that client and thus confirm that he was still alive. Even though he wasn't.

More objectively: could I have *been* any more mindful? Breitner's book had begun to hold a mystical significance. Now all I had to do was make sure the police didn't arrest me for murder, and that neither Dragan's gang nor its competition suspected what had really happened to Dragan.

Breathing the air of freedom, I walked home through a city in bloom to check if all was right with Dragan's right thumb.

I had put the silicone thumb mould in my bathroom. The material felt like it had firmed up pretty well. And the thumb was definitely ready to come out – that much was clear from the smell. Unfortunately, I had no idea how long silicone takes to dry out completely. Appropriately enough, the internet offers a rule of, well, thumb. Each centimetre of silicone requires twenty-four hours of drying time. Since I had simply pressed the thumb into the tube, the layer of silicone was quite thick on all sides. So to be on the safe side, I'd have to wait at least three to four days.

But the internet also offered plenty of tips on how to speed up the drying process. A room heated to around 20 degrees with high humidity would help things along. So I ran the shower a bit and implored my heater to keep the foggy bathroom at a happy 20 degrees. I wanted to give the silicone one more day. Mindfulness is not a one-way street, silicone has needs too.

It wasn't even Monday afternoon, and a lot of the worries I'd woken up to had already evaporated all on their own. Sure, there were still a few calls to take care of. Wanting to put those behind me, I called Peter Egmann at Homicide Command. I just wanted to tell him I had nothing to tell him, but it turned out he had a few things to tell *me*.

'Björn, thank you for returning my call. I imagine you must have your hands full right now.'

Cradling my phone between my ear and shoulder, I looked at my hands, which had been full when I was packing up my office just a few hours earlier, which had carried the plaster, and which had just given the silicone mould a tentative squeeze. Now they were full of exactly nothing, and I picked my phone back up again.

'You certainly have a vivid imagination for a copper. Why should I have my hands full?'

'Well, your boss is wanted for murder and has gone into hiding. And this morning, one of his soldiers was found dead in the woods. Shot in the head.'

My stomach cramped up again. I had just solved almost every one of my problems, and now suddenly someone had been shot in the head. Setting aside the fact that a layperson like myself was apparently the only person who could properly dispose of a corpse, more bodies just sounded like more trouble for me. Was this the beginning of a gang war with Boris? Perhaps I shouldn't have put off calling him back.

I plastered a smile over my dark thoughts.

'My bosses run a law firm. I just sat down with all three of them earlier. If you want to arrest one of them, go ahead. Yet you probably don't mean my boss, but my client. And I don't know anything about any headshot.'

'Murat Cümgül, a bouncer at one of Toni's spots. A passer-by found him dead this morning on a bench near the feed dispenser at the deer park.'

I didn't have to play dumb: I actually had no idea who was responsible for Murat's death. All I knew was that Murat had tried to reach me the day before. Had he reached me and convinced me to meet, I'd have been sitting on that bench next to him this morning. A chilling fear grabbed a hold of me. It looked like my digital fast had saved my life. But that didn't mean my life wasn't still in acute danger. In front of me on the table was my mindfulness guide. I leafed through it until I found the right section:

When fear arises, focus on your breath. Calmly in- and exhale. Feel your breath moving through your body. At your nostrils, for example, or in your abdomen. Keep your mind on your breath, do not judge your fear, and try to appreciate the here and now.

'Do you have a cold?' Peter's question broke the silence.

'Why do you ask?'

'You're breathing so heavily.'

I was just breathing consciously. And soon I was consciously feeling better: with every breath, more of my self-confidence returned. Unlike some people in my professional circle, I was still able to breathe, which was clearly a positive. Was there anything else to appreciate about this situation? Well, at least the deceased died in a scenic environment, that was also positive. And I hadn't shot him, that was positive insofar as it meant I could have a completely clear conscience when it came to Peter. So whatever was going on with this murder, here in the present I was fine. The rest would reveal itself in time.

I did not respond to Peter's observation, but posed a question of my own: 'Hunting accident?'

'Must have been a pretty blind hunter if they couldn't tell a fully zip-tied Turkish guy from a roaring stag. Especially considering they shot him in the back of the head at close range.'

'Tragic, but what does it have to do with me?'

'Well, let me put it this way – the number one of Dragan's gang eliminates the burning number two of Boris's gang. Subsequently, said number one disappears without a trace, and the deputy of Dragan's number two is shot in the woods. This could lead to legal complications for all parties involved.'

'Not *all* parties.'

'Who do you mean?'

'The dead are obviously off the hook.'

'The real question is: why are they dead in the first place?'

In other words, the police knew as little as I did. I'd have to discuss that with Dragan. Oh right, he was dead too.

'Maybe you could discuss it with Dragan,' Peter suggested.

'At the next opportunity.'

'When might that be?'

'You know that's none of your business, that's covered by confidentiality.'

'Björn, we know Dragan left town.'

'Then you know more than I do.'

'He cannot have done so alone.'

'If you say so.'

'You're the only one he called.'

Hm, the only way they'd know that was if they were illegally tapping my phone, which they'd never do, of course. 'Help me out – what did he say to me?'

'That he wanted to go for ice cream with you.'

'How romantic, and what did I say?'

'You said you wanted to take your daughter to the lake.'

'And what did I do next?'

'You drove to the office with your daughter and she had an ice cream there.'

Bloody hell, I hoped Peter wasn't about to charge me with perverting the course of justice just because that Möller moron saw Emily's ice-cream-covered face.

'OK, guilty as charged. My daughter had ice cream at the firm. Any other grounds for suspicion?'

'We know you then drove to the lake.'

'And how do you know that?'

'We were watching you.'

'You tailed a lawyer and his barely three-year-old daughter the whole weekend? On what legal basis, illegal enjoyment of ice cream?'

'We weren't tailing you. I'll put it this way – a colleague happened to be boating and happened to snap some lovely landscape shots with his telephoto lens.'

It must've been the boat that had dropped anchor on the lake that night. If Emily hadn't helped me shift to mindfulness mode, I'd not have been at the home improvement store this morning, but in prison: both if I'd let myself be spotted on the jetty with a live Dragan *and* if I'd taken the dead Dragan out of the boot on Saturday instead of Sunday.

I summarised the new information.

'So Dragan called me to go get ice cream. After that, you saw me at my office and at the lake. Yet you didn't see Dragan, neither at my office, nor at the lake. And it wasn't me who had an ice cream, but my daughter. I'd like to see you try and get a search warrant for my office or the lake house on that evidence.'

'Well, there's one more minor detail . . .'

'Which is?'

'The people living next to the lake house called the police this morning. They found a severed finger with a signet ring on their patio table.'

This was anything but minor. Correctly interpreted, it was actually a clue to the murder I committed. Surprisingly, this didn't fill me with fear right then, but anger, anger at that bloody bird. Did she have to drop the finger in such plain sight? And where are all those fucking cats when you need them? Why hadn't the finger been gobbled up?

'And what does that have to do with Dragan?' I asked, hopefully sounding bored.

'The ring on the finger bears a striking resemblance to the one Dragan pressed under the little boy's chin in the video. This suggests the finger is also Dragan's. So the finger must have come to the lake either with Dragan or with you – or, in the dumbest possible case for you, with both of you at the same time.'

'The consequences of which being?'

'The first consequence being that a judge was of the opinion that said finger would certainly justify a search of the lake house. Ten colleagues of mine are scouring the property at this very moment.'

Fuck! One ring finger doesn't even make up one-thousandth of a person's body weight. I'd chipped up 99.9 per cent of Dragan without any difficulty, yet this one silly detail led to a search warrant.

But it needn't be cause for panic. I had chopped up Dragan precisely because there was the possibility of a search, otherwise I could've just left him in the boathouse. I was pretty sure that, except for the finger bit, I had done a thorough job. I just had to have faith now.

'Then I hope your colleagues make sure to leave every-thing neat and tidy. If anything turns up missing afterwards, Peter, I'll hold you responsible.'

'If anything more than this finger turns up, Björn, I'll hold you responsible.'

We hung up. The consequences of my mindlessness con-firmed my need for mindfulness. I breathed in and out for another two minutes and organised my thoughts. As for the search of the house, I just had to wait and see. Off the top of my head, I couldn't think of anything dramatic the police might find. And it'd take a few days before any DNA results came in on the finger. Of course, I could immediately start racking my brain over whether the police now assumed

Dragan was dead; whether that meant they were now look-ing for his murderer; and whether I was a suspect. But I could also let it go. After all, what did one severed finger really mean? Its former owner would have difficulty becom-ing a concert pianist, nothing more. I had more pressing matters to contend with, questions I should clear up quick. Above all, I needed to meet Sasha to talk about the hit on Murat – also to determine whether it had been intended to be a hit on me.

Boris I would deal with last. If he had already launched a gang war, a phone call from me couldn't avert it anyway. And if Boris wasn't behind Murat's murder, then he could probably wait a little longer before embarking on a murder spree of his own.

It's a familiar issue for anyone who suspects or knows their phones are being tapped: conversations are always tense, as you're always aware of who might be listening. Using disposable prepaid phones is only a semi-solution. After all, you first have to get the other person's prepaid number without the police finding out.

Dragan and I had developed a method that his entire gang, including Sasha, made great use of. You send an eleven-digit sequence via SMS from your tapped phone to the other person's tapped phone. Then they simply add those individual digits to those of the sender's number, and the resulting number is that of the new number they need to call.

So I used the mobile phone I now knew the police were monitoring to send Sasha a text with the numbers

00177489032. Anyone who doesn't know my number would have no way to crack this message. And though the police did know my number, they didn't know how these digits were connected to my phone number, so they wouldn't know what to do with it. As Sasha knew both, he called me a short time later from a heretofore unknown number.

'It's me,' he said.

'Thanks for calling me back.'

'How's the boss?'

'Alright, given the circumstances.'

'Where is he now?'

I almost answered: *His thumb is in a tube of silicone, his ring finger in an evidence bag and the rest is being digested by a school of fish . . .*

I managed to stop myself and instead said: 'For your protection and that of everyone involved, he wants no one to know.'

'But you do?'

'Not directly,' I improvised.

'But you are in touch.'

'Of course. He wants business to keep going. We need to meet.'

'Where and when?'

'Why don't you suggest someplace?' It was always good to let the other person make some decisions. In this case, it would even come in handy. I had no real experience in choosing places to meet conspirators, Sasha did.

'You know the playground at the Schlosspark?' he asked.

'Of course.'

'Tomorrow morning, half past eleven.'

That would be during working hours, of course, but for now I would just consider myself 'on leave'.

15

Letting Go of Prejudice

Mindfulness requires the unprejudiced attitude to life that we admire so much in children. Children live in the moment. Lost in play, they simply enjoy themselves. Learn to be as unprejudiced as a child.

Joschka Breitner, *Slowing Down in the Fast Lane: Mindfulness for Managers*

The silicone would dry fine on its own. I had called back Sasha, the police, and my bosses. As for the press, the firm would keep them off my back until my official departure at the beginning of next week. I was hoping the waters would've calmed somewhat by then. And now I no longer needed to call Murat back. I didn't know whether a gang war had started on Friday, but if it had, there was nothing I could do about that now. Before I could have a clarifying conversation with Boris, I needed the necessary background information from Sasha. And I wouldn't see him until the next morning. So at the moment, I had nothing more urgent to do than to be good to myself.

I decided to go see my daughter. If I could be closer to Emily while successfully keeping all this violence away from her, then all my effort made sense.

Since Katharina had suggested we discuss the preschool situation anyway, I called her up. She answered after the third ring.

'Hi Katharina, it's me.'

'Did something happen?'

I searched myself to see if I wanted to say anything like 'shredded my client', 'threatened my bosses' or 'was almost shot at the feed dispenser' – but I didn't want to. And since I didn't have to do what I didn't want to do, I said, 'No, why?'

'It's Monday afternoon and you have time to talk on the phone?'

'I have a little free time on my hands right now.'

'I thought you must be fighting a five-alarm fire, what with your favourite client on every front page.'

Katharina and I had already had every single conceivable argument about the moral intricacies of my work. But since our separation, any discussion of the issue was blessedly no longer laced with bitter irony.

'The front page is currently his only known location. And a client who's not around also requires no work.'

'Sounds like the calm before the storm.'

'Probably, but I'd love to enjoy it with Emily, if you wouldn't mind.'

'Of course not, come on over. I need to talk to you anyway.'

I hung up and got out the parrot toy.

When I said, 'Off to Emily!' into the hidden microphone, its silly voice parroted me.

'Emily is my everything.'

The bird repeated it.

I took it to my coat rack.

'I'm the greatest dad in the world.'

The bird felt just the same.

'I chopped up my client and now I'm free.'

Unfortunately, that's when I stumbled on my way to the front door and dropped the bird before it could answer.

I picked it up again and repeated: 'I said: I chopped up my client and now I'm free!'

The bird remained silent. The fall must've damaged its memory chip. But what durability did I expect from a toy given away with a Happy Meal? I stuck the bird in my jacket pocket and decided to buy Emily a new one.

I drove to our old house. A beautiful detached 1960s build with a great garden, a great terrace and a great many majestic trees. Emily greeted me with enthusiasm.

'Did you bring any work, Daddy?'

'No, sweetheart, not this time.'

'I'm playing lake house!'

She showed me how she had lined up all her stuffed animals on the edge of the terrace so they could watch the fish in the grass and feed them with nut spit. I envied my daughter's ability to relive beautiful moments through play. And I envied her knowledge gap: her re-enactment didn't include a chainsaw and a wood chipper.

Katharina and I sat down on the expensive teak chairs I had splurged on after I'd gotten Dragan off in a complex case of human trafficking.

I earned my money through gangsters and then basically had the rainforest cut down to provide seating for our terrace.

I never understood how Katharina could criticise my job, but still unselfconsciously enjoy the fruits of that labour. Fortunately, our relationship had now reached a point at which such questions no longer mattered. We didn't feel any hatred for each other; we'd known each other too long for that. And in everything that concerned Emily, we had now simply and touchingly become a team. A great team.

That was also why Katharina wanted to talk.

'We have to come up with a preschool for Emily,' she began.

'But we applied to thirty-one preschools . . .'

Regardless of the fact that being with other children was developmentally necessary and important, Katharina also planned to go back to her insurance job from the summer onwards, at least part-time. So getting Emily into preschool was urgent from both perspectives. Thanks to my mindfulness course, I'd managed to be at least physically present during most of the admission interviews. However, I had rather lost track of what was supposed to happen next.

Katharina nodded. 'Right, and each preschool awards its spots in April. And April's almost over! So far, we haven't heard back at all from twenty-five preschools and five have said no.'

'No response doesn't automatically mean rejection, does it?'

'All the kids from Emily's dance class have already received at least one acceptance. And no acceptance means rejection. You know how it is: preschools don't send rejections because they're afraid lawyers like us will sue.'

'But the registration deadline hasn't passed yet.'

'The deadline is the thirtieth of April. If we don't have an acceptance for Emily by then, she won't get a spot for another year.'

'OK, twenty-five preschools that didn't get back to us, five rejections. That's thirty. What about application number thirty-one?'

'That's what I wanted to talk to you about.'

Katharina handed me a letter. The premium organic envelope and stationery were a luminous white with a big fat recycling logo on it. The letterhead was emblazoned with a deranged dolphin clearly drawn by a child: the logo of the co-operative preschool Little Fish. Wouldn't you know it, this was the co-op I was supposed to scare off to make room for Dragan's fancy new brothel . . . We'd originally ranked it twenty-nine on our wish list, but I got the uncomfortable feeling that it had just shot to number one. And that the contents of this letter very probably presented a major obstacle.

In order to understand just how dire finding a preschool spot in our city had gotten, you have to know that the registration process was a complete joke. First you had to register your child on the city's central online platform. True to the creative spirit of civil servants, the platform was called Smart Initiative for Childcare and Kindergartens – SICK for short. The corresponding URL actually was 'sick. de', and only by registering there could you assert your claim to a preschool place. SICK's user interface was so user-unfriendly that, due to various pages crashing and inputs not saving, a large percentage of children would've already left the city for university before their parents could fully complete their preschool registration.

Yet registering on SICK did not automatically register you at any preschool. You still had to make appointments at each individual one and re-enter the exact same data you'd already painstakingly managed to enter at sick.de in the respective institution's own questionnaire.

These ludicrous basics had to be mastered before you could even get to the decisive phase of the preschools' selection process: admissions interviews. This was when you sweet-talked each head of early years, telling them how much you loved their 'childcare concept' – all in the hopes you could choose the best preschool out of your acceptances later.

Of course, each German preschool has its own ideological orientation. This starts with the difference between Christian and secular preschools: Christian preschools teach children the importance of Easter, Christmas and Martinmas; secular preschools celebrate the Spring Festival, the Winter Festival and the Lantern Festival – contributing to integration by pretending to shun tradition.

In addition, parents have to decide what kind of nutritional fascism they prefer: do you want your preschool to feed your child organic, vegetarian or vegan food before you stop for McDonald's on the way home anyway? There are preschools that discriminate against pork so as not to be suspected of poisoning Muslims, and preschools that like to explore the woods. Others emphasise that they integrate disabled children into the group, while yet others might have no disabled children, but at least thirty per cent Spanish speakers.

Every preschool claims their selection process is absolutely non-discriminatory. Religion, nutrition or nationality do not affect the allocation of spots: having been baptised is not mandatory for a Catholic preschool, nor a vegetarian diet for an organic one or a Spanish parent for a bilingual one. Officially, at least. In practice, your child should always be baptised both Protestant and Catholic, and to get into a secular preschool you should be ready to abandon that faith at the drop of a hat – just as quickly as you lost faith in the selection process. Make sure your child has at least one trendy food allergy and/ or intolerance when you take them to the interview. They should be word-perfect on 'The Tidying Up Song' in at least three languages. And of course, Mummy and Daddy should be happily married, even if they've just come to blows in family court.

Yet even when you and your child have endured all this nonsense, every single preschool manager will ultimately still have free rein to de-centrally decide which child to take – and which not.

If it wasn't for my mindfulness course, by the second interview I'd have insisted on just handing them my business card and simply suing Emily's way into preschool without going through the whole fawning 'childcare concept' charade. But how did Breitner so beautifully put it?

Mindfulness requires the unprejudiced attitude to life that we admire so much in children. Children live in the moment. Lost in play, they simply enjoy themselves. Learn to be as unprejudiced as a child.

On whom better to apply this childlike lack of prejudice than on the people whose job it quite literally was to exercise that very lack of prejudice in preparing Emily for primary school? So I went to every admissions interview and tried my best to maintain an unprejudiced perspective, despite knowing the whole deceitful game was rigged . . .

Katharina snapped me out of my ranting reverie. 'Just read the letter.'

I nodded, took the letter and read:

Dear Mrs Diemel,

You and your husband applied for a spot at our co-operative preschool for your daughter, Emily. The final decisions were made at a meeting this past Thursday, and we have decided not to accept your daughter. The decisive factor was the fact that your husband threatened us with an eviction suit because one of his clients wanted to turn our space into a brothel. We do not want to have anything to do with parents who represent such clientele.

Kind regards,

I looked at Katharina, she looked at me. This couldn't be happening! Here I was, having only just restored my work–life balance by murdering my client, and now a preschool was throwing it back out of whack?

'I need you to know that this whole eviction situation—' I started, but she wouldn't let me finish.

'Björn! It's none of my business how far you're willing to go for Dragan, but this isn't about him, it's about Emily!'

She was rearing up like a lioness, and you don't mess with lionesses. Raising my hands in a placatory gesture, I tried to bring her paws back to solid ground:

'Katharina, we ranked that preschool twenty-nine out of thirty-one. The chances that it might become a last resort for us were one in thirty-one. I couldn't very well predict that there might be some professional conflict—'

Again, I didn't get very far.

Katharina snarled at me. 'So we suffered through this endless admissions insanity only for it all to fall apart again because of that fucking gangster of yours!'

'I really do try to separate the personal from the professional—'

Katharina tore the letter out of my hand and almost poked a hole in it with her index finger. 'Unlike you, the softies at this preschool obviously cannot separate the personal from the professional. After all, they rejected our daughter because they don't like what her father does for a living. Maybe they should find out just how good you are at your job.'

The lioness had extended her claws. Yet for once they were not directed at me but at the co-op. Though I was apparently no longer the only bad guy, I was still a little overwhelmed by the question of what consequences this would have for me.

'And what do you want me to do?' I asked.

Katharina looked at me with a wild determination in her eyes: 'I want you to fix this. Whatever you need to do.' She pushed the letter back at me. 'Anyone who rejects our girl because they don't like her father should find out just who her father is.'

'What . . . would that look like?'

177

'You're asking me? Ask that client of yours, Dragan certainly owes you.'

'Excuse me?' I couldn't believe what I was hearing.

'You managed to turn these people against our daughter because of Dragan,' Katharina continued. 'So now you can convince them they made a mistake, just like you always do for Dragan. Isn't that your job, "convincing" people?'

That *was* my job, and I was good at it. I had just begun to take issue with the kind of people I was doing it for. Convincing people for Emily's sake, however, seemed like quite a positive experience. But this positive turn was quickly undone.

'Either you secure Emily an acceptance letter by the thirtieth or . . .'

I looked at her in shock. 'Or what?'

'Or . . . I'll move somewhere else with Emily. Somewhere I'm not expected to perform an Olympic gymnastics routine on the monkey bars just to get a preschool spot. At some point, I'd like to get a say over my own time again, go back to work, and if that's not possible here, I'll just need to go somewhere else.'

This was a serious threat. If she moved away with Emily, I'd be left behind. Katharina was basically threatening me with less Emily time. And I had just killed my main client and blackmailed my bosses in order to secure the exact opposite – though of course Katharina didn't know that.

Here I had been briefly under the impression we might actually be able to see eye to eye for once. Still, I was almost grateful she'd managed to sour the mood after all: a sudden surplus of peace and harmony might've also been hard to accept.

16

Impatience

To avoid impatience distracting you from your mindfulness practice, it is helpful to become aware of any impatience when it arises and to acknowledge it. But don't judge the impatience. Simply assert the state of mind you desire: 'I am calm.' Do not let your restlessness escalate.

Joschka Breitner, *Slowing Down in the Fast Lane: Mindfulness for Managers*

The visit then relaxed after all, because Katharina suddenly announced she was going out for a coffee by herself. This put me in the liberating position of getting to spend the rest of the afternoon playing with Emily out in the garden.

When I got back to my apartment early that evening, I felt completely happy. Spending this one free Monday afternoon in the garden as a father had been more meaningful and inspiring than spending the previous fifty-two Monday afternoons in the office as a lawyer.

I was (and to be perfectly honest, still am) a person who likes to have something to do. Not too much, of course. After years in the fast lane, Breitner had taught me as much. But doing nothing proved impossible too. Yet that is exactly the crux of mindfulness: the twinge you feel in your conscience whenever you have nothing to do often gets in the way of your own needs. My mindfulness guide has something sensible to say about this:

Don't look for things to do. Let them find you.

In other words, if a client decides to vanish in a lake somewhere, another problem is sure to arise somewhere else.

Seen in this light, Katharina had simply gifted me something new to do. My task was to 'fix this'.

Or more professionally phrased: I had to get Emily a preschool spot by the end of the month or her mother would move away with her. Katharina obviously didn't care how I fixed it; she only cared about the result.

While Emily and I had been playing in the garden, part of my brain was already trying to find a solution. I had spent a lot of time over the last few years trying to convince Dragan that eliminating a competitor was only half the battle; it made more business sense to take over their customers. Shooting one Albanian drug dealer doesn't win you a single new customer, but once you take over *all* a drug dealer's customers, he can be free to shoot himself.

An idea started to emerge: wouldn't it make more sense to take over the co-op on Dragan's behalf than to fight it? In any case, it'd require Dragan's approval. Not least because I'd need to somehow convince his officers and ruffians that this idea for them, of all people, to take over a preschool really came from Dragan. Since Dragan was dead, his thumb would have to do the heavy lifting instead.

So I went into the bathroom and studied the silicone mould. The thumb had completely lost its former colour and even its shape. The silicone, on the other hand, was unchanged and apparently almost completely dried – yet I wasn't quite sure. I really wanted to pour plaster into the mould, but didn't dare do so yet, for fear I might damage or destroy the silicone mould out of sheer impatience.

Since I couldn't decide, I went into the living room and picked up my mindfulness guide. I impatiently riffled to the page that covered the topic of impatience.

To avoid impatience distracting you from your mindfulness practice, it is helpful to become aware of any impatience when it arises and to acknowledge it. But don't judge the impatience. Simply assert the state of mind you desire: 'I am calm.' Do not let your restlessness escalate.

I was fully aware of my impatience, otherwise I would have just relaxed into my waiting state and not had any reason to frantically riffle through the book. How could I *not* judge my impatience? It was really getting to me. But maybe impatience might actually be a good thing? Maybe there was no need to wait so long for the silicone to dry. Maybe waiting was just the wrong move. I shouldn't let a tube of silicone and a few DIY tips online dictate how I spent my evening. Mindfulness means taking in each moment with love – with love for myself, that is, not for a tube of silicone. I would instantly reach my desired state of mind – 'I am calm' – if I could finally dispose of this rotting thumb and just start on the plaster cast. Whether or not the silicone still contained some residual moisture hardly seemed relevant.

As waiting any longer was probably completely unnecessary, my impatience was completely justified.

I in- and exhaled deeply, feeling my breath in both of my own thumbs.

So as not to get sucked back into my restless state, I took the now entirely useless thumb out of the mould, threw it into the toilet and flushed.

Suddenly, my restlessness was gone.

I picked up the silicone tube and studied the shape of the thumb. It looked really good: the fingerprint was fully visible, and the scar in the form of a D also clearly stood out.

I cleaned the mould of any lubricant or thumb leakage and mixed the plaster I'd bought that morning.

Lightly shaking and tapping the mixture, I poured the viscous mass into the silicone mould – and started waiting again. But this time the wait made absolute physics-based sense.

I used the time to study the website of the co-operative preschool. I already knew these people from the admissions interview and from threatening them with an eviction lawsuit. Both times, however, I hadn't given much thought to the history of the co-op or the individuals involved. If I wanted to use my mindfulness to put a stop to these people's mindlessness as successfully as I had done with Dragan, perhaps I should learn more about them.

In Germany, a company is considered a non-profit if it serves a non-profit purpose and exclusively uses its profits to achieve this purpose. Legally, it turned out Little Fish had been established as a non-profit company rather than an association. That was good news. In an association, the committee members make all the decisions, so they need to be convinced individually. In a non-profit company like this, however, it's the shareholders that make the decisions. Whoever has the most shares has the most power. Those shares, however, can be bought without anyone having to be convinced – though the decision to offer those shares up for sale may require supporting arguments.

Little Fish had only three shareholders. These three men had founded a start-up together five years earlier that turned old car tyres into flip-flops. But the founders soon realised that their crawling children were getting in their way at work, and since they were in the founding spirit, they co-founded this offshoot for their offspring.

The three founders were in their mid-to-late thirties. As I learned from their tyres-to-flip-flops website, they aimed to 'commercially explore the important issues of sustainability and recycling' – a roundabout way of saying their lucrative business imported Third World garbage.

Though these chaps didn't come from army families, they wore WWI-style beards with WWII-style haircuts. They were vegan, drove hybrid cars, and shot more CO_2 into the atmosphere with a single business-class flight to Asia than their cars could save in a decade.

These self-described 'change agents' bought old tyres in Pakistan, where children without protective clothing pulled tyres off rims on metres-high mountains of trash. Then they had the tyres delivered to Bangladesh, where other children without gloves cut them up into soles and straps. Those were then taken to Sri Lanka, where yet other children without any respiratory protection stuck them together into footwear.

So these three gentlemen had no time for their own children at home because they were too busy organising Third World child labour instead.

The flip-flops were then shipped from Sri Lanka to Hamburg. By the time they reached Germany, each shoe – including material, child labour and shipping costs – had run them up just 2.39 euros. The eco-conscious entrepreneurs sold their tyre-wear for 69.95 euros a pair at hip boutiques and online. Bearing the lower-case brand name 'untrd', this rubbish was touted as 'sustainable streetwear', a contribution to reducing waste in the Third World. Meanwhile, what with the additional packaging, the actual amount of waste had tripled. Interestingly enough, even though this hazardous waste couldn't have made its way from overseas without globalisation and its attendant child labour, the folks wearing these flip-flops were often vocal opponents of globalisation.

These three chaps were also the sole shareholders of Little Fish. They were the ones responsible for rejecting Emily just because her father earned his money as a bleurgh-lawyer, not through child labour. For now, this was sufficient information.

After an hour of research, I had a rough plan. After another, the plaster had dried. I carefully peeled it out of the silicone mould: a perfect copy of Dragan's right thumb, a stamp to put on all future orders. Having cleaned the silicone mould, I hid it in my cleaning cupboard. I took the thumb into the living room and pulled out the tabloid I'd bought that morning. It was time to flesh out my plan and let Dragan sign his first set of instructions.

17

Uncertainty

Certainty and uncertainty are irrational feelings, and you can control them yourself . . . Start by imagining you are somewhere that gives you a sense of certainty, surrounded by people you trust. You will soon realise you have given yourself a sense of certainty.

Joschka Breitner, *Slowing Down in the Fast Lane: Mindfulness for Managers*

After my first breathing exercise the next morning, the firm's severance offer was already in my inbox. It essentially covered what we discussed. As a matter of principle, I made a few changes to the draft and sent it back, asking to have the amended contract countersigned on my desk by three that afternoon. I then wrote a statement on behalf of Dragan stating that he would indemnify the firm of Von Dresen, Erkel and Dannwitz from any claims and that he wanted to be represented exclusively by me in the future, as he had been in the past. I printed this letter on some of the blank letterhead Dragan had signed and put it in my briefcase.

It was time to meet Sasha at the playground. That day, too, I decided to leave the A8 outside my apartment and explore my new freedom on foot. I'd already taken my office stuff from the car and decided to drop the car keys at the office later. The firm was free to pick up the car and return it to the leasing company. I was no longer letting anyone else determine how I made my way through the world.

As it turned out, the Schlosspark playground had three enormous advantages for clandestine meetings. Firstly, as mornings saw it busy with mums, nannies, nanas and children, there was a permanent noise cover created by shrieking Elijahs and Amelias, as well as by mums calling out 'Elijah, Amelia, stop that please'. Amid this tumult, someone sitting just two metres away wouldn't be able to overhear even a fragment of your conversation.

One supposed disadvantage of this particular playground: two men stood out like two drag queens at Sunday service. Yet this also resulted in the second advantage: we'd be able to spot anyone tailing us immediately.

The third advantage was content-related. Admittedly, when we'd made the appointment, what I had wanted to discuss with Sasha largely revolved around dead bodies and hand grenades. Since the previous afternoon, however, my list of discussion topics had expanded a little: now we would also be talking about children.

And when it came to children, Sasha was the perfect person to talk to.

Sasha was twenty-nine. He wasn't very big, but wiry. He looked shrewd, sly and always a little sloppy – not dirty, but like he'd jumped out of bed ten minutes earlier, like he hadn't yet brushed his teeth or his hair and was still wearing his superhero pyjamas under his clothes. As a result, people usually underestimated him, which for some had turned out to be a fatal mistake.

He had come to Germany from Bulgaria six years earlier. For the first few years, he'd worked for Toni, first as a bartender, then as deputy managing director. Sasha was smart, and soon he knew every bouncer, dealer and sex worker at Toni's club. Though not a nerd, he also turned out to be good with computers, so within a very short time he'd become the bloke to call for any virus and network issues.

What no one knew was that, during the day, Sasha was taking university classes to get a German degree. After three years, however, he realised it was unsustainable for him to leave his job at the club at eight in the morning and then attend lectures at nine.

He dropped out of university. Instead, and to prevent the gangster lifestyle from dumbing him down, he decided to pursue a qualification he could do part-time and without as much effort. Sasha decided to train as an early years educator and asked Toni for a job with more daylight. As Dragan's driver had just been caught going seventy-five mph past a primary school, Toni vouched for Sasha and took the opportunity to place one of his confidants in Dragan's immediate vicinity. That's how Sasha and Dragan met. As Sasha was always loyal to his direct employer, however, he proved unsuitable as an informant for Toni, so their relationship cooled down considerably.

The job suited Sasha perfectly. As Dragan liked to sleep late and manage his affairs from home during the day, Sasha was usually only needed by the afternoon and could devote himself to his classwork in the mornings. After three years, he got his degree and didn't tell Dragan about it until he got the actual certificate. Dragan laughed himself half to death. Sasha and I were the only people close to the boss who had degrees. Since Sasha had his early years educator qualification, Dragan made fun of me for lacking any pedagogical qualifications, which even his driver had. That's how I learned about Sasha's additional training.

When I got to the playground, Sasha was already on a bench watching the children rollicking around. I sat down next to him.

'Nice place,' I said.

'It's easy to relax when innocent children are romping around.'

'Are there even any children who aren't innocent?' I asked.

'No, just as there aren't any innocent adults. Every experience burdens you with the weight of its own guilt.'

'Are you an educator or a philosopher?'

'Working with children, there's not much of a difference.'

'My little one has certainly taught me that. Yet it's usually her who's more of a philosopher.'

'Wonderful girl, your Emily. How is she doing?'

I really appreciated Sasha remembering her name. 'Great, she really enjoyed our weekend at the lake.'

'And Dragan?'

'He's fine too. Since he never officially got into my boot, he also doesn't want anyone to know where he got out of it. But we're in touch and I have his first instructions with me. And Dragan told you he wants the business to continue as usual.'

'Though that'll be more difficult than expected,' Sasha noted.

That was the stupid thing about people who weren't familiar with mindfulness: their judgement got in the way.

'What's the issue?'

'Well . . .' Sasha hesitated. 'To be honest, there's a whole lot of issues.'

As a student of non-judgemental perception who appreciated single-tasking, I asked Sasha to list every issue he deemed problematic in order.

'In order? OK, so the facts are that Dragan was almost killed, I was almost killed, Igor was killed, and Murat is also dead. Toni has a real attitude right now, and if we do nothing, we're heading straight for a real gang war with Boris.'

That Dragan and Sasha were almost killed was news to me. But even without that, Sasha's sketch of the current landscape didn't quite mesh with my state of deepest relaxation.

'OK, let's start with the last one: what's the gang war situation?'

'Boris is furious that Dragan grilled and killed Igor. He's especially furious that Dragan won't reach out to apologise. As Boris couldn't reach you either, he has told me that he expects to hear from either you or Dragan in person by tonight. Otherwise, he will shoot one of our officers every day until Dragan deigns to talk to Boris. Though to be fair, he also wouldn't have any problem shooting you, Dragan or me – he's really fucking furious.'

This was to be expected, but Boris could be appeased. He was a businessman. For him, every human life had a price. And Igor's could be paid in cash, drugs or some new turf.

'Though that's not great to hear, it's understandable. Before I meet with Boris, however, I'd like to know exactly what happened at the lay-by. Don't leave anything out.'

'Of course. For a few weeks now, Toni's numbers haven't been adding up. His earnings are going down. Not dramatically, but still enough that it's hard to ignore.'

'And what's causing this?'

'Toni claims someone on his turf is selling stuff at half price. It's ruining his trade.'

'And what did Dragan think?'

'Dragan suspected Toni is selling some of his stuff on the side. But as he had no evidence, he was going to bring it all up at the next officer meeting if Toni couldn't come up with a better explanation.'

'And has Toni come up with a better explanation?'

'An explanation, yes. But after what happened on Friday, I doubt whether it is any better.'

'What did Toni tell you?'

'Toni said he'd find out what the word on the street was: lean on a few dealers, break a few bones and so on. And on Friday night, Murat called me and told me it'd become clear who's behind it: Igor. He supposedly had Boris's approval to set up his own distribution network on our turf. And he was about to get a fresh supply of drugs in a lay-by that same night, which made for a great opportunity to catch Igor in the act. It would also be proof that Boris was messing Dragan around.'

'I see. And why wasn't it Toni who told Dragan? Why did he send Murat instead?'

'I wonder about that too. Probably so he could still deny everything if need be, if anything went wrong. Which it did . . .'

'How did it happen?'

'So, we were on our way to Bratislava, Murat called me, and we drove to the lay-by shortly after. In the van were Igor and this bloke. Dragan started yelling at Igor, I splashed petrol on his trousers, Dragan set him on fire. Light a little spark under his bum, the usual routine. That should've done it. I was already holding a blanket to put him out. But then this supposed courier all of a sudden pulls out a hand grenade and wants to jump out the vehicle. So instead of putting Igor's fire out, I threw the fire blanket over the bloke and kicked the un-pulled grenade out of his hand. Igor seized his chance and leapt out, still burning. The van caught fire, and Dragan ran after him. I saw the coach full of kids coming, knocked out the grenade guy and went to get our car. You know the rest from the video.'

'So your plan was just to light a little spark under Igor's bum, that's it?'

Sasha nodded. 'Yes, then we'd have taken Igor to Boris and had a little chat about how Boris could apologise for pulling this shit.'

I shook my head. 'Best-laid plans, eh?'

'Depends how you look at it.'

There was a strange undertone in Sasha's voice. 'What do you mean?'

Sasha hesitated. 'Maybe the plan was really someone else's. Dragan was so furious, he must have missed it, but the way I saw it, the guy with the hand grenade was not at all surprised we showed up. Igor was, but that bloke looked like he'd been just waiting for us, waiting to get rid of all of us.'

Yikes. Though I had mindfully eradicated the queen wasp, I guess someone else had rather mindlessly stuck his finger in her nest.

'Who was the guy?'

'No idea, never seen him before. And the way that van exploded, nobody'll ever see him again.'

'And what about the drugs?'

'That's the thing: there weren't any drugs, none whatsoever. Igor must have been there for an arms deal, hand grenades.'

'And what was the point of luring you and Dragan into an ambush? Who stood to gain?'

'Toni, of course, and no one would've even suspected him. Aside from Dragan and me, no one knew he was in trouble with Dragan. Had Dragan been killed, he would've probably claimed Dragan's throne and sped things along by starting a gang war with Boris.'

'But that plan – if it was one – didn't work either. Dragan survived.'

Sasha shrugged. 'But everything else *did* work: Igor is dead, Boris is furious, Dragan is in hiding, and Toni is in the clear. As long as Dragan thinks it was Boris who lured him into a trap, everyone will forget all about Toni's bad numbers.'

Fuck, the situation was more complicated than I'd thought.

'OK.' I squinted my eyes shut. 'If Toni wants to start a gang war, how does Murat's killing fit into the picture?'

Sasha shook his head. 'No idea,' he admitted, 'but after it all went down in the lay-by, Murat called me, all meek-like. Absolutely had to speak with Dragan, didn't want to say what it was about though. He was fully bricking it, sounded like. I told him to call you, you're Dragan's mouthpiece.'

'He did. He left a message on Sunday night. He wanted us to meet at the deer park Monday morning.'

'Maybe he was kicking himself for sending Dragan into a trap, maybe he wanted to confess.'

'If he was shot for trying to snitch on Toni, it means that Toni knew what message Murat had left me. I was already afraid my phone was being tapped, but – by the police.'

Sasha paused, clearly trying to put it all together. 'What if Toni has a dirty cop on his books?' he said finally. 'Then he would have access to your voicemail and the whole thing would make sense.'

I nodded. 'Quite possible, and if I'd shown up I would've probably been killed right along with Murat. Toni doesn't need me, and he must be scared that I'll find out, or that Dragan smells a rat.'

Shooting me a worried look, Sasha asked, 'Should I call Walter to get you a security detail?'

Walter was Dragan's officer in charge of arms trafficking. His legal cover was a security company. And his boys and girls were very effective when it came to personal protection.

But round-the-clock security was the last thing I needed at the moment.

'Not yet,' I said quickly. 'I . . . I'll see how the talk with Boris goes. Besides, I first need to discuss everything you just told me with Dragan. I'll let you know.'

There was a small pause. Mainly due to the fact that, after all this talk of intrigue, murder and revenge, I was struggling to segue into the topic of a hostile preschool takeover.

Luckily, Sasha took it out of my hands by asking, 'So, what instructions does Dragan have?'

I tried to keep my nerves in check as I handed Sasha the scrawled-up tabloid from the previous day. The page had numerous circled words connected by lines – and a perfect Dragan thumbprint.

Sasha deciphered the artwork: 'Brothel plans changed. Take over preschool co-operative. Within a week. Do not develop knocking house, but preschool. Everything else see lawyer.'

Sasha gave me an irritated look. 'Did Dragan get hit on the head when I closed the boot lid on him? What the fuck's all this supposed to mean?'

The playground noise seemed to drop away. It felt like all the kids were suddenly waiting for me to answer the question, and all the mums were offended that I was keeping their kids waiting. Even the birds seemed anxious, silent. Above all, however, Sasha was waiting for an answer, and he would not be put off with excuses.

The takeover of a preschool by an organised crime network was certainly a great opportunity for a father who worked for said network and wanted his daughter to receive the best possible childcare. But it didn't exactly solve the question of how to react to an impending gang war over a gang leader who was in hiding.

In short: I was overcome by a feeling of uncertainty as to whether or not I'd actually be able to reconcile my work and family life.

'Certainty and uncertainty are irrational feelings, and you can control them yourself,' is what Breitner had to say about that.

Mentally take yourself out of the situation about which you feel uncertain. Start by imagining you are somewhere that gives you a sense of certainty, surrounded by people you trust. You will soon realise you have given yourself a sense of certainty.

So I mentally took myself out of the playground. I imagined sitting next to Emily on the jetty at the lake. The warmth of the wood animated my body and relaxed my muscles. The lapping of the waves against the wood calmed my nerves. The shimmer of the sun on the water tickled my senses.

'Well, the idea isn't that outlandish when you really think about it,' I improvised. 'For one thing, Dragan is not yet aware of all this Toni intrigue. Like you said: he probably didn't pay much attention to the guy.'

'But he still knows we're not playing around here,' Sasha interjected.

'Exactly, and that's why . . .' I mentally took Emily on my lap and crunched another nut. 'That's why Dragan wants to take matters into his own hands. He doesn't want to hand over control to anyone else, especially now he's in hiding. He wants to act, not react.' You have to agree that didn't sound half bad. 'And confidently,' I continued, 'as if nothing happened. The upmarket brothel Dragan has been planning is a long-term project. In the short term, the preschool is fighting our eviction suit. So we should gain control of them first: preschool instead of a gang war. It projects confidence. Ignoring this ongoing project just because someone wants to instigate a gang war would send the opposite message.'

'Someone is sure to see this differently.'

'That's what Dragan wants: that same someone would expect Dragan to halt all long-term projects and exclusively focus on some impending gang war. They'll have to go through Dragan though.' I threw it back to Sasha. 'When you're teaching preschool, what do you do with children who cross a line?'

'Sometimes it is actually helpful to simply ignore them.'

'There you go. So if Dragan wants to take over a pre-school instead of being forced into a gang war, we'll see soon enough whose feathers get ruffled over his unruffled response.'

'But what does he want with a preschool? Aren't we in the business of drugs, weapons, prostitutes?'

'Of course, but those don't require any new instruc-tions. That'll all go on as always. The preschool and the brothel are a political issue. Possession proceedings to evict the preschool for our personal use might take years, not to mention getting all the permits for the brothel in place.

But if we take over this co-op, we can simply and quietly close it down in due course.'

I didn't quite believe that last part myself and I felt my train of thought was about to derail.

'I see. So taking over this preschool is now our most pressing problem and the only thing on Dragan's mind?'

'The only thing Dragan needs to communicate in writing. The preschool didn't show the proper respect . . . Look, if a competing drug ring doesn't show the proper respect, we don't kill them either, we just take over. The customer base is worth cash.'

My comparison of the preschool to a drug ring made the jetty I still imagined myself sitting on wobble so much that I started slipping towards the lake.

'But is a preschool's customer base worth anything?'

'Well, it's quite simple really . . . Because . . . For example, every child usually has two parents. So each preschool spot involves three people: two parents, one child. Parents are just as dependent on a preschool as . . . as junkies are on dope. They'll do whatever you need to secure a spot.'

Like a cat burglar dangling from a gutter, I clung to the jetty with my very last strength. But Sasha didn't seem to notice.

'Good,' he said suddenly, 'then we'll take over the preschool.'

I could only look at Sasha incredulously.

'I'll handle it. No problem.'

'Excuse me?' It was only then that I realised I could save myself any more stammering. The jetty was level once again.

'I'll talk to the people from the co-op.'

'Now, Dragan wants this to be over and done with by the beginning of next week, so that conversation should happen this week.'

Relieved, I got up and gave Sasha a note with Little Fish's name, address and phone number.

Sasha got up too. 'I still don't understand what's so pressing about this, but I know it's just how Dragan is. It'll be done within the week, but please tell Dragan I have one request.'

I looked at him questioningly.

'If we're getting into the childcare business, I want to be the head of this division.'

'You want to . . .'

'Do you see any other trained educators around here?'

Sasha was even smarter than I thought. As head of a division, Sasha would become an officer – on the same level as Toni. Which wouldn't be a disadvantage if Toni had been the one behind the attack on Dragan.

'That won't be an issue. I think Dragan wants that anyway.'

Looking at Sasha, I could tell this made him proud. Finally, his qualifications were being recognised – albeit by the plaster thumb of a minced-up mob boss.

'Dragan wants me to schedule a meeting with all the officers this week to set out our new course and reassure everyone that otherwise everything will stay as it was.'

'I'll set it up. Any particular day?' Sasha asked.

'Thursday at the earliest. I first need to be able to discuss your Toni theory with Dragan and perhaps prepare any necessary measures.'

Sasha moved over to the metal litter bin next to the bench, set fire to the newspaper page and dropped its charred remains into the basket. Pensively, he stared at the smouldering ash. He seemed to be moved by something.

'This preschool thing might be some consolation to Natasha,' he finally said.

'Who's Natasha?'

'Someone I know.'

'Is she connected to the preschool?'

'No, to the building. Natasha was going to work at the brothel, which won't open for a while now.'

'So why would she be happy about the preschool?'

'If I'm running the preschool, she can put her two little ones there during the day. As you said, it's the parents who are dependent on these preschool spots, not the kids.'

I nodded. 'Who's looking after her kids now?'

Sasha smiled. 'Me.' At that, he turned to the playground. 'Alexander! Lara!' he called. 'Come on, time to go.'

Alexander and Lara obediently trotted over and left with Sasha, the first eager customer for my new drug: preschool spots.

18

Shamelessness

Some people communicate openly, others with restraint. The latter are often quick to consider the former rude, brazen or shameless. Instead of getting pointlessly upset about other people's shamelessness, you can address the discrepancy between communication styles instead. Be less cautious in expressing what you want and respond to any shamelessness with clarity. The best response to an unjustified request is: 'Thank you for openly expressing what you want. Unfortunately, I cannot fulfil your request.'

Joschka Breitner, *Slowing Down in the Fast Lane: Mindfulness for Managers*

To organise my thoughts, I went for a walk in the Schlosspark. I needed to contact Boris and I needed to find out what had really happened in that lay-by.

Aside from me, only two people would've had an interest in killing Dragan: Boris and Toni. Boris because he wanted to eliminate his competitor, and Toni because he wanted to take Dragan's place. So we were facing either a gang war or an insurrection. As a newly minted king slayer, both scenarios could go properly pear-shaped for me, especially if I wasn't 100 per cent sure who was behind it. If I made a move against the wrong guy, the consequences could be nasty. If I didn't do anything, the consequences could be even nastier. So I based my rough plan on simply letting Boris and Toni eliminate each other.

Once, Boris was Dragan's best friend. Once, Toni was Dragan's protégé. Now, Dragan was out of the game. Now, Dragan was . . . me. Though I'd resolved my own issues with Dragan quite mindfully, as the new Dragan I'd taken on *his* issues too. Still, I'd be able to cope with those as well.

While letting my gaze wander along a lane of poplars in the park, I got a text from Toni: 'Where's Dragan?' It was phrased like Toni himself: rude and demanding.

Who asks a question like that? Either Toni was behind

Friday's ambush, in which case the question couldn't be more brazen, or he wasn't, in which case the question couldn't be more stupid. Especially sent unencrypted to a phone that was monitored by the police or *from* one that was being monitored – possibly even both.

Before I could rashly and angrily respond, 'Have you gone completely barmy?', I found a quiet seat on one of the benches lining the lane, took three deep breaths, and pulled out my mindfulness book. A few weeks earlier, when Dragan was getting on my nerves, I had already found a passage about dealing with the shamelessly brazen:

> *Some people communicate openly, others with restraint. The latter are often quick to consider the former rude, brazen or shameless. Instead of getting pointlessly upset about other people's shamelessness, you can address the discrepancy between communication styles instead. Be less cautious in expressing what you want and respond to any shamelessness with clarity. The best response to an unjustified request is: 'Thank you for openly expressing what you want. Unfortunately, I cannot fulfil your request.'*

I found it a nice approach, but if I would write back to Toni, with the police reading along, 'Thank you for asking where I hid Dragan. Unfortunately, Dragan told me not to tell anyone where he was', then I might have responded mindfully to Toni's rudeness, but I'd also ensure that the investigators both mindfully and rudely reading along would have a lot of questions for me. I chose to split the difference: communicate so openly that Toni and the police could both interpret my message any way they pleased. I texted back:

'Thanks for asking so openly. Dragan is at Hermannstraße 41, 2nd floor, "Ms Bregenz" (ring twice), but he wants to keep that under wraps.'

Let the police, Toni and Ms Bregenz decide among themselves what this text meant. And if this got Ms Bregenz into trouble . . . I'd welcome that too.

While still on the bench, I called the office and asked whether the termination agreement was on my desk. It was.

I set off on foot to sign it. From the park, the office was just half an hour's walk away. To keep up my new habit, I drank a quiet coffee at McDonald's and bought a newspaper before going up to the office. At three o'clock on the dot, forty-five minutes after I got Toni's text, I was in my office. The termination agreement – including the changes I'd requested – was ready for my signature. I countersigned and added Dragan's statement to the folder. Starting the next day, I would no longer be an employee of Von Dresen, Erkel and Dannwitz. As my final goodbye to this firm that had cost me ten years of my life and perhaps also my marriage, I wanted to personally hand Ms Bregenz the folder, my key card and the car keys – along with the address where the car was parked.

But Ms Bregenz wasn't behind the desk. When I'd gotten to the office, her grumpy self had still been there to ignore me. Now she was on the ground behind the desk, her face pale, breathing shallow, surrounded by two paramedics and all the employees who were around – Clara, the trainee, among them.

'What happened?' I asked her.

'Ms Bregenz collapsed,' Clara replied.

'Clara, considering you've got an oral exam coming up soon, it would be helpful for you to practise summarising the key points of a complex issue. I can see for myself Ms Bregenz has collapsed, but can you tell me *why*?'

'She got a call and then she collapsed.'

'Who called her?'

'The police did.'

'How do you know that?'

'Because when I picked up the phone to call an ambulance, the police were still on the line.'

'And what did they tell you?'

'That they would call the ambulance themselves.'

'Thank you, Clara. Now, did the police perhaps also tell you what upset Ms Bregenz so much that she collapsed?'

'So, they told her that a hand grenade had exploded in her apartment, right before a specialist firearms unit was about to storm in.'

Another hand grenade.

'Thank you, Clara, wasn't that easy?'

I focused on my breathing and on the one indubitably positive thing I had just learned. My mindful text had apparently reached its destination and been read by both Toni and the police. To actually carry out an attack on Dragan – supposedly staying with Ms Bregenz, of all people – was as ludicrous as it was desperate. Boris was neither of these things; Toni was both. This meant that, unless Boris had a mole with the police, only Toni could be behind this new attack. I had gotten exactly what mindful people appreciate most: clarity. Now I knew who was behind all these problems. Yet this did not necessarily make those problems any smaller.

Since Ms Bregenz was no longer available for my ceremonial handover, I put the folder and the key in the internal mail drop-off. I realised this was probably the last time I would leave the office as an employee. As I breathed away the hand grenade exploding in Ms Bregenz's apartment, I started to feel cheerful, elated even. What did I care about the personal lives of my former employer's employees? I had a six-figure sum in cash, a contractually guaranteed severance payment almost twice as high and, from now on, plenty of time to spend with my daughter and live a stress-free life. No hand grenade had exploded in *my* apartment. Sure, to prevent one from exploding there in the future, I'd still have to pit Toni and Boris against each other, but it would all work itself out.

Of course, I had no idea then that the waves I'd just ridden were actually heralding a massive storm that would drown me if I didn't step up to captain the ship I'd been about to disembark.

19

Time Pressure

Time is relative. How we perceive it depends on our subjective assessment of the situation we find ourselves in. Time pressure, therefore, is nothing more than an expression of tension.

Joschka Breitner, *Slowing Down in the Fast Lane: Mindfulness for Managers*

Barely had I left the firm when a new text from Toni came in: '00035247315.'

After the 'Where's Dragan?' text and the hand grenade in Ms Bregenz's apartment, this was truly shameless. Who did this guy think he was? I certainly wasn't about to call him on any prepaid number; he should be calling *me*. These formalities still mattered. I decided to let him stew a little longer before I sent him the cypher for my new prepaid phone.

At that same moment, my official mobile rang: Peter Egmann. He wanted to meet, right away. We arranged to meet at McDonald's – I hadn't gotten much further from the office than that.

Within ten minutes, Peter walked up to the table where I was calmly nibbling a McMuffin and enjoying an imaginary lake shimmering behind the McCafé counter. Peter, on the other hand, looked very upset for a copper who usually kept his cool.

'Björn, what is all this shit?'

'This? This a very successful fast-food restaurant.'

He sat down. 'I'm not talking about this place, but the state of your Ms Bregenz!'

I shrugged. 'Apparently she had a little fainting spell.'

Peter glared at me, furious. 'After I told her that a hand grenade was tossed through her living-room window. Who's behind this?'

'How would I know?'

'You sent Toni a text saying that Dragan was in her apartment!'

'And was he?'

'Of course not.'

'Setting aside for a moment the legality of you having read my text – did you seriously believe what it said?'

'You know we have to follow up on every lead.'

'If you really want to know what this shit is about, why don't you ask whoever threw that hand grenade?'

'He's on the run.'

'Oh really? I thought the SCO19 unit was already on site because of the text. Did the SCO19 unit call another SCO19 unit to catch the guy?'

'Björn, this situation is serious. In four days, there've been three deaths and two grenade explosions – and all of them directly connected to Dragan.'

'But I'm not.'

'You're not? One day after you spent the night at the lake house with your daughter, both Dragan's ring and his ring finger turn up on his neighbours' patio table. Can you explain that?'

'Are you even sure it is Dragan's finger?' I countered.

'It's obviously the signet ring Dragan is wearing in the video, a bespoke piece. It's as tasteless as it is unique.'

'Wait a minute,' I objected, 'Dragan's ring is not unique,

but one of a bespoke pair. Boris had the exact same ring made at the time.'

'Yet Boris has informed us that he's still in possession of all ten fingers.'

'Fingers that haven't worn that ring for years.'

'What's that supposed to mean?'

'Well, if you don't even know whose ring it is you found, how can you be sure whose finger it's on? Who's to say that at this very moment Dragan's not sunning on some beach with his tasteless ring on one of his ten intact fingers, while you've got an evidence bag with Boris's ring on some unlucky other person's digit?'

As a criminal defence lawyer, you don't have to stick to the truth, you just have to sow doubt. I've always been quite good at that.

'Granted, that point still has to be clarified, yet the DNA report will certainly help us do so. Unfortunately, the laboratory is completely backed up, but I hope to get the results by the end of the week.'

'For a DNA examination, you would need a sample of reference DNA from Dragan. Let me give you a little expert tip: take a saliva sample – those stand up best in court. But . . . if you're poking a cotton swab in Dragan's mouth anyway, you can just ask him yourself if any of his fingers have gone walkabout.'

As a lawyer, I'd always been able to talk circles around anyone. Admittedly, my entire argument would fall apart the second an incontestable sample of Dragan's blood, sperm or saliva could be compared to the finger's DNA – but no sooner than that. Right now, however, Peter was clearly itching to get back to safer ground.

'Don't you want to know what we found during our search of the lake house?'

Had I failed to wipe out all traces of the corpse disposal? A chill came over me, my throat felt parched, my neck tensed up. I tried to go over it all again in my mind.

'Oh, right, sure. What did you find?'

'In front of the boathouse, divers found a gold watch and a belt buckle, both also visible on the video.'

Boundless relief surged through me: both watch and buckle were mass-produced. So, except for the finger thing, I didn't seem to have made any mistakes getting rid of the body, all thanks to my intentional centring.

'Congratulations. And if the divers had kept on their search, they'd probably have discovered some antique amphoras, or relics from Atlantis. What does this have to do with Dragan?'

Peter looked at me like I'd lost my marbles.

'Björn, your client is the focus of a murder investigation. And it's not entirely impossible he has become the victim of a crime himself – at a time and place that puts a spotlight on you! I really don't understand how this could leave you so cold.'

'Mindfulness.'

'Excuse me?'

'Breathing exercises, time islands, mindful action: you should give it a try some time.'

'I've got no time for that.'

'At some point, you'll be ready to make time for mind-fulness. Until then, let's summarise: you've got nothing concrete on the finger yet. As soon as Dragan reappears, he can pay you a finder's fee for a watch and a buckle. What else? No leads on who threw the grenade?'

'Only that it was probably the same type as the one in the lay-by on Friday.'

'I don't want to tell you how to do your job, Peter, but the attack can only have been committed by someone who knew what my message to Toni said. So you should prob-ably first clarify whether anyone among your ranks might've passed it on to Boris.'

Peter was about to object, but I continued, 'And if that would prove not to be the case, the only remaining suspect is Toni.'

With that, I got up. I picked up my tray. Peter stayed seated. He looked exhausted and emaciated.

'You should really eat something,' I said. 'I can recom-mend the Happy Meal. The toy of the week is a parrot that talks – your son's sure to enjoy it. Watch out, though, it's not very sturdy. But then, nothing's perfect.'

The copper just growled and waved me off. By the time I'd dropped off my tray and made my way to the door, he was already gone. I hadn't told him about leaving the firm, but that wouldn't be official until the next week anyway.

I set off for home. As I strolled through the city centre, I decided to pay Boris a visit that evening. I had to talk to Toni beforehand though: I'd ignored his message long enough. I sent him an eleven-digit text and promptly got a call on the prepaid phone. I sat down on a bench facing a frothily babbling but otherwise unadorned 1970s fountain.

'Björn, why didn't you call sooner?'

'Mum, is that you?'

'Cut the crap, mate. It's all hitting the fan up here. Dragan's not around, and you're the only one in touch with him. Decisions need to be made right fucking now, you hear?'

'Sounds like you're under some pressure.'

'Pressure? Fuck right off with you. It's all going to blow up in our face if Dragan doesn't make some decisions, and sharpish too.'

'There will be an officer meeting on Thursday, that's when Dragan will tell you what we need to do.'

'Fuck Thursday. Thursday is a long fucking way off. We don't have that kind of time! I need to talk to him right now. Right fucking now!'

My mindfulness guide had a few very helpful things to say about time pressure:

Time is relative. How we perceive it depends on our subjective assessment of the situation we find ourselves in. Time pressure, therefore, is nothing more than an expression of tension.

Or a sign that someone had fallen flat on his face trying – for the second time – to kill his boss and was furious with himself about it. I could imagine how he must be feeling. Still, I had succeeded at what he had screwed up – and on my first attempt. That's why I was on that bench feeling zero time pressure as I watched the bubbling fountain with its crown of foam, a stray floating chip and a random pigeon.

'Tell me, Toni, is it possible that you are feeling a bit tense?'

'Of course I am!'

'Why is that?'

'Because . . . because . . . because for the second time in four days, my boss was almost blown up. . . Because my closest employee was shot in the head in the woods . . . Because Boris is massacring our whole operation . . . Is that enough for you?'

I followed the small, dirty-white crown of foam along the edge of the fountain as it drifted away from the chip.

'Try to set up a time island, it really helps.'

'Are you kidding me?'

'I just want to be helpful.'

'You want to be helpful, mate? Take me to Dragan, right now.'

I had no intention of letting myself be pressured by Toni's pressure. As the pigeon tried to peck the soggy chip out of the fountain, I went on the attack.

'Maybe you can explain to me how this apartment blew up less than an hour after I texted you.'

'Of course I can. Even a numpty would understand: the police intercepted our fucking texts.'

'And then tossed a hand grenade in there?'

'Boris obviously has a mole that passed it on to him, and

then one of Boris's people threw the fucking hand grenade. We need to act against Boris right now.'

I was reaching my quota of right nows. 'That's still Dragan's call, and Thursday at the earliest.'

'No, take me to him first!'

'That's definitely not up to you.'

'Excuse me, mister lawyer man. You spent a peaceful weekend at the lake with your little one, fishing, swimming and toasting fucking marshmallows, while I'm up to my neck in shite here, trying to save the business. I'll tell you one thing: if you don't set up a talk with Dragan right now, next weekend your daughter will be splashing around ten centimetres below the surface of the lake. Have I made myself clear?'

The foam around the edge of the fountain was suddenly nothing compared to the foam starting to form around my mouth.

Of course he had made himself clear. By threatening my daughter, he had just clearly made himself my enemy for life. In the last four days, others had died for less. In addition, Toni had just revealed to me that he obviously had a mole with the police, otherwise he wouldn't know so much about my weekend. And if this mole also had access to my voicemail, they would've also told Toni that Murat wanted to meet with me. And if this mole knew that a finger wearing Dragan's ring was found on the neighbouring property, then sooner or later Toni would find that out as well. The fact that Toni hadn't mentioned the finger led me to conclude that either he didn't know about it yet or he wanted to keep it up his sleeve.

But above all, my by-now-familiar mindfulness routine kicked in:

1. I took in the purpose of what I was about to do: threaten Toni.
2. I took a deep breath in and out.
3. I calmly and centredly started verbally castrating Toni.

'Did you make yourself *clear*, mister barman? Let me sum it up: you want me to tell Dragan you don't give a fuck about his explicit order to stand down and wait for his instructions. You want me to tell Dragan to get in touch with you ASAP. And you want me to tell dear old Uncle Dragan that you'll kill his favourite lawyer's daughter if he doesn't do exactly what you want. If I understood all that correctly, then the best advice I can give you as a lawyer is to cut off your own dick and cook it up however you prefer before sticking it down your own throat. Otherwise, it'll be up to Dragan to determine the time and the recipe. Have *I* made myself clear?'

Toni had never met this Björn. But then he'd also never threatened my daughter before.

After a long silence, he finally said, 'I . . . Well . . . It's just that . . . Maybe you can just ask Dragan to be considerate of the circumstances we're in over here. I just want . . .'

'Excuse me?'

'I just want . . .'

'You don't get to "want", you "would like".'

'OK, well I would just like Dragan to tell me what I need to do.'

'There's a good boy. And now just wait for Dragan's instructions – or you can insert the next hand grenade as a suppository.'

'I . . . I . . .'

'Anything else?'

'Listen, Björn, if Dragan is alive and you speak to him, then I would like to formally apologise to him.'

That's how it's done. Unusually compliant for that muppet, but unfortunately, he didn't leave it at that and struck up a much less compliant tone. 'But if Dragan is no longer alive or you're not speaking to him at all, then you are dead. You have until the end of the month to take me to Dragan. If you don't, you'll be in pieces by the first of May.'

I hung up.

Now I had another ultimatum to deal with. By 30 April, I also needed to secure a preschool spot. Somehow, my new mindful lifestyle was putting me under a very centred time pressure.

The first possible solution that occurred to me was: Toni needed to go.

I didn't have to make that decision just yet, however. First, I had to pay a visit to Boris.

20

Enjoyable Eating

Mindfulness is also the art of enjoying the everyday. Eating, for example, stimulates all the senses. Pick up an everyday food item and imagine you are experiencing it for the very first time. What does it look like? What does it feel like? What does it smell like? Does it make any sound when you bite into it? What feelings can you perceive when your body ingests it?

Enjoy the process with all your senses. Have an experience that is entirely your own. This experience is perfect just as it is.

Joschka Breitner, *Slowing Down in the Fast Lane: Mindfulness for Managers*

Getting in touch with Boris was relatively easy. He dined at his own Russian restaurant at the same time almost every night. Above it was his office, and below was a club. You could only get into the restaurant with a reservation, a search warrant or an invitation from Boris. The bouncers outside the restaurant frisked me and brought me to Boris.

Boris and I had a pretty good relationship. I even liked him a little. Unlike Dragan, he wasn't temperamental – which didn't make him any less cruel. On the contrary, Boris knew exactly what he was doing. He didn't inflict pain on anyone impulsively, he did it intentionally. Boris was Russian-German and grew up in the same part of town as Dragan. Both outcasts in school, the two had become friends. They fought the same knobheads, chased the same skirts. They committed their first criminal offences together, bought and sold their first drugs together, and pimped out their first girls together. They'd had the signet rings made with their first earnings.

The reason for their split was the usual: Dragan had stolen Boris's girlfriend. What was more unusual was Boris's reaction: he had the girlfriend beheaded and then nailed her torso to Dragan's front door. As a result, the police completely turned Dragan's life upside down. From then on, they went their separate ways. Boris took the ring off, which unfortunately wasn't an option for Dragan. They divided up their territory between them. Though Boris knew that Dragan was willing to cross any line at any time, Dragan knew that, if he did, it would come back to haunt him in ways he couldn't even imagine. This established a balance of terror and mistrust.

In order to maintain that balance, they met every six months. Since becoming Dragan's lawyer, I'd been attending these consultations. Boris appreciated my work, not least because I'd snuck him a few tips on how to legalise parts of his business. This helped preserve the peace, but Boris would never steal me away from Dragan. In this business, you didn't do that with lawyers any more than with girlfriends. This was something that had really reassured me over the years – I wouldn't have liked Dragan to nail my headless body to Boris's door in retribution.

If Dragan was a man built like a tree, Boris was built like a bear: tall, massive, hairy. He looked stout and good-natured, but consisted of nothing but muscle, and behind his rounded face lurked an ice-cold intelligence.

Boris was at his table, having dinner. There were plates and bowls everywhere. I'd never been able to get the hang of Russian food. It honestly disgusted me a bit to see Boris stuff himself with all these strange dishes.

I remembered an exercise Breitner had about eating. Food is particularly well suited to stimulating all your senses. To experience this, we had both eaten a slice of apple and paid attention to how it sharpened each individual sense. It'd felt a bit silly, but I had found it relaxing. So as to get something positive out of my negative associations with watching Boris eat, I tried to repeat the exercise through Boris and his dinner.

Pick up an everyday food item and imagine you are experiencing it for the very first time. What does it look like?

To me, Russian food always looked like a Chinese person had eaten Italian food and then vomited it over a plate of traditional German cuisine. Massive ladles of sour mush laced with dough and vegetables, and here or there a chunk of meat or potato peeking through. I'd never been a big fan of stews; Boris loved stews.

What does it feel like?

Judging by the liquid dripping apparently unnoticed down his chin, it had to feel like a second skin: soft, supple, warm.

What does it smell like?

It smelled like a Sunday afternoon in a big apartment building's stairwell: countless smells that didn't mesh.

Does it make any sound when you bite into it?

Yes, or at least when Boris did. It sounded like a suede boat shoe stepping into pretty low-viscosity cowshit. You really had to listen carefully, but that was the exact sound.

What feelings can you perceive when your body ingests it?

A feeling of gratitude came over me: my body was *not* ingesting this.

Enjoy the process with all your senses. Have an experience that is entirely your own. This experience is perfect just as it is.

Thanks to my little mindfulness exercise, this experience had at least stretched and warmed up my senses.

'Björn! I appreciate you stopping by in person.' I knew Boris meant it. 'Would you like something to eat?' he asked, pointing to the dishes on the table.

'No, thank you. I . . .'

'Don't tell me you've already eaten.'

'I haven't, I just hate Russian food.'

Boris laughed. 'You know I prefer a brave truth over a craven lie, but you're really missing out!'

I smiled politely.

Boris turned serious again. 'Let's get straight to the point, why didn't that spineless dog come himself?'

'Dragan . . . had to scatter.' That wasn't a lie: I'd scattered him myself.

'He's hiding from me.'

'He's hiding from the police.'

'And hiding from me.'

'And hiding from you, yes. But I brought this for you.'

I gave Boris a page from the previous day's newspaper covered in circles and lines. It was signed at the bottom with the 'D'-branded fingerprint. Boris disdainfully picked it up.

'Like in the good old days?'

Boris had a 'B' branded into his right thumb. Dragan and he had developed the newspaper method back when they were still close.

'If this is one of Dragan's crossword puzzles, then he can get the following solution tattooed on his arse: "Burn in hell!"'

Still, Boris started deciphering the squiggles into three sentences:

'Igor's death unfortunate. Lay-by was a trap. Lawyer has full authority to negotiate.'

Boris picked up the newspaper page, touched it to the table's candle, and held it up in front of me.

'If I remember the video correctly, Igor burned much longer than this newspaper.' Boris let the ashes flutter down into a wine cooler. 'Plus, he was beaten to death while still on fire. "Unfortunate" indeed.'

Boris shovelled a forkful of food into his mouth and chewed for a while.

'Alright,' he said finally, looking me in the eye. 'So Dragan claims to have been lured into a trap?'

I nodded.

'And he didn't mean to kill Igor, that was just collateral damage.'

I nodded again.

'OK.' Boris put on a false smile. 'If he's sure of this, then . . . Let me think . . . Yes, then he can't help it that Igor has been turned into a pile of smashed-up cinders and the matter is settled. Please tell Dragan he can come out of hiding, so we can get together and make some blini.'

'You mean those little Russian pancakes?'

Boris turned serious again. 'Those little Russian pancakes will be the last thing Dragan puts in his mouth, before I cut off his head.' Looking almost bored, he devoured another forkful.

'Boris – let's discuss retribution later. If Dragan was ambushed, then the person responsible is also responsible for Igor's death. As soon as that person is caught, you can both take your revenge on him together.'

Boris stopped chewing. He swallowed, put his fork aside and dabbed at his mouth with a napkin. I finally had his attention. 'Let's pretend Dragan and I have interests in common. What do *you* think happened in this lay-by?'

That question was a good sign. I took a deep breath. 'For weeks now, someone on Dragan's territory has been selling drugs at half-price.'

'I had no part in that,' Boris responded. It sounded like a factual statement, not a justification.

'Sasha got a call from Murat,' I continued.

'Who's Murat?' Boris looked at me, clearly in the dark.

'One of Toni's little soldiers, no reason you should know him. Anyway, Murat said Igor was about to receive a drugs shipment for Dragan's territory from a guy on this lay-by. Sasha and Dragan went over. Igor was there, the guy was too.'

'And were there any drugs?' Boris enquired.

'No, but there was a crate of hand grenades.'

'Then you should ask this Murat why he's spreading such shite.'

'Dragan would love to, but Murat was found shot dead yesterday morning.'

Boris picked up his napkin with both hands and folded it twice. He was thinking. 'And what does Toni have to say about that?'

'He wants Dragan to start a war against you. He has already threatened me that something will happen to my daughter if he's not put in touch with Dragan.'

'And what does Dragan think?'

'He doesn't really like it when his lawyer's daughter is threatened – incidentally, I don't either.'

'Perhaps anyone looking to talk to Dragan should just kill you: if he no longer has a mouthpiece, he'll have to come back.'

I hadn't thought about it like that. This was not ideal, but for now Dragan still spoke through me. So I spoke.

'Dragan sees you as the priority, not Toni. Dragan doesn't want to go to war with you, Boris. He wants clarity between you first.'

Boris looked at me. It was obvious what he had concluded from what I just said: Dragan is alive, Dragan is scared, Dragan is dealing with an internal problem.

Boris pushed his plate aside, as though clearing the table between us.

'Since you were so open and honest with me, dear

Björn, I want to be open and honest with you. Igor got a very cheap deal on French hand grenades. Not usually our kind of thing, as they're no good as a tool of war. But when we throw them into a competitor's club where we'd like to be selling our drugs, they occasionally come in handy. Igor had never seen the guy or his goods. It was their first meeting.'

'And Igor's last.'

I shouldn't have said that.

Boris shot me a menacing glare. 'Igor was one of my most important men. And I still have no proof that Dragan wasn't trying to meddle in my affairs.'

I raised my hands in a placatory gesture. 'Boris, Dragan was ambushed just like Igor. We have to assume that all three of them – Dragan, Sasha and Igor – were supposed to have died that night. The guy with the hand grenades was supposed to make sure of that. But then the coachload of kids showed up.'

'Who's responsible for this? I need a name.'

It was the one we both knew we were really talking about, Toni. But officially saying so would have immediate consequences: Boris would pick him up. To save my own skin, however, I first needed to convince the rest of Dragan's officers Toni had to go. I needed proof for that, and to get it I needed time.

'If you give me a little time, I—'

Boris did not let me finish. 'I'll give Dragan six days. Then he will give me a clear answer as to who I've got to thank for my dead officer. You will then serve up the pig with an apple in his mouth. I'll then personally stuff him with a few hand grenades, or else . . .'

I was all ears.

'Or else I'll hang a few hand grenades around your neck. Maybe that'll get you motivated.'

'Within six days?' I pretended to think it over, pretended two other people hadn't already given me 30 April as a final deadline. 'That'd be . . . next Monday.'

'Exactly. Next Monday you hand over the traitor or else you're dead.'

Six days. It wouldn't be easy, but it was doable. I felt a degree of relief. 'Don't worry,' I said. 'I'll bring him to you. Anything else?'

'And then you take me to Dragan.'

Any relief I'd felt evaporated. 'Excuse me?'

'I need to have a little chat with that coward. So something like this doesn't happen again.'

'Yes, but . . . how do you imagine that happening? He's wanted by the police.'

'It's your job to make it happen. If I haven't spoken to Dragan by next Monday, you're dead.'

By now I was wondering if my life wouldn't have been a lot easier if I'd had Dragan just kill me the previous Saturday. But oh well, just another problem that needed to be solved by Monday.

'Well, now we've covered all things business,' Boris beamed at me, 'how about a nice slice of Leningradsky cake for pudding?'

21

Panic

A panic attack can be alleviated through the following mindfulness exercise: first, find a quiet place in your apartment, house or office where you will not be disturbed. Ideally, it should have a view of a garden or a tree. Before starting, loosen any tight clothing, belts or shoes.

Take in the world around you. One by one, silently list five things you can see. After that, focus on five things you can hear (e.g. different sounds or voices).

If possible, keep your eyes fixed upon a single area. Now notice how the ground supports your feet, how your legs rest firmly on your feet, how the rest of your body is supported by the ground, your feet and your legs. As you feel your weight on the ground, you will realise that nothing has the power to knock you over.

Joschka Breitner, *Slowing Down in the Fast Lane: Mindfulness for Managers*

The next morning, due to my new lack of professional obligations, I could really have slept in. Unpleasantly, however, I was awakened at eight thirty by an explosion outside my building. Careful to maintain my mindfulness practice, I first sat up in bed and took three deep breaths. Then I opened the blinds and looked down at the street. My former company car was on fire. Its entire rear end was torn apart and burning, black smoke all aswirl. Though the rest of the car had been unharmed, with each passing second more and more of it was falling victim to the flames. In front of the blazing wreckage stood Clara, paralysed, pale as chalk and wearing ill-fitting designer clothing; her traineeship apparently included retrieving the firm's leased vehicle. This was the third explosion in five days. The first two were meant for Dragan, and I had to assume this one wasn't meant for Clara, but for me. Toni apparently wanted to underline his threat from the day before. He had succeeded. My heart was racing, my whole body soaked with sweat. This wasn't fear – it was panic.

I quickly reached for my mindfulness guide and opened it to the chapter with an exercise on how to deal with panic:

Find a quiet place in your apartment, house or office where you will not be disturbed. Ideally, it should have a view of a garden or a tree. Before starting, loosen any tight clothing, belts or shoes.

That was easy. I was already standing at the window of my bedroom, which was quiet – until the explosion, that is – and looked out on a quiet, green street. I saw a front yard scattered with smoking debris. On the other side of the street, one burning rear tyre was stuck in a tree. I was barefoot, wearing comfortable boxer shorts and a T-shirt. I kept reading.

Take in the world around you.

I was in a quiet apartment with a pleasantly cool granite floor. My room was minimalistically furnished and very tidy. Outside, however, it looked like a bomb had gone off – because a bomb *had* just gone off.

One by one, silently list five things you can see.

I saw a burning tyre in a tree. I saw the burning back end of a car. I saw a warped boot lid. I saw an ashen trainee, and I saw broken glass scattered as far as twenty metres from the car.

After that, focus on five things you can hear (e.g. different sounds or voices).

I focused on the countless car alarms that'd been triggered by the explosion. I heard the crackle of flames devouring the A8's back seat. Now I heard the gas tank explode, the burning tyre drop from the tree, and finally a feverish shriek from the trainee.

If possible, keep your eyes fixed upon a single area.

I first wanted to fix on the trainee. But then she started randomly running around, so I fixed onto the car wreck itself – which wasn't easy, as its outline kept being subsumed by black clouds of smoke.

Now notice how the ground supports your feet, how your legs rest firmly on your feet, how the rest of your body is supported by the ground, your feet and your legs.

I noticed all of this. A beautiful feeling.

As you feel your weight on the ground, you will realise that nothing has the power to knock you over.

It was true: I felt like nothing could knock me over.

Now turn your attention to your breathing. Breathe calmly and evenly.

For two minutes, I breathed calmly and evenly. My panic

subsided. The car alarms stopped beeping. The trainee had been tackled to the ground by passers-by who were now trying to talk her down. A simple mindfulness exercise had resolved the situation, and I could devote myself to practical matters again. What needed to be done first?

Since I'd been wanting to tell Peter from Homicide Command that I'd left the firm, I decided to use that call to also inform him that an assassination attempt had obviously just been made on one of the firm's leased cars. Peter answered after the second ring:

'What's up?'

'There's something important I forgot to tell you yesterday afternoon.'

'Hit me.'

'I quit the firm. I've been on leave since yesterday and will officially be out of that place on the first of May.'

'And you're calling me before nine in the morning to tell me that?'

'Yes, because that information might make your work easier.'

'How so?'

'Insofar as about eight minutes ago a car blew up outside my apartment.'

'What car?'

'A black Audi A8.'

'Your company car?'

'Not exactly. I returned the papers and keys to the office yesterday afternoon. Legally and factually, I am neither its lessee nor its owner. And if there are any questions: as the explosion woke me up, I can't say anything about the sequence of events leading up to said explosion.'

'Is Dragan behind this?'

'I can say even less about that.'

'So you represent Dragan independently now?'

'Someone has to do it.'

'Well, then . . . Thanks for letting me know.'

'Catch you later.'

I hung up.

Next, I called Sasha and told him what had happened. I asked him to tell Walter to dispatch a personal protection detail after all, a very inconspicuous one though, watching first and foremost to find out who'd been watching *me*. Sasha assured me that a team would be available within half an hour. He also told me that we could swing by the co-op that night. I agreed, the sooner we could the better. The officer meeting was scheduled for the next day.

I already felt much better. This was my first day in over a decade without any professional commitments. I had traded a lucrative permanent position for the freedom of a freelance father. Hans in Luck would've been proud. Sure, I did still need to deal with a few investigations against me for perverting the course of justice, not to mention one death threat against my daughter, two death threats against myself and the power-plays of at least one psychopath – two, if you counted Boris. In addition, my erstwhile company car had just blown up outside my apartment. Yet Hans in Luck also didn't keep the horse; he simply kept exchanging it. But that hadn't stopped him from being happy in the moment, and it shouldn't stop me either.

I did a few more breathing exercises at the window and decided to tell Katharina about my career change. After all, our daughter was the reason I'd wanted a change in the first place. I called Katharina and asked if she'd mind if I took Emily to the playground.

'On a Wednesday morning?'

'Yes. In fact, this one in particular.'

'What happened? Did Dragan give you the boot?'

I spared myself explaining to her the intricacies of the complex relationship between an employed lawyer, their employer and their client. Instead, I imagined that my future ex-wife had the best intentions. That the entire universe had the best intentions for me. That even everybody on the subway had the best intentions . . . And that was enough.

'Listen, Katharina, my mindfulness training has made me realise that I cannot continue working the way I have. My workload at the firm has gotten to be too much for me. I have come to a mutual termination agreement with Von Dresen, Erkel and Dannwitz.'

'But that's . . .' Katharina was speechless.

'Financially, nothing is going to change for now. They agreed to a very nice severance agreement.'

'So you finally won't have to deal with all those criminals any more?'

'Not with those at the firm. As far as the others . . . Well, I'll have to earn money one way or another. Criminal law is my speciality, so I can't rule out that I won't have to—'

That wasn't a complete lie.

'What about Dragan?' Katharina interrupted.

'I don't even know where he is, but I'll certainly have to wrap things up with him too.'

That our daughter's life had been threatened as part of this wrapping-up was something I decided not to share with her at this point.

'The main thing is that all this round-the-clock drama has come to an end, you'll be happy to hear.'

'Emily will also be happy to hear that.' As long as Toni didn't deliver on his threat.

'Can I pick her up right away?'

'Of course, come on over!'

Since I no longer had a company car, I didn't need to feel angry that it'd been blown up. So I took the bus to Katharina's completely by choice.

Emily was thrilled to be going on another outing with me.

Katharina seemed very relaxed, and she reiterated how happy she was I'd finally quit my job. 'Could it be that that glimmer of hope on the horizon is slowly turning into full-on daybreak?'

I didn't want to explain that this glimmer on the horizon might be accentuated by a series of grenade explosions – which I'd hesitate to interpret as daybreak. But I also didn't want to deprive her of her joy. Who knows, maybe all these explosions around me were heralding a new day. I decided to be optimistic.

'Possibly, but right now I'm just trying to enjoy the moment as it is. Plus, I'll have more time to take care of the preschool thing.'

Katharina grabbed my arm and gave me a kiss on the cheek. She hadn't shown that much tenderness in months – apparently, mindfulness was sexy.

22

Bitterness

Bitterness is an expression of prolonged disappointment. This disappointment may have been due to outside forces, but how long it stays inside you is entirely up to you.

Joschka Breitner, *Slowing Down in the Fast Lane: Mindfulness for Managers*

When sufficient harmony had been established between Katharina and myself, I prepared to set off with Emily. Before we left, Katharina asked me to rub Emily's chest with Vicks every two hours, as she showed signs of a slight cold. I took Emily and the ointment, and we caught the tram to the playground at the Schlosspark. I'd liked it there the day before: there were tons of climbing frames, slides, swings, and lots of sand all around. Plus an espresso cart plentifully supplied with oat milk for the growing number of yummy mummies suffering some kind of intolerance.

Emily wanted to go on the slide by herself, to show me how great she had gotten at it. So I leaned against the playground fence and watched Emily and the other kids, and the other adults.

Anyone who sweepingly states that all children are great is lying. Your own child, yes, they're the greatest child in the world. And fortunately there's quite a number of other children who seem likeable enough. Quite simply, though, there's a whole bunch of kids that are just arseholes. Looking at them, you can immediately tell how profoundly unlikeable their parents are. Arsehole kids, however, are not exclusively defined by the way they look: they are also demanding, repetitive, unpleasant and exhausting. At this playground, these children were recognisable by their monotonous whining.

Except for me, one half of a couple and another lone man, all the adults at the playground were women. The couple was one of those aggressively happy ones: attractive, sporty, successful – it was obvious that since the day they were born they'd been living off their parents, who probably also took care of the grandkids seventy per cent of the time.

The other dad looked a little sad and lost, probably another infrequent playground-goer, visibly uncomfortable at being surrounded by women. Maybe he was a divorcé compulsively staging a scene from his previously carefree life for his kid.

Aside from these three outliers, there were basically two types of women: mums and childminders.

The mums were usually overwhelmed, lethargic-looking women with forced smiles who were each taking care of one overexcited child.

The childminders, on the other hand, were upbeat women single-handedly pushing open-plan prams with up to five lethargic-looking, overwhelmed toddlers.

In Germany, childminders can take in up to five children. If there is even one arsehole child among them, the other four will basically be left to their own devices while the childminder tries to prevent the arsehole from biting, beating or scratching the other children – or to make them stop sulking.

As my eyes swept across the playground, I suddenly realised that instead of enjoying my time with Emily I'd been thinking bitter thoughts about the mums, child-minders and children around me.

After just three minutes on the playground, my mood had changed from 'Oh, how beautiful!' to 'I'm surrounded by morons!' – all without any change to my external circumstances.

My mindfulness guide had something to say about bitterness too:

Bitterness is an expression of prolonged disappointment. This disappointment may have been due to outside forces, but how long it stays inside you is entirely up to you. Once you have decided that you do not want your quality of life to be affected by old disappointments, ask yourself the following questions:
1. *How did the disappointment first arise?*
2. *Do you really want to give those reasons so much power over your life that they turn it bitter?*
3. *How would you feel if you realised that your happiness does not depend on anything outside yourself?*

What was I so disappointed about that was making me so bitter? The answer was very simple: unlike all of the women around me, I'd never spent a weekday at a playground with my daughter in both of our lives.

For two and a half years, I had completely stayed out of my daughter's care because I'd been working like a maniac. All those years, I'd never found myself exhausted at a play-ground, never had to put all my needs aside for days or weeks at a time just to be there for one single small person. This made me not only terribly disappointed in myself, but above all terribly angry that I'd never stepped up. Two and a half years I'd wasted, years I'd never get back. And it definitely wasn't the fault of any of these mums and children that I'd just been winding myself up about: it was nobody's fault but my own. I no longer wanted to give this bitterness any power, especially since I'd already radically changed my life. From now on, I would find my happiness myself.

I got up and went to Emily, took her in my arms, threw her in the air and caught my happiness with both hands.

To celebrate, I was just about to treat the other bitter-looking father and even the pointedly happy couple to a latte when my phone rang.

It was Sasha. He told me that the security detail Walter sent to shadow me had just disarmed someone who'd been following me. He'd apparently followed me from my apartment to my ex-wife's house to the playground. The security team, disguised as a couple, had unobtrusively removed him from circulation when he'd gone behind a tree to make a phone call. In addition to the latte in his hand, he'd also been armed with a pistol and two French hand grenades, but he was now cuffed in their boot.

I looked around: both the happy couple and the sad man had disappeared. Considering my apparent inability to read people, I quietly congratulated myself on the fact that I'd become a lawyer, not an HR consultant. I'd sooner have thought three of the childminders were professional killers than that one mousy chap. And I could never have imagined that the happy couple were my protectors, not parental antimatter.

I told Sasha to ask the team to give me a little more time. Surely a few hours in the boot wouldn't harm the guy, Sasha and I could deal with him together later. Sasha assured me that this wouldn't be a problem. In addition, the co-op had confirmed that evening's proposed appointment through their appointment management platform. Sasha only had to confirm by email. We ended the conversation there, and for the rest of the morning I happily and safely enjoyed my little ray of sunshine. On our way home, instead of a latte, we got chocolate milk and a newspaper at McDonald's.

23

Actionism

Of course, you *could* try pulling on the grass to make it grow faster, but you could also rest your head on it; neither will affect the grass's rate of growth. But only one of these two options leaves you rested well enough to mow the grass later on.

Joschka Breitner, *Slowing Down in the Fast Lane: Mindfulness for Managers*

The Little Fish co-op was very motivated to talk to us. Financially speaking, an eviction action – however unfounded – is a disadvantage for any business: no one is prepared to put their child in a preschool for three years if a brothel is scheduled to open in the same building within the first year. So these self-described innovators wanted to avoid any such trial. On my behalf, Sasha had confirmed the innovative meeting set through their innovative appointment management platform with an almost as innovative email.

I remembered the Little Fish space from our admissions interview with Emily. The co-op had rented the ground floor of a stately and stunning but severely run-down town house. Until recently, the upper floors had housed an architectural office, a yoga studio and a start-up for instant-noodle subscriptions. All three had since responded positively to my suggestion they vacate the premises immediately and save themselves a world of trouble.

Of all the admissions interviews Katharina and I had been through, the one with Little Fish had been particularly absurd. When two parents need to visit a preschool together because they're looking to place their child, any normal-thinking person would ask: who takes care of their child during the interview? Katharina and I had arrived at the very logical solution of taking Emily with us. Where else can you feel confident to bring your child if not to a preschool?

But when we got there, we were almost indignantly asked if we wouldn't rather leave Emily in the car, so as to ensure the 'assessment' could proceed undisturbed. They said the parking spaces out front were quite clearly visible from inside – for me, however, clearly visible parking wasn't even a minor criterion when deciding on a preschool.

This meant that the interview was basically over, at least for us: within thirty seconds, it was clear that our Emily would be in completely the wrong hands with these people. Nevertheless, we stayed, and Emily did too – if only because we had a legal right to a preschool spot. That also gave us a right to get a closer look at this ludicrous place, and it was worth it.

The three innovative founders had turned the admissions interview into a kind of assessment. In total, there were four sets of parents and one mum. The other three sets of parents had been able to place their child with grandparents. The lone mum had left her child with her 'better half'. Everyone looked at Emily as if bringing a child to a preschool in the evening was a sign of parental neglect.

First, we had to complete a written quiz on what we knew about Little Fish. The parents on either side of us were furiously writing. When I wanted to copy off one of the mums, she in all seriousness turned her back to block me. Since all Katharina and I knew was that the preschool was within a ten-minute drive from our two homes, we gave the paper over to Emily to colour on.

Afterwards, there was a creative-slash-motivational group discussion in which every parental unit was supposed to explain why the child of the parents to their *right* – none of whom were present except Emily – would enrich the preschool's community. At that point, neither Katharina nor I were taking the whole procedure very seriously any more. That's why we pointed out to the parents to our *left* that Emily had psychic powers: she had a unique ability to identify stupid people. As we explained, however, that unfortunately was also precisely why we had to leave immediately – so as not to overwhelm Emily's paranormal powers in this particularly triggering assembly.

The next time I found myself dealing with the preschool was when I learned Dragan had bought up the building. I'd therefore had no hesitation about kicking these pre-school posers out. At that time I'd of course assumed Emily wouldn't need to rely on this preschool for a place. How quickly things could change.

24

Communication

If you want to optimise your own communication skills, the way to get there is through emotional intelligence. This intelligence can be trained by targetedly training your attention: develop a better impression and understanding of your interlocutor by gaining insight into what they *need*.

Joschka Breitner, *Slowing Down in the Fast Lane: Mindfulness for Managers*

After all their hypocritical hoodoo around the application, I really didn't like the fact that these guys thought they could exact retribution on my daughter just because they didn't like what I did for a living.

Mindfulness had done me good by helping me get my problems with Dragan under control. I wanted to continue down this path. So I didn't have the slightest inhibition against going over there with Sasha and tearing these self-righteous arseholes some new ones. In fact, I was looking forward to it – for Emily, for me and, yes, for Katharina too.

Of course, I had mentally prepared for the appointment.

My mindfulness guide was very instructive when it came to communication:

If you want to optimise your own communication skills, the way to get there is through emotional intelligence. This intelligence can be trained by targetedly training your attention: develop a better impression and understanding of your interlocutor by gaining insight into what they need.

So I trained my emotional intelligence by considering what my counterparts might need. I knew they were self-righteous bleeding hearts. They spent a lot of time in front of the mirror and in front of their Apple devices, using social media to weave a lovely set of lies around their tyre-wear company. First and foremost, they needed to see *themselves* reflected, specifically in some utopia of peace and harmony.

So the main question was how much peace and harmony we'd need to offer them in exchange for their utopian preschool.

Of the three innovators, one had a business management degree and considered himself a financial genius. Another had a law degree and considered himself a lawyer. The third had dropped out of first a business management and then a law degree, and therefore considered himself a creative. In all their narcissism, none of them had felt they needed any external support in this conversation. I had.

We were meeting in the preschool's administrative office. Sasha and I had brought a sixty-something gentleman who was so inconspicuous that he could quietly sit on a children's chair outside the office without raising any enquiries. The atmosphere was frosty. Unconventional as these three bros were, they waived the handshake customary everywhere else, even among adversaries. Instead, we were offered an espresso from a 5,000-euro portafilter. It was a sign of their tendency to blow their own trumpet that these three bros wanted to show off their innovative preschool was able to afford an espresso machine with a 5,000-euro portafilter.

The five of us sat at a small meeting table that had really only been designed for four. Everything in the office was contrived to show off. It looked like an advertising agency specialising in design products for children, not a space where children's needs were ever discussed. While bro number three lit an honest-to-goodness electronic pipe by pressing the 'on' button in the pipe's bowl, I took the floor and started the conversation.

'We asked for this meeting to clear up a few misunderstandings. You already know who I am, but you might want to get to know this man over here.' I pointed to Sasha. 'This is Sasha, Little Fish's new managing director.'

Irritated disbelief showed on all three faces. Bro number one spoke.

'I see. Since when?'

'Soon. I guess in about . . . twenty minutes.'

'I don't know what you think you're on about.'

I tried to understand his need to understand what was happening and, in simple terms, explained to him what would transpire:

'What'll happen next is this: we will offer you one and a half times the face value of your shares in Little Fish. Those shares will then be transferred to a different company, Sergowicz Preschool and Fishing. The preschool will continue to operate and every child will retain their spot. For your part, you'll have a little more money and considerably more free time. That little guy outside is a notary, and he will wrap up the formalities. In ten minutes, my friend Sasha will be the new managing director, and then we can all go home.'

Bro number one asked about the only bit he'd apparently grasped.

'Didn't you say this would all be over in twenty minutes?'

'Right, I took into account a certain amount of time for questions.'

Sasha stepped in. 'Any other questions, or can we call in the notary?'

The notary had come to Sasha's attention a few years earlier when he found the man upside down on a St Andrew's cross in the basement of one of Dragan's brothels, completely naked but for a red ball-gag in his mouth. Sasha was there to warn all customers they were about to be raided. Since then, the notary had been grateful to him for not having to be put right-side-up by the police. He felt a little indebted – also because Sasha had documented the man's before-and-after states on his phone.

None of these bros wanted to wrap things up quickly, however. Bro number two took the floor.

'What are you on about? You need to turn our preschool into a brothel for your gungy boss and now you want us to sell our shares to you?'

'No, as I have just explained, my client will continue to operate the preschool. So this is no longer about the children, only your egos. And I just made you an offer for those.'

It was bro number three's turn.

'Listen here, we were under the assumption you were here to apologise for your behaviour. Threatening us with eviction, turning this children's paradise into a brothel – that's not on. But if you want trouble, go for it. You obviously have no idea how well connected we are on social media. We'll start a shitstorm you'll never forget.'

Though I had planned to keep the conversation at a friendly and not overly emotional pitch, it appeared I'd have to take it there.

To me, a social-media shitstorm was and remains so insignificant it's not even worth ignoring. The concept is neither meaningful nor measurable. Yet for those who worship at the altar of all things online, even just waving the word around is proof enough of its validity. A statement like 'Don't do that, otherwise there will be a shitstorm!' should be taken as seriously as someone telling their child: 'Finish your plate, otherwise a child in Africa will die.' Children die every second, all over the world. And every second, some idiot posts shite on the internet. None of this will improve if you just ignore all causality and threaten to lay the blame on someone else instead.

The shitstorm bro apparently felt the need to start a brawl. Mindful as I was, I'd make sure he'd get one. Once that need was satisfied, he might find he had a need for peace after all.

25

Forgiveness

Forgiveness is very liberating, especially to the one who forgives. Anger and thoughts of revenge can really get in your way. When you forgive the person you are angry with, the greatest freedom you generate is your own. Once you see that the person you are so immensely angry with is just a wounded soul like you, forgiving them is all the easier.

Joschka Breitner, *Slowing Down in the Fast Lane: Mindfulness for Managers*

Sometimes, people need to be forced to be happy. And in any case, I no longer wanted to stand in the way of what these three apparently needed most.

I gave Sasha a quick look and struck up a tone that was friendly, yet full of conviction: 'In fact, I *would* like to apologise for what's about to happen.'

'Why, what's going to happen— Mmmpf.'

Without warning, Sasha had grabbed the head of bro number two next to him and slammed it onto the table. Blood was dripping from his nose. The three bros were speechless with horror.

'Now that I've apologised for this incident, we can get down to business.'

Finally, bro number two found his voice again. 'That guy bwoke by nose!' he shouted, looking at his fellow shareholders. 'Caw the police!'

'You are welcome to call the police. But if you do, maybe you should erase your hard drives first.'

'Our hard drives? Why, what do they have to do with this?' asked bro number three.

'For a preschool, your hard drives contain rather a lot of Nazi child propaganda,' I replied.

'Nonsense, how would you even know what's on our computer?'

'Because I'm the one who downloaded all that funny business onto it, boyos,' Sasha said calmly, 'through that nifty confirmation link for your innovative appointment management platform.'

Bro number one turned to the computer over on the desk. He clicked the mouse and the desktop appeared on screen. As a wallpaper, the bros had chosen a selfie of the three of them on a beach somewhere in Asia: three straw hats, three pairs of Ray-Bans, three globalised bleeding hearts.

'See that folder named "Siegheilbigsmile"?' Sasha asked him. 'That's where you're storing all that filth. Very badly hidden, if you ask me.'

By hijacking the appointment software, Sasha had been able to send the posers the Trojan horse that was now on their desktop. Out of disbelief as much as curiosity, bro number one clicked on the folder with a trembling hand. An .exe file opened and installed something on the computer.

'You must be joking,' the bro said, clearly disturbed. At that very moment, hundreds of pictures, ebooks, movies and posters were being stored and distributed on the preschool network, all of them dedicated to the darkest pedagogical corners of twentieth-century German history. From children's books like the anti-Semitic *The Poisonous Mushroom* or the anti-French *Hans and Pierre: A Cheery Tale of the Trenches* to films such as the anti-communist *Hitler Youth Quex* – the broadest possible range of the previous century's politically incorrect children's entertainment.

I looked over at Sasha. 'Well, I'll be damned. That numpty really clicked on the file.'

'Told you: you can only gain access to someone's computer if they open the door for you. After that, you can just walk in.'

Bro number three was the first to regain his composure. 'Nazi child propaganda? What's the point of putting that garbage on our computer?'

I was happy to explain.

'It's very simple. To end this meeting, we're now left with two courses of action. In the first, the guy with the ouchy nose calls the police. He then tells them your story about the evil brothel operators who broke your noses. We then tell them our story of the arseholes we caught wanting to revive fascist educational methods. Let's see which story the press sinks its teeth into first.'

'And what's the second course of action?'

'I wasn't quite done with the first one. As part of the investigation into your fascist ideas about child-rearing, they're bound to come upon the story of Taruk.'

'What's that?'

'Taruk, my friend, is your employee of the month. A seven-year-old boy with a respiratory disease working in a Sri Lankan factory. For the past two years, he's been soldering and gluing together trendy flip-flops for you without the proper protection – for fifteen cents a day.'

'That's not true.'

'Isn't it? I'm not the one here who's been reaping the rewards of this post-truth world. Whether Taruk's story is true or fake won't change the fact that one call to the police will send both your preschool and your footwear business down the drain.'

'Considering how well connected you are on social media, the story is bound to make the rounds, mister shit-storm,' Sasha said.

'With registrations dropping, the preschool would probably become an upmarket brothel after all, but since you three are so smart, you'll probably invent some trendy way to turn Third World tyres into climate-neutral condoms.' I added. 'Wouldn't that be a sustainable business model?'

'You can't do this.'

'Yes, we can, but we don't need to. There's still course of action number two.'

'Which would be what?' the bro with the bloody nose wanted to know.

Now we had finally arrived at the point where I'd wanted to be. 'You transfer your shares in Little Fish to Sergowicz Preschool and Fishing. The preschool will continue to operate. We will pay you half the face value of your shares and you can continue to have children's fingers stitch together your silly little flop-flops.'

'But you said the offer was one and a half times the face value . . .'

'That was before we discovered the Nazi propaganda on your network. So, are we agreed?'

Bro number one wasn't. 'What would you have done if I hadn't accidentally opened the folder? Then those pictures wouldn't have been downloaded onto our computer.'

I cleared that up for him. 'First of all, you didn't click on that file by accident, but out of stupidity. Secondly, if you hadn't, Sasha would not have broken one of your noses, but at least one leg each. By that point, any one of you would surely have hobbled to the computer to click on the file.'

Bro number three switched back on.

'We'll need to talk about this first, just the three of us. I mean, this is nothing but mafia intimid— Grmmpf. Arghhhhh!'

Sasha had grabbed bro number three's head and slammed it into the table, unfortunately on the exact spot where he put down his e-pipe. The tabletop broke his nose. The pipe lost him a tooth.

'Can we bring this meeting to a close now?'

'Yes. Yes . . . Let's do that.'

I stepped out and brought in the notary.

'This is Mr Derkes. Mr Derkes, these gentlemen would like to transfer their shares in Little Fish to the Sergowicz Preschool and Fishing company – at a quarter of the face value.'

Bro number one wanted to say something, but then seemed to place a greater value on his intact nose than on a fair price.

Signing and notarising the contracts took no more than five minutes. Fewer than twenty minutes had passed since we arrived.

We now faced three profoundly humiliated former shareholders. Fathers who had financed their children's luxury childhood with the slave labour of children in the Third World. Entrepreneurs who got off on posing as responsible and sustainable. Arseholes who arbitrarily denied my daughter a preschool spot because they didn't like what I did for a living. Two of them already had a broken nose. While the notary packed up his things and Sasha printed out one last document on the computer, I realised that there really were three deeply wounded souls standing in front of me. That's when I understood what my mindfulness coach meant by forgiveness:

> *Forgiveness is very liberating, especially to the one who forgives. Anger and thoughts of revenge can really get in your way. When you forgive the person you are angry with, the greatest freedom you generate is your own. Once you see that the person you are so immensely angry with is just a wounded soul like you, forgiving them is all the easier.*

My resentment had vanished. I no longer felt any hatred for these bros who had wanted to unleash their hatred of me at my daughter's expense. I felt loosened, liberated. I had forgiven them.

So I was able to say goodbye in correspondingly relaxed fashion.

'Oh, right,' I remembered. 'Since our paths will diverge at this point, I should tell you about the second official act of the new managing director of your former preschool.'

Bro number one bewilderedly asked: 'What's that?'

'He will revert your rejection of my daughter's application and offer her a spot. You remember what her name is?'

None of the three did, they could only shyly shrug. To them, Emily had always been just the nameless child of the bleurgh-lawyer.

'OK, then I think it's time for the managing director's *first* official act. Sasha, whenever you're ready.'

Sasha stood in front of the bro whose nose was still intact and changed that with a targeted blow.

'His little girl's name is Emily, arsehole. And now please sign this.'

Apparently, Sasha wasn't quite as ready for forgiveness.

26

Overcoming Internal Resistance

Internal resistance has a positive purpose.
And to be able to deal with internal resistance
constructively, it is important to recognise and
appreciate this purpose.

> Joschka Breitner, *Slowing Down in the
> Fast Lane: Mindfulness for Managers*

After successful negotiations, I always felt a bit like a marathon runner crossing the finish line: exhausted but happy, bursting with endorphins. In this exhilarated state, Sasha and I drove over to the headquarters of Walter's security company to have a chat with the man who'd been caught tailing me that morning. He was still in the boot of the security team's VW Passat, which was parked in the underground car park of a featureless commercial building on the outskirts of the city.

My guardian angels were there to greet us, not a loveydovey couple but total professionals. Even in the car park's fluorescent glare they still looked sporty and attractive. No longer passing for the spoiled children of rich parents, they looked like people you should only joke around with if you were signing their pay cheques.

I thanked them both for their excellent work. Sasha opened the boot. There's a significant difference between leaving someone in a boot for thirty-six hours (twenty-four of them in the blazing sun) or just eight. Unlike Dragan, this guy hadn't yet developed rigor mortis or started to decay. He did evince a stubbornness that bordered on rigidity and wasn't willing to say even a single word. Luckily, the number he'd been about to dial before he was loaded into the boot was still stored on his phone, at least the digits he'd already entered. The last four were missing, but the first seven matched Toni's most recent prepaid number.

In the basement of Walter's security company was what they called the conference room. That designation was deliberately misleading: instead of plates with assorted pastries to create a conversation-enhancing atmosphere, there was a shop-bought generator with custom-made finger clamps. In addition, there was a state-of-the-art video conferencing system through which intimate interviews could be shared with interested parties online if necessary. This wonderful set-up also allowed for the results of any conversation to be recorded.

There were a lot of questions I wanted this boot guy to answer. For example, who was his client, what was behind all this, and whether he was also responsible for Murat's death, the ambush in the lay-by and blowing up my former company car.

I did, however, feel some internal resistance to connecting a total stranger to a generator.

When I had dealt with the co-op bros mindfully, I'd come to the conclusion that the only way to meet their internal need for a brawl was to have Sasha break their noses. And it was precisely this solution that made it possible for me to forgive these wounded souls that had come upon my path.

But I didn't even know this guy. Only the information he might be able to give me would help determine whether I liked him or not.

As I watched Sasha and the couple skilfully secure the guy to a metal garden chair with handcuffs as well as a heavy-duty iron chain, I started to feel uncomfortable. When I spotted a bucket of water with which the young man's clothes were likely to be drenched to enhance conductivity, my internal resistance actually coated my forehead with a thin layer of sweat. Everything in me resisted what I was seeing.

I briefly excused myself and went to the toilet to consult my mindfulness handbook on the topic of 'Overcoming Internal Resistance'. It said:

Internal resistance has a positive purpose. And to be able to deal with internal resistance constructively, it is important to recognise and appreciate this purpose. In just six steps you, too, can constructively deal with your internal resistance.

I memorised Breitner's advice and quickly went back to the conference room. Since they still had a few things to set up before the generator's electrodes could be clamped to the young man's fingers, I used the time to go over the steps I had just learned.

Step 1: Mindfully take in what is happening.
Objectively describe the situation you are in.

Well, I was about to clamp a generator to the fingers of a guy I didn't even know; what was difficult for me about that was clamping a generator to his fingers.

My motivation was that I wanted to live in peace and quiet.
I didn't want my life to be determined by a few gangsters' power games. I didn't want to spend my weekends
using an infrared thermometer to see if my client was
fully cooked yet. I didn't want anyone to get shot if
I missed an appointment with them. I didn't want a
joking text about a secretary I hated to blow up her
apartment. I didn't want to be woken by cars exploding.
I abso-fucking-lutely didn't want any arseholes threatening, endangering or surveilling my daughter. And
I wanted this guy to tell me who was responsible for all
this crap.

My internal resistance was due to having learned
and internalised that you're not supposed to hurt other
people – at least, not if you don't even know them. That
wasn't easy to reconcile with sending ever-stronger electric
surges through the drenched body of a stranger before even
knowing his name. I didn't want to torture anyone.

resistance. Ask what bothers it so much, then ask what it would prefer instead.

Alright then: 'Dear Internal Resistance, why don't you want me to send electricity through this guy's body?' To my surprise, my internal resistance responded promptly and without hesitation.

'*Hello,*' it said. '*Well, I imagine the parts of him that'll be hooked up will start to smell quite a bit. You'll never get that stench out of your nose and it'll always remind you that you're a torturer – with a very guilty conscience.*'

Alright, noted and understood. Now for the second question: 'Dear Internal Resistance, what would you prefer instead?'

'*Can't you just offer the guy some conference-room pastries, so he'll tell you everything without having to resort to electricity? That way you'll get your answers without also getting a guilty conscience.*'

There it was – I'd discovered my internal resistance's positive purpose: it simply wanted to save me from a guilty conscience.

Step 4: Renaming your internal resistance.
Give your internal resistance a positive name that is connected to its positive purpose. This makes it easier for you to appreciate it and integrate its positive purpose into the next step.

As my internal resistance wanted to save me from a guilty conscience, I called it The Conscientious.

Step 5: Get your internal resistance on board.
Your motivation has a positive power. As you have just
discovered, your internal resistance also stems from a
positive idea. If these two things are positive, they are not
fundamentally different. They do not need to disagree;
they can also support each other. See if there is a path that
works for both your motivation and your resistance.

It was now clear to me that a guilty conscience was standing in the way of my looking a stranger in the eyes and sending powerful currents through their body. But I'd have a much guiltier conscience if this guy harmed my daughter, me, or anyone else around me just because I wasn't willing to put up with the smell of burnt skin. I'd feel better about keeping a loved one safe than I'd feel guilty about hurting someone I don't know. So that any guilt would not diminish my good conscience too much, I even saw two solutions that combined my motivation and resistance. I would first offer this guy some pastries before asking if he'd be willing to answer my questions. If he wasn't, I could jump-start him without a guilty conscience. Any resulting smells could be combated with my daughter's Vicks, which I'd forgotten to give back to Katharina.

Step 6: Follow this path consistently.
Once you have found a path that works for both, follow
it consistently. It is quite possible that your motivation or
your resistance will still urge you to deviate from this path.
When that happens, briefly speak to them, take their needs
seriously – but remain consistent.

286

So before Sasha and the couple could get started, I turned to the man in the chair, gave him a firm smile and politely offered him a pastry. He didn't want any. Alright. I asked if he'd be willing to answer a few questions. He wasn't. Fine then. I rubbed some Vicks under my nose. Sasha and the security team gratefully also each took a fingerful.

I asked my internal resistance if it was now OK with me clamping the electrodes onto the pastry-refuser's fingers. My internal resistance not only agreed, it also pointed out that it would make sense to first pour the bucket of water over his upper body so as to ensure better conductivity.

After the guy was soaked, Sasha took over with the finger clamps. The five marked negative were put on the fingers of his right hand, and the ones marked positive on his left. I turned to the generator's current regulator with interest.

Meanwhile, the security team sat discreetly in a corner of the room, playing a quiz game against each other on their phones.

After ten minutes, we knew everything. It only took two electric shocks to find out that the guy's name was Malte and he was from Chemnitz, in East Germany. After those first answers, getting the next was remarkably more energy-efficient. Malte was a nephew of Toni's, a former soldier in the French Foreign Legion who hadn't worked for Dragan's organisation before. Toni had hired him to – in his words – 'clean up'. What that meant, he couldn't say. After another electric shock, he could.

Toni had made Murat lure Dragan into the lay-by. The guy with the hand grenades was some petty criminal, also from Chemnitz, whom Toni had hired to sell the grenades to Igor. The guy's actual mission, however, was to blow up Dragan, Sasha and Igor. After Boris got blamed for the attack, Toni would've taken Dragan's position, Murat would've become an officer, and the ensuing gang war would've been used to consolidate those new positions. Then the coachful of children foiled those plans.

'May I?' Sasha asked. Of course. He turned up the regulator as far as it would go. Malte screamed like a banshee. Sasha turned it off again. Didn't he have any questions? He didn't, he just wanted to hear the idiot scream again. I proceeded.

It took another electric shock to learn that it was only on Sunday that Toni had tasked him with shooting Murat and me. Unfortunately, I hadn't been there at the deer park on Monday. Arghhhhh . . . Why did he get electrocuted again? He had answered the question, hadn't he?

'For saying "unfortunately".'

Sasha asked him how Toni knew that Murat wanted to meet with me. Well, from the voicemail message. After all, my phone was being tapped.

By whom? No idea. Arghhhh . . . Another shock. Now he remembered. By the police. Toni had an inside source. And their name?

'No ide-arghhhhhh . . . Möller. The guy's name is Möller . . . works for homicide.'

'I see. And the hand grenade in Ms Bregenz's apartment?'

'Whose apartment?' He looked at me in honest astonishment.

'The dragon guarding the reception desk at my firm.'

'Dragon? No ide-arghhhhhh . . . I don't know nothing about any dragon. Really . . . Arghhhhh.'

OK, we believed him. No matter, I tried a different approach. 'Did you throw a hand grenade into a woman's apartment on Tuesday?'

'Yes.'

'Did you blow up my car this morning?'

'Yes.'

'Why?'

'To teach you not to threaten Toni.'

'Good, no further questions. Do you guys have any?'

'What is the source of kombucha's unique flavour?' the woman from the security team enquired. Malte didn't immediately understand this question had nothing to do with Dragan or Toni, but came from the quiz game she was playing against her partner. Sasha and I figured it out a little sooner and jogged the young man's memory with a little juice.

'What? Huh? No ide-aaaaarghhhhh . . . A scoby! You need a scoby to make kombucha.'

'Well, fermentation was the word we were looking for. But you're right about the scoby, so we'll give you a pass.'

'Uh, thanks . . .' Malte tried to interject.

'Which category next, "Out in the Countryside" or "Food and Drink"?' the security guy enquired.

'I would very much like to get off this chair . . . Aaaaaarghhhh. "Exploring Nature"! I'll take "Exploring Nature".'

'Saffron is extracted from which flower?'

'Hibiscus? . . . Aaaahhhh . . . A crocus, it's a crocus!'

Sasha and I left the quiz contestant and the generator to the security team. We'd agreed to leave the young man in the conference room until further notice. If it was just for a few days, this kind of thing wouldn't raise any questions. Until then, not a word of this interrogation would leave the room without my consent.

Sasha and I finally knew for sure: Toni was the traitor, Malte was the murderer and Möller was the mole. We both had many good reasons to do something about all three: Sasha because Toni had tried to kill him and his boss; me because I'd killed Sasha's boss and now Toni wanted to do the same to me.

However different our reasons, Sasha and I agreed that Toni had to go. But *we* couldn't make that decision – only Dragan could.

27

Brainstorming

The first step to a good solution is having a problem in the first place. Many great solutions fail simply because the problem they are meant to address does not actually exist.

The second step is to avoid searching for one single solution. There are countless solutions for every problem. The right solution will find *you*.

To ensure this happens, do the following:

Take a walk – both physically and mentally – and invite your problem along. Now wait until the problem tells you what it needs in order to disappear. Do not judge what it offers you, as each of these offers is a solution. Invite each of the solutions to walk with you for a while and engage them without any bias or prejudice.

Having several solutions walk alongside you, however absurd they may be, and finding out which one suits you best is what we call brainstorming.

At the end of the walk, there will be three of you: you, your problem and the right solution.

Joschka Breitner, *Slowing Down in the Fast Lane: Mindfulness for Managers*

On Thursday morning, I woke up feeling refreshed. I was well on my way to being able to meet Katharina's ultimatum. As of the previous night, I also knew that if I could deliver Toni on a platter by Monday night, I'd be able to meet Boris's ultimatum – which would in turn dispatch Toni's ultimatum.

To do this, Sasha and I needed to get all the other officers on board and convince them that Toni had to go. Because Dragan himself wouldn't be able to communicate this very personal instruction personally, we'd have to be all the more convincing.

But Toni's clique also included the corrupt copper and the young East German.

And I had to make sure that Toni couldn't rain down any more grenades on my mindful parade before Boris made him join Dragan in gangster hell.

This meant that I only had until that evening to find solutions to the Toni, Möller and Malte problems – and present them in a way that would convince Dragan's officers. In addition, I also had to come up with responses to Boris's demand to meet Dragan and Peter Egmann's questions about where the ringed finger had come from.

Without my mindfulness practice, I'd never have been able to manage this without suffering stomach, head and neck aches. I first clarified one thing to myself: the only one who was making demands on me right now was me. And if that was the case, then I was also fully in control of how I phrased these demands.

So I started by rephrasing things:

That evening, I would have the great opportunity to discuss solutions to all my problems with my officers, at least to the extent that these solutions had revealed themselves to me by then.

That sounded better already. On with the next step. What was the thing about solutions again? Breitner had written a whole chapter on the subject.

The first step to a good solution is having a problem in the first place. Many great solutions fail simply because the problem they are meant to address does not actually exist.

The second step is to avoid searching for one single solution. There are countless solutions for every problem. The right solution will find you.

To ensure this happens, do the following:

Take a walk – both physically and mentally – and invite your problem along. Now wait until the problem tells you what it needs in order to disappear. Do not judge what it offers you, as each of these offers is a solution. Invite each of the solutions to walk with you for a while and engage them without any bias or prejudice.

Having several solutions walk alongside you, however

absurd they may be, and finding out which one suits you best is what we call brainstorming.

At the end of the walk, there will be three of you: you, your problem and the right solution.

Well, there you go. I had already completed the first step: I knew what my problems were. Since the officers' meeting was only scheduled for the evening, I had all day to take a walk. I put on comfortable jeans and an old pair of hiking boots, walked to the bus stop past the burnt-out parking bay where my old company car had blown up, and took public transport to the outskirts of the city, to a recreation area where I had last gone for a hike over a decade earlier.

Aside from me, the two security minders disguised as a couple were the last and only other passengers to get off the bus at the final stop in the middle of the forest. At nine o'clock on a Thursday morning, no one else seemed to be going for a walk. There was a single vehicle in the car park, but it had already been there before the bus got there. I asked the two of them to wait for me at the bus stop. I didn't have a phone on me and no one had followed me, so no one could have known I would be here right then.

I picked a well-marked circular trail that would take about two hours and set off. Soon enough, the Toni, Möller, Malte, Boris and Peter problems mentally fell into step alongside me. I greeted all five and first engaged the Peter problem. It stood out among the other four simply because I didn't know how big of a problem it was. With the others, it was clear: Toni wanted to kill me; Boris wanted to kill me; Malte had tried to kill me; and Möller had provided Malte with the information he'd needed to do so. When it came to Peter and the finger, however, I didn't know what else might come my way: at worst, that signet ring could seal my fate as a convicted murderer; at best, they'd have no recoverable DNA from Dragan to compare it to, thereby settling the matter. If Boris and Toni found out about the finger and realised that, despite my assurances to the contrary, Dragan was dead, then a police investigation against me would be the least of my problems. But maybe there was a way I could affect whether and when Toni and Boris would find out about it. Perhaps . . . at best . . . at worst . . . What it came down to was that as long as I didn't know the extent of the problem, looking for a solution was useless. So I kindly said my goodbyes to the Peter problem and turned to the problems that had already materialised.

I asked the Toni problem to tell me what it needed in order to disappear. As if I had pushed a button, solutions bubbled out, anything from 'Take me to Dragan' to 'Make me the boss' and 'Just kill me'.

Those were already three possible solutions to the Toni problem, and I'd only walked five hundred metres.

'Take me to Dragan' would basically equate to 'Just kill me'. 'Make me the boss' would mean that I'd be dead soon after, so 'Just kill me' was the easiest walking companion.

The Boris problem was a little simpler. This one was either 'Take me to Dragan' or 'Kill me or I'll kill you'. The killing solution, however, seemed a little more complicated than it had with Toni. If I went about it the right way, Toni was pretty much alone, whereas Boris had a whole crime syndicate behind him. Still, I did not want to judge this proposed solution just yet. After all, I was glad it showed up so quickly.

The Malte problem was similar: 'Offer me a job', 'Offer me money' and 'Beat me so badly I'll never dare do anything bad ever again' were all possible solutions. But here, too, the most promising solution was 'Just kill me'.

The Möller problem was slightly different. Since Malte's interrogation, I'd been racking my brain about how I could take the mole out of circulation. At first glance, this might hardly appear necessary. Möller didn't present any immediate danger. He only heard whatever I communicated through my tapped phone and what he learned from Peter through the chain of command. Those were the only things he could pass on to Toni. I could have just left it at not communicating on my usual phone and pointing Peter to the leak in his own ranks. But I hadn't completed twelve sessions with a mindfulness coach to just avoid conflicts; I wanted to actively resolve them. And I did, in fact, have a conflict with that utter idiot Möller, who had thought my ice-cream-smeared daughter was proof enough that I helped a murderer escape – especially since he'd been right, so he couldn't be such an utter idiot after all. But this was the guy who had passed on to Toni what the police had learned from shadowing my weekend with Emily. This guy had told Toni that Murat wanted to meet me at the deer park, which made him partly responsible for Murat's death – not to mention mine if I'd gone to the meeting.

I didn't want a guy like that to prescribe how I could use my phone. In other words, this guy really presented a problem.

The problem suggested the following options: 'Report me to the police', 'Blackmail me and threaten you will report me to the police' and 'Just kill me'.

Reporting Möller to the cops would mean a lot of work. Especially because they'd then scrutinise every one of my calls and messages, making me as much a focus of the investigation as Möller. Again, 'Just kill me' was the most appealing solution.

After spending less than fifteen minutes in the forest, I'd already found several solutions to all four problems. The most optimal solutions had automatically kept pace with me, while less optimal ones had gone away by themselves.

Although I was completely alone in the forest – aside from the solutions – I suddenly got the feeling I was being watched. I also noticed a quiet mechanical whirr somewhere above me. When I looked up, there it was: a small drone, the modern pest of our lowest airspace, hovering about three metres over my head. When I went left – the drone flew left. When I turned back – the drone followed. I had no idea which of my problems would be interested in tracking me with a drone.

Since I had left the security team at the start of the trail, I had to take out this disturbance myself. I picked up a large stick and tried throwing it at the annoying craft.

It was a direct hit. The drone cracked in the air and shattered into dozens of small pieces on the ground. As it turned out, the drone had a wingspan of almost half a metre, four rotors and a small HD camera.

While I was wondering who exactly was putting so much effort into tracking me, an angry guy ran out from behind a tree.

'You destroyed my drone!' he shouted furiously.

'You were harassing me,' I replied. 'Where'd you get the stupid idea of using annoying gadgets to spy on people enjoying a nice hike?'

'I got it as a toy for my son. Where else am I supposed to practise flying it? In a pedestrian zone? Besides, you only spotted it when I brought it further down. At ten metres up, you didn't even notice it.' As the man collected the debris from the ground, he was clearly close to tears.

'Hold up,' I said. 'That's a toy? With a camera and all that? How long were you watching me with that?'

'Only about five minutes.'

'And why didn't I see *you*?'

'The camera transmits everything to my surveillance monitor. I can see you, but you can't see me.'

'And how much did you pay for a high-tech toy like that?'

'This one cost over four hundred euros, for which you will be reimbursing me.' He looked at me indignantly as he stood back up. 'Otherwise, I will call the police.'

To shut the bloke up, I gave him five hundred in cash and advised him not to stage his flight exercises directly over strangers' heads in the future. After he disappeared, I was alone in the woods again. Yet the drone didn't disappear, at least not from my head, where it had left a hint of an idea.

I resumed my hike. Soon the solutions rejoined me, all four of which came down to 'Just kill me'.

It's so obvious in retrospect: if a person's life is the problem, their death is the solution. But the most obvious solution is often the most elusive. Less than a week ago, when I was solving the Dragan problem, I'd already learned that it can be liberating to simply kill a problem off. I had overcome that initial inhibition. And with Murat's assassination – in which I should've been killed as well – Toni, Malte and Möller had forfeited any right to my moral scruples. Getting rid of all three bastards felt right. And just because Boris had nothing to do with the deer park murder was not nearly reason enough not to kill him before he killed me.

Still, I needed to work out the exact details of their elimination. These four men who were all connected, at least through Toni, all needed to die. Ideally without anyone finding out what they had in common. On the other hand, it'd be worth seeing if the four targets' relationship to each other might present some kind of synergy that could save me work. I wanted to have Toni killed by Boris anyway, that much was clear. But maybe I could ensure Toni would take care of Malte or Möller for me first?

As I brainstormed my way through the forest, I considered each of the four men, their backgrounds, their preferences, their strengths and weaknesses. And if problems and solutions had feet, there would've been places on my trail where the path was marked with hundreds of footprints. But fewer and fewer the closer I got to the end of the trail. And when I got back to the bus stop, I was left with just four slender solutions that were carrying the Toni, Boris, Malte and Möller problems on their shoulders.

The pair of bodyguards and I rode back to the city. Once we got downtown, I couldn't resist treating them to a coffee at my new favourite chain restaurant. I used the opportunity to pick up the latest tabloid edition as well.

And once I got to my apartment, I began to put the solutions into action by signing them with Dragan's thumb stump.

28

Give and Take

We can give and we can take. This is a cycle. As long as this give and take remains balanced, we are doing well. Yet those who only give, but cannot take, feel drained – and those who only take, but cannot give, feel bad.

> Joschka Breitner, *Slowing Down in the Fast Lane: Mindfulness for Managers*

The rest of the morning I elaborated the targeted solutions I'd found off-site so I could implement them in Dragan's name at that night's all-hands officers' meeting – but fuck that stupid corporate lingo. I just looked for ways to present the solutions from my walk in a way that rang the most true – which required Dragan's thumb and a few pages of newsprint.

I spent the rest of the afternoon at home, planning my own professional future.

As a fully qualified lawyer, you can be anything you want – at least, that's what every first-year law student imagines. And it is true in that a fully qualified lawyer can be anything they want as long as they have wealthy parents. As long as you have wealthy parents, you can also be anything you want if you have a degree in technical illustration, an apprenticeship as a track inspector or even no qualifications at all. Still, there's a far higher percentage of children of wealthy parents at any first-year law lecture than among technical illustrators or track inspectors.

I myself was not a child of wealthy parents. I only knew how to be a lawyer, particularly one specialised in business and criminal law. As I had just spent ten years trying to see whether I would enjoy salaried employment –

I hadn't – starting my own firm looked appealing enough to try. If I survived 30 April, I'd rent a nice office space of my own on 1 May, preferably near my apartment, my daughter's house and her future preschool.

The building where Little Fish was located not only met these requirements geographically; thanks to my old skills at eviction negotiation, it was also practically empty. So I decided to catch a bus and take a closer look at the unoccupied upper floors.

These turned out to be beautiful office units with high ceilings, stucco details, sliding doors and great parquet floors. As an upmarket brothel, it would've been hard to beat. Dragan had a deft hand at these things. Now I had a plaster cast of that hand's right thumb at home, however, so I could decide the property's fate myself. And what could be better than having my own law office right above Emily's preschool?

As I strolled around the three empty floors, I envisioned how I might set up my office: a conference room, a playroom for Emily . . . I was just imagining a TV lounge with a comfy sofa when my phone rang: it was Peter from Homicide Command. I fervently hoped the call would be about hand grenades, not fingers.

'Hi Peter, what's up?'

'I just wanted to update you about your company car.'

'I don't have a company car.'

'Alright, your *former* company car. The explosion was triggered by a hand grenade.'

Though relieved, I acted surprised. Which was difficult

to do, as a few electric shocks had already made me realise the night before.

'A hand grenade?! But how?'

'They're primitive but effective ignition devices. This one was duct-taped to the rear wheel cover, the safety pin connected to the rim by a wire. The slightest movement of the tyre would pull out the pin and then . . . boom.'

'Sounds technically simple, but emotionally complicated.'

'I can tell you three things: first, the grenade was the same type as the ones in Ms Bregenz's apartment on Tuesday and at the lay-by on Friday.'

So Peter could now work out that Toni was behind the grenade attack on me. But he had no proof.

'Second, the grenade was installed in such a way that it couldn't have killed the driver. If someone had wanted to kill you, they would've stuck the grenade under the front wheel cover.'

'And third?'

'Third, I'd like to talk to you in person.'

'Sure, where?'

'Where are you right now? I'll come to you.'

'I am currently in one of Dragan's properties, Herder-straße 42. I don't know if there's a café around here somewhere—'

'Which floor?'

'What do you mean, which floor? Third, why?'

'I'll be there in ten seconds.'

Puzzled, I was just putting my phone away when I heard

footsteps on the wooden stairs. Five seconds later, Peter knocked on the open door and walked in.

'What are you doing here?' I asked, astonished.

'I could ask you the same thing.'

'Like I told you, I'm looking at a client's property.'

'And I'm looking into your client's victims.'

'I may be the victim of a hand-grenade attack, but I'm certainly not a victim of my client.'

'Other crimes do happen in this city, crimes that have nothing to do with grenades.'

'Oh, really?'

'Crimes like assault, harassment, libel, computer fraud . . .'

It was absolutely out of the question that the chaps from Little Fish had filed a complaint. They knew they still had until the weekend to pack up their personal belongings and tell their parents about the preschool's new proprietors. If they deviated from our agreement, they would find themselves firmly cancelled.

I nodded. 'I see. And that's what took your investigation to a preschool, of all places?'

'I guess it must've been a false alarm. The wife of one of its shareholders contacted us this morning and wanted to talk to the inspector on Dragan Sergowicz's case. Which happens to be me.'

'What did she want?'

'She told me that two employees of Mr Sergowicz had threatened and horribly beaten her husband last night. His nose had been broken and a tooth knocked out. In addition, they threatened to break his leg and destroy his company's reputation if he didn't transfer his shares in the preschool to Mr Sergowicz.'

Broken nose and lost tooth . . . Must've been the bro with the e-pipe. I was unsurprised he was the kind of muppet who went crying to his wife.

'That's quite a number of unpleasant claims. Are there any witnesses?'

'Now, that's where it gets a little weird. I came out to see the guy – he's just cleaning out his office in the preschool downstairs – and he can't remember any of it.'

'So he doesn't have a broken nose?'

'He does, and he's missing a tooth too. But he's absolutely adamant he just fell down the stairs to the cellar.'

'Any witnesses for that?'

'Yes, the other two shareholders – who both happen to have broken noses as well.'

'Fell down the stairs too?'

'Fell down the stairs too.'

'I'll have to have a word with my client about the state of those stairs.'

'Fine, fine. Then there's just . . .'

'Please don't worry about it. My client and his employees will refrain from filing a criminal complaint against the wife for defamation.'

'That's fine too, fine.'

It was clear Peter had something else on his mind. Finally, he came out with it: 'While I was down there, I saw some pictures of the kids and their parents on the wall. Funny coincidence: one had Paul and Mary on it.'

'Who are Paul and Mary?'

'They're the kids of Karl Breuer, head of the building control department. I often play squash with him. He's always saying great things about Little Fish.'

Would you look at that: the head of the building control department. Whenever Dragan needed anything expedited, Mr Breuer would bring up some concerns, maybe about environmental protection or animal welfare, only for them to blow over once Dragan made sure Breuer had been thoroughly entertained at one of his brothels. And this fine gentleman's children went to my preschool? Good to know.

'Possibly, I don't know the man, but then it's not my preschool.'

'Yet the three former shareholders all said they have transferred their shares in the preschool to a subsidiary of Dragan's. Do you know anything about that?'

'Of course, I was the one who drew up the deal. But as you know – I'm just a lawyer, not an early years educator. Sasha, however, does have the required qualifications.'

'And Sasha is the preschool's new managing director?'

'Correct. Why do you ask?'

'So . . . Don't get me wrong, but . . .' Suddenly, Peter looked downright miserable. He mustered the nerve: 'Do you still have any spots available?'

I almost couldn't believe that the plan I'd basically improvised in front of Sasha was actually working. Preschool spots attracted parents, which made them dependent on that preschool – and, by extension, us. I'd already been wondering why Peter would spontaneously share the results of the investigation into the grenade attack on my former company car. But it was quite simple: life was all about give and take. Peter wanted something from me, a preschool spot.

Though the change agents behind 'untrd' hadn't even left the building, I already had three people hooked on my new drug: Sasha, the head of the building control department and now the head of Homicide Command. I couldn't imagine a better first day.

For mindfulness reasons alone, I couldn't deny Peter's request. My handbook clearly said:

We can give and we can take. This is a cycle. As long as this give and take remains balanced, we are doing well. Yet those who only give, but cannot take, feel drained – and those who only take, but cannot give, feel bad.

I wanted neither Peter to feel drained, nor to feel bad myself. Of course I would give his son a spot – but only if he gave me Dragan's finger in return.

'You're asking about spots in general? Or specifically for your little Lukas?'

'For Lukas, yes. You wouldn't believe how difficult it is to get a spot nowadays. They've got this awful online registration platform . . .'

'SICK. Yes, I'm familiar.'

'We sent out twenty-eight applications.'

'We did thirty-one.'

'And not a single acceptance.'

'The same with us.'

'So I just thought I'd ask if you saw any possible way a spot might be available.'

I looked at him appraisingly. 'Now, just to make sure I understood that correctly. You're tired of bringing your three-year-old son to work so he can colour in arrest warrants half the day, and you're asking if Lukas might be admitted to Dragan's preschool instead?'

'I'm just asking. Children are children, and work is work. Plus, this isn't Dragan's preschool, it's run by a non-profit company whose sole shareholder is a subsidiary of Dragan's. After all, I can still have a beer in one of Dragan's bars even as a copper, just as long as I pay my own tab.'

'And you would put up with the fact that Lukas might end up in a group with Emily, whose father is suspected of having kidnapped a finger wearing a ring that looked similar to one worn by the preschool's main shareholder?'

'Who on earth is even saying that?' Peter countered indignantly. 'There are almost ten times as many fingers as people in the world – no wonder one finger is occasionally confused for another.'

'Could you please clarify what you mean by "confused"?'

Peter cleared his throat. 'I took a closer look at the file. The finger was clearly found on the neighbouring property. So that in itself already makes it clear you had nothing to do with it. Unfortunately, I also didn't find any reliable DNA from Dragan I could compare it to. And as per usual, the lab is completely backed up, So I think this finger probably has no bearing on our case . . .'

That sounded better already. Relaxed, I stuck my hands in my coat pockets.

'I completely agree. So, Nemo or Flipper?'

'Sorry, what?'

'Would Lukas rather be in the Nemo or the Flipper group? Downstairs, all the groups are named after fish.'

'But dolphins are mammals.'

'If you want a spot at the most innovative preschool in town, you really should be a little more open-minded. But welcome to Little Fish!'

As I shook Peter's hand, I accidentally pulled the parrot toy out of my pocket. As it fell to the floor between us, its absurd falsetto screeched:

'*I chopped up my client and now I'm free.*'

Great that the piece of crap was finally working again, not so great that it'd done so now. There was an embarrassing break in our conversation.

'What was that?' Peter demanded.

'*What was that?*' the toy parroted.

'That's that parrot toy I was telling you about.' I put the bird back in my pocket. 'So: Nemo or Flipper?'

Peter briefly hesitated before declaring, 'Flipper. Lukas should join the Flipper group.'

'Great decision. You won't regret it.'

'*Won't regret it,*' my pocket repeated.

29

Convincing People

If you want to convince someone of something, here's a handy bit of wisdom: people who feel at ease are more open to trying new things, whereas people who do not will automatically raise their defences. So create an atmosphere in which you feel at ease yourself, then convey that ease and openness to the person you are trying to convince. Really surprise them, make them curious, explain what your proposal might bring them. You will probably no longer need to convince them at all, for they will have already been convinced.

Joschka Breitner, *Slowing Down in the Fast Lane: Mindfulness for Managers*

The meeting was scheduled for nine that evening. All the officers had confirmed they'd be there. So far, Dragan's illegal empire had consisted of four clearly defined areas: drugs, prostitution, arms trafficking and smuggling of all kinds.

The drugs division was led by Toni, disguised as the director of a managing company for bars and clubs.

Prostitution was the domain of Carla, a former sex worker and former girlfriend of Dragan's. Officially, she was the managing director of a casting agency. Carla hated Toni's guts because he only ever saw her as a former prostitute.

Walter oversaw the weapons business. He was a former career soldier from the Franco-German Brigade whose official title was director of the security company.

Smuggling of all kinds – which included both goods and people – was handled by Stanislav, who publicly acted as the director of a shipping company.

There were a lot of synergies between these companies: Stanislav transported Toni's drugs; Walter's security staff were sent to clear up any confusion when people didn't take Carla seriously; Carla's casting agents were loyal visitors to Toni's nightclubs; and every officer could shop from Walter's arsenal at wholesale prices. In short, each officer could rely on the services of every other officer.

And since Dragan's disappearance, in addition to officers in charge of drugs, arms, hookers and slaves, there was now also Sasha, charged with the childcare unit.

At the officers' meeting, four goals needed to be met.

First, I had to convince the officers that just because Dragan was going to be in hiding indefinitely and running the business remotely, he wouldn't be any less in charge. The key to this was convincing everyone that Dragan was still alive.

Apart from Toni, no one seemed to be in any doubt about that.

The second goal was related to the first: I had to convince all the officers that it was both Dragan's decision and best for everyone that we keep calm and carry on. In other words: any gang war with Boris should be prevented.

Apart from Toni, nobody would contest that either.

As for the third goal, I had to convince a former prostitute, a former career soldier and a smuggler-slash-trafficker that our most urgent piece of business was taking over a preschool, which also involved promoting Sasha from driver to fully fledged officer.

As it was already clear to me I wouldn't be able to convince Toni, that couldn't be my goal.

Oh right: and my last goal was to convince everyone – except Toni – that we should let Boris kill Toni.

On the subject of setting goals, Breitner had given me some very wise advice:

Mindfulness means also recognising partial successes. If you always aim for 100 per cent, even reaching 90 per cent means

you are 100 per cent a failure. If you only aim for 80 per cent,
reaching 90 per cent means you are 100 per cent successful.

So I didn't have to rack my brain trying to convince *every-one*. I only had to figure out how to convince Carla, Walter and Stanislav. After all, Sasha was already convinced.

I wouldn't have to waste any energy trying to convince Toni. To the contrary, if everything went as planned, him being the only naysayer could even be a huge help.

As I wanted to turn the others against him anyway, it would be good if it looked like he was already turning them against him all on his own. This way, the Toni problem could be part of its own solution.

Now I just needed to be as convincing as possible. In my mindfulness handbook, under the heading 'Convincing People', it said:

> *If you want to convince someone of something, here's a handy bit of wisdom: people who feel at ease are more open to trying new things, whereas people who do not will automatically raise their defences. So create an atmosphere in which you feel at ease yourself, then convey that ease and openness to the person you are trying to convince. Really surprise them, make them curious, explain what your proposal might bring them. You will probably no longer need to convince them at all, for they will have already been convinced.*

Dragan's officers' meetings were usually held in a cordoned-off area at some upmarket restaurant that was as lavish as it was lifeless. The atmosphere would start off anxious, and by the end be one of boundless relief. Each officer came fully prepared for Dragan to shower them with either praise, fury or profanity without warning. The best thing about the meetings had always been that they happened so rarely.

I wanted to change that. Compared to that familiar state of all-consuming apprehension, creating a veritable feel-good atmosphere was not impossible. Even just foregoing fury and profanity would already mean a quantum leap in atmospheric terms. For the rest, Sasha and I were banking on the element of surprise. That's why we'd decided to hold the meeting in the Moby Dick room at Herderstraße 42. We had pushed the activity tables against the walls and created a circle of six chairs in the middle. On each chair was a name card in the shape of a fish. During the day, Sasha had familiarised himself with the preschool's records and asked the caterer to bring six extra lunch portions for the evening. The vibe couldn't have been further from that of a fine-dining restaurant.

By 7.12 p.m., five convicted criminals were looking around in wonder as they plonked down on colourful wooden chairs designed for children under the age of six.

All of them were expecting unpleasant announcements about agenda items like gang warfare, violence and treachery, but nothing in the Moby Dick room suggested any of that. You could almost make out the question marks hovering over Carla, Walter and Stanislav's heads – above Toni's head was a pitch-black thundercloud.

If you want to throw already unsettled employees completely off their game, here's a sure-fire trick: thank them for no specific reason. So I opened proceedings as follows:

'On behalf of Dragan, I would like to thank you all for coming here on such short notice.'

This kind of greeting was a surprise, and a positive one at that. The closest to gratitude Dragan had ever gotten when it came to addressing his officers was by choosing *not* to shout.

'In light of recent events, Dragan will be unreachable for the foreseeable. He would have so loved to be here, if only to see you sitting on these silly chairs.'

At this, a tentative hint of exhilaration.

'I have a large number of messages from Dragan, so perhaps we should just start with the first.'

I opened an insulated box that stood next to me and passed each of the officers a covered plastic plate. A puzzled murmur went around the room.

Then I took a copy of the previous day's tabloid from the box and unfolded it. It was stamped with Dragan's thumb. Only two words were circled and connected.

Any cheerfulness vanished. Each of the officers was afraid they'd find Boris's ears on their plate. As I lifted the cover from my plate, I read out the newspaper's message: 'Bon appétit.'

Each plate had peas and carrots, twisty pasta and fish fingers as well as a little box of organic apple juice.

Carla, Walter and Stanislav were visibly relieved. As expected, only Toni was disappointed not to find any body parts on his plate.

321

'The fuck's this supposed to be?' he demanded, a disgusted expression on his face.

I was about to answer when Stanislav stepped in.

'Dude, those are fish fingers. Do you know how long it's been since I've had fish fingers? It must've been . . . I must've only been fifteen!'

'And the last time I had this twisty pasta was back in military training,' Walter added. 'That takes me back, that does!'

The stomach is not just the way to a man's heart, but also a way to make them feel at ease. Upmarket restaurants are great if you want to impress outsiders, but there's one thing they can never do and that's satisfy you – neither physically nor emotionally. Fish fingers with twisty noodles casually create a completely different, more open atmosphere.

'Is there any Capri-Sun as well?' Carla asked as she poked her straw into the juice box. 'I always loved those when I was small.'

With the help of children's chairs, name cards and fish fingers, Sasha and I had just turned four sceptical criminals into one pissed-off criminal and three enthusiastic children in the bodies of hardened criminals.

'I don't know what to do with this shite. Can we finally get down to business?' Toni said, torpedoing the other officers' reminiscing.

There is a very simple way to create an atmosphere where everyone but one person feels at ease. This is called bullying. From a mindfulness standpoint, bullying can be very enjoyable, at least for the bullies. They're free to have a good laugh at someone whenever they fancy a laugh, and they're free to not do a thing for that person if they don't fancy it. As soon as bullies start bullying, they can rest easy, content in the knowledge they're not being bullied themselves.

Since I was in charge of the meeting, I needed to get the bullying going.

'Well, if you're not hungry, Toni, maybe you can just get me my briefcase with the remaining instructions,' I said, as I pointed to my briefcase next to the door and dug into my noodles.

So as not to fully take on the role of a sulking toddler, Toni had to get up and fetch me the briefcase, like it or not. Have you ever in your adult life tried getting up from a child-sized chair without embarrassing yourself? You haven't, because it's impossible. Toni's rugged, muscular body couldn't help but look entirely lost and ridiculous as he tried to get up from the much-too-small seat. He failed miserably. There was just no room to place his legs at the right angle, so after three unsuccessful attempts he finally had to pull himself up by grabbing Sasha and Carla's shoulders. And when he was up, he couldn't immediately find his balance. As the others couldn't help but giggle, their comfort increased at the same rate as Toni's decreased. Furious, he trudged to the door, fetched my briefcase, slammed it down in front of me, and sat down again.

'Thank you, Toni, but I'm afraid that's the wrong brief-case. Mine is at the back door.'

Toni looked dismayed. The rest snickered.

'Just joking, this is the right one, you stay seated.'

I wiped my mouth, put down my plate and pulled a set of newspaper pages from my briefcase.

'As you all know, since Friday night there have been some incidents that could be considered interruptions to our usual course of business.'

Although everyone already knew what'd happened, I briefly summarised the events, starting with Dragan and Sasha being ambushed on Friday night all through Dragan's escape, the death of Murat and the respective hand grenades in Ms Bregenz's apartment and my former company car.

'And Boris is behind all of it,' Toni cut in.

'Do any of you remember "quiet coyote", by any chance?' I asked. The fish fingers, colourful chairs and collective thirst for Capri-Sun had opened up the group to yet more childhood memories.

Sasha and Carla made the 'quiet coyote' hand signal in Toni's direction.

'What does that mean?' Walter enquired.

'Whoever gets the quiet coyote has to shut the fuck up,' Stanislav explained, showing Walter how to do the quiet coyote: place the middle and ring fingers on the thumb, pointing up the index and little fingers like ears.

Now four quiet coyotes were pointed at Toni.

Toni looked on, speechless. Used to dealing with weapons and fists, he had no idea what to do with quiet coyotes. I proceeded.

'Dragan wants everything to continue as usual. He won't let himself be forced into a gang war until he knows why and by whom.'

The quiet coyotes disappeared and gave way to relieved nods.

'Why doesn't Dragan just tell us this himself?' Toni now demanded.

The quiet coyotes popped up again, joined by four reproachfully shaking heads. I did not respond to Toni's question directly.

'If there are any disagreements with Boris, Dragan and only Dragan will sort those out. Specifically, through me and only me. All other business will continue as usual. Understood?'

Four nodding coyotes, one quiet Toni.

'Good, then on to Dragan's personal instructions. There's one for *all* of you and then one for each of you personally. I'll read the message to everyone first.'

Everyone anxiously leaned in as much as their little chairs allowed.

'I'm doing well. I've had a lot of time to rethink my life. I won't let anyone drag me into a gang war. Until we have facts, everything continues as usual. To show that things are back to normal, I ordered the preschool you're in to be taken over. Direct any questions about this to Björn.'

I showed everyone the page from yesterday's newspaper signed with Dragan's thumb and covered all over with squiggles and lines.

After that, I gave each of the five, including Sasha, their own page from the same newspaper. There was also one for me.

To enhance our group dynamics a little, I'd thought up a fun twist.

'Dragan asks that everyone pass their page to the person on their right, who will then read it aloud. This way we'll all hear what Dragan has to say to each of us.'

Six newspaper pages rustled as they changed hands. I had deliberately chosen the seating arrangement so Toni had to read the instructions for Sasha, Carla those for Toni, and Sasha those for me.

'Toni, why don't you start.'

Very slowly, due to his severe dyslexia, Toni sullenly deciphered Dragan's instruction for Sasha: 'You are . . . hereby appointed . . . officer . . . For years of . . . loyal . . . service, you will be . . . director of . . . Little . . . Fish.' Toni looked up. 'What the fuck is this?'

'Toni, before we clear up any remaining questions together, please let's finish reading all the messages first,' Sasha asked him, on equal footing now that he was a newly appointed officer.

Carla read out Toni's message. 'There are three instructions for Toni: "First, shut your mouth and stay put. Second, your next threat is your last. Third, when we find those responsible for this shite, you will be in charge of interrogations."'

With her amused, angelic voice, Carla almost crooned the message. It sounded like Dragan, the psychopath-in-chief, had smacked the junior psychopath in the mouth while simultaneously pouring honey in his ear. By now, Toni had turned red with anger, but he didn't dare interrupt the others' messages.

Stanislav read the one for Carla: 'The fancy knocking shop is still happening, but not in the preschool as we planned. Looking for a replacement.'

Walter had the message for Stanislav: 'You may have to send a few extra packages soon. Await instructions from Björn.'

I read the message for Walter: 'From now on, your security will monitor Boris and provide personal protection for all our officers. Suspects are to be taken to Toni.'

Sasha was last, reading the message for me: 'Until further notice, you will be my mouthpiece in all matters. If someone wants something from me, they go see you. They can assume anything you say to the others comes straight from me.'

Four of the five officers were relieved – and convinced that Dragan was alive. That he didn't want a war. That lying low seemed to be doing him good. That I was the big guy who'd made it possible for him to lie low in the first place and that I had his full confidence. Without Dragan, the atmosphere was much more pleasant. For the majority of those present, the first two issues on my agenda were thus more than satisfactorily resolved.

Only Toni could no longer restrain himself: 'What about Boris? When do we hit back?'

'What about Boris?' I asked, acting surprised.

'Murat, who I know is totally solid, he found out that Boris wants to take over my territory. Now Dragan has disappeared and Murat is dead, shot by Boris.'

'Was there anything about it in any of the instructions?' I parried.

'No, that's why I'm asking.'

'Carla, what did it say again in the instructions for Toni?' I asked her.

She relished reading it out again: 'Shut your mouth and stay put.'

I looked around the room. 'Any other questions?'

Carla raised her hand. I nodded to her.

'What's going on with the plans for the brothel? Wasn't it supposed to be in this building?'

'Yes, it's happening, but not here.'

'Can I ask why not?'

Thanks to what Peter had told me that morning, the answer was very simple:

'The head of the building control department has two kids at this preschool. If we closed it, we'd never have received approval for the necessary renovations. But if *we* run the preschool, he'd be all the more open to our suggestions anywhere else.'

'I didn't know about that,' Sasha whispered to me.

'Won't happen again,' I whispered back. 'After all, you're the officer in charge.'

'Oh, good old Mr Breuer?' an amused Carla interjected. 'My girls were usually enough to convince him . . .'

'That's the whole point of taking over this preschool,' I continued. 'When people's kids are involved, they can be convinced even more effectively. This morning, for example, none other than the head of Homicide Command registered his son here. And that's exactly the kind of thing Dragan aims to do with this preschool. He believes that we should be trying to reach people emotionally, not just through whores and heroin. In fact, this preschool is so important to Dragan that it'll be an independent arm of the business run by an officer familiar with the field. In this case, that's Sasha.'

Three heads nodded admiringly at the sheer perceptiveness of their absent boss. I could check off the third item on my list of things I needed to convince the officers of.

'Does that mean there are still spots available?' Walter enquired. Walter had three children by two women: two of them were grown up and lived with his ex-wife in France, one illegitimate daughter was fifteen and lived here.

'Of course. Do you have another toddler running around somewhere?'

'I don't, but my sister does. You have no idea how difficult it is to get into a good preschool in this city . . .'

'That SICK website is outrageously awful,' Stanislav concurred.

I stared at Stanislav in amazement. 'How do *you* know about SICK?'

'My new girlfriend's daughter needs a spot . . .'

'What about Natasha's Lara and Alexander, don't they need someplace?' Carla asked Sasha.

'Already on the list,' he replied.

Creating a pleasant atmosphere had worked. I had convinced the entire group – except for Toni.

Just one day after the takeover, Sasha and I not only had five new preschool registrations, but we had also got the head of Homicide Command, the head of building control and our officers for weapons, prostitution and human trafficking on side. Plus, I'd driven a wedge between Toni and the others without making a single accusation against Toni myself.

'Well, if all questions have been answered, we can move on to more pleasant things,' I concluded. The meeting was over, but unfortunately Toni didn't think so. The evening's humiliations had probably been a little too much for him after all.

Though he was fuming, he sounded ice cold when he said: 'Everyone stay seated. I have some information. On Monday, the police found Dragan's ring finger at the lake. That lawyer prick is trying to fool us.'

The time had come. Möller had told Toni about the finger. Backed into a corner, Toni played his final card. And even though the finger was no longer a problem for the police, Toni had now made it a problem for the officers.

An icy silence hung in the room. All the officers were looking at me. Since an attack is the best defence, I addressed Toni directly.

'And why are you only sharing this important information now?' I barked at him.

'Because I wanted to see what kind of monkey show you'd put on to try and fuck with us. Dragan is dead. His ring finger is in a plastic evidence bag, and his thumb can sign off on anything before it rots. You killed Dragan.'

Walter was the first to recover his speech. 'Björn, is this finger business true?'

'Of course it's true,' I replied. The officers looked at me in surprise. 'At least insofar as the police found a finger with Dragan's ring on it – but it's not Dragan's finger.'

'Quit mugging us off and just tell us the truth,' Toni shouted.

I remained utterly calm. 'The truth? The truth is that, unlike you, I'm doing my job. Dragan needed to go into hiding, disappear from the scene. Unfortunately, there is a very strong investigation underway against him for man-slaughter. There are basically only three ways to end such an investigation: firstly, by being convicted, which Dragan did not want. Secondly, by getting the case dismissed, which is completely unthinkable given the evidence presented in the video. And thirdly, by the death of the accused. So when the police find a finger with Dragan's ring by the lake, it's because Dragan wanted that finger to be found, so the police would believe he's dead. And rest a-fucking-ssured, you prick: the ring is Dragan's, the finger isn't.'

At least I'd managed to prevent Carla, Walter, Sasha and Stanislav from immediately moving over to Toni's side. My argument made some sense to them, though they didn't seem entirely sure whether I was a murderous traitor or a genius hero.

Toni didn't let up. 'Oh? And how did Dragan get that ring off of his sausage finger?'

'Just like how you've been brown-nosing Dragan for years: with a lot of vim and a big bucket of Vaseline.'

Toni blustered out of his seat and had to be restrained by Walter and Stanislav before he strangled me on the spot.

'Fuck you, you wanker. There is no evidence that it wasn't you who lopped off Dragan's finger and who's playing us all for mugs with this newspaper rubbish.'

However coherent my arguments may be, Toni's asser-tion was entirely correct. There was no one who could testify that Dragan really was alive. And since I couldn't think of anything to say, I stayed silent. The others were looking back and forth between Toni and me. Obviously, they were expecting me to clear this up. They wanted hard evidence – which I didn't have.

OK, I thought, why don't I just try to look at this situation without judging it. I managed to kill my boss and get away with it from Saturday to Thursday. This is probably where it ends. Enough with the lies, enough with the stress. It's done. So relax.

And right when I was thinking I had mindfully stamped out the stress this whole charade had caused as soundly as I had apparently stamped out my own chance at survival, a voice spoke up in my defence.

'But he does, there's evidence.' The voice was Sasha's. All eyes turned to him. 'Dragan spoke to me on the phone just this morning. So you, arsehole . . .' he pointed at Toni, 'you can fuck right off.'

Toni gave me a scathing look and hissed in my ear, 'You've got until Monday. I see Dragan by Monday or you can forget about this whole preschool.' He turned and left.

Everyone breathed a sigh of relief.

I put on a brave smile and was about to dismiss the others, but Carla, Walter and Stanislav still wanted a tour of the rest of the preschool.

30

Delegating

If subjectively you feel that everything is getting too much for you, objectively there can be one very simple reason for that: everything actually always is a little too much. So do not just subjectively let go of what you feel you need to do, let go objectively as well. Letting go is good! 'Letting go' does not mean 'losing your grip', nor does 'handing over' mean 'losing'. The magic trick is to *delegate*. If you hand over parts of your work to someone else with love, they will take up that love along with the work. Then, in half the time it would have cost you by yourself, you will both get double the end result.

> Joschka Breitner, *Slowing Down in the Fast Lane: Mindfulness for Managers*

'What did that dildo say to you at the end?' Sasha asked when we stood in the outside play area twenty minutes later. He was smoking a roll-up, I was drinking the organic apple juice Toni had scoffed at. Carla had gone to the loo. Walter and Stanislav were in the office, stocking up on promotional material for their sister and girlfriend.

'Exactly what you'd expect. He gave me until Monday to set up a meet with Dragan or I'm dead.'

'That craven cunt. But everything else went brilliant, don't you think?'

I was glad Sasha brought it up himself. I knew he couldn't have spoken to Dragan on the phone, but I didn't know whether Sasha knew that I knew. Why had he lied? Just to spite Toni? Or did he know the truth?

My curiosity won out.

'So you spoke to Dragan this morning,' I said neutrally.

Sasha gave me a piercing look before he spoke. 'Björn, I have no idea what you're playing at with all this. All I know is that we'll all benefit more from your game than from Toni's. So don't ask that type of question and I won't either.'

'Understood, Officer Sasha. Then I'd finally like to officially congratulate you on your promotion.'

'Thank you, Counsellor Björn. And by the way: the

335

others think you're a hero for coming up with that finger thing. I do too. Making the police think Dragan is dead is a genius move.'

That was good. I needed everyone's support, because there was a lot to support: Toni had to be eliminated, Boris had to be reassured, Möller had to be silenced, Malte had to be scrapped – and all of it by Monday. A lot for me to do alone, and a lot even for Sasha and me together. In all mindfulness, I didn't know how I would do it without the support of the rest of the officers.

Fortunately, mindfulness doesn't mean doing only what you're willing or able to do. Mindfulness also means dividing what you need doing into things you are capable of doing and things others are much more capable of. Those things can then be confidently handed over to people you trust.

I had already discussed with Sasha how we wanted to divvy up the tasks, promising him I'd discuss it with Dragan. And Dragan had miraculously agreed to the distribution of tasks and even suggested one or two improvements.

'When do we tell the others?' Sasha asked, stubbing out the ember of his rollie against the tile floor but holding on to the butt.

We had decided to show Carla, Walter and Stanislav the footage of Malte's interrogation once Toni had left. The three of them had already witnessed how far out on a limb Toni had gone when it came to blaming Boris. It wouldn't take too much effort now to push him off the limb entirely, especially not after his last freak-out.

Sasha and I stood next to the fire pit over which the founders probably made the preschoolers cook campfire twists in the autumn. I made a mental note to order proper sausages for the same occasion next autumn. When Carla, Walter and Stanislav joined us outside, Sasha was just burning the signed newsprint in the fire pit.

'Too bad we always have to burn them,' Carla said. 'In a few years, they'll be historical documents.'

'That'd get you banged up for historically long sentences if they ever end up in the police archives,' I couldn't help noting. 'But I still haven't read out tonight's most important historical document.'

I waved around another newspaper page.

'But what about Toni?' Carla enquired. 'Doesn't that buzzkill officially have to be here too?'

'He's what it's about. Listen up.'

I unfolded the newspaper signed with Dragan's thumb. The date confirmed it was from today's edition, meaning it was a whole day fresher than the instructions from earlier. The page was almost illegibly cluttered with squiggles and strokes.

I read aloud: 'If Toni, as expected, left the meeting early, please watch the video Björn sent me this morning.'

The three looked at each other, unsure. On my iPhone, I showed them a recording of Malte's interrogation from the previous evening.

The footage caused an uproar. Not because of the electric shocks, but because of the information they'd revealed: that it was Toni who was a traitor, that Toni had also wanted to eliminate Dragan, Sasha and – with Malte's help – Murat and me too. That he'd succeeded in Murat's case, not in mine. Yet just half an hour earlier, in front of the assembled officers, Toni had put his hand in the fire for Murat, the colleague he'd had shot. He had blamed Murat's death on Boris because he wanted to start a gang war.

He had betrayed us all.

'I was the one who got the prick those hand grenades,' Walter said, giving me a sad look. 'But I had no idea what that traitor was planning to do with them.'

'Let's drive down to his dive right now and take the wanker out on the spot,' Stanislav fumed.

'We should clip those electrical clamps to his tiny brain,' Carla suggested.

I raised my hands in a placatory gesture. 'Let's first hear what Dragan has to say about this.' With that, I unfolded another newspaper page.

It was a lengthy text with specific instructions, delegating various tasks to various officers so that together we could achieve the perfect result.

We spent another half-hour discussing the details of Dragan's plan. Once each of us knew what to do, Sasha burned this last newspaper page too, and the meeting was over.

31

Gratitude

There is one feeling that can be generated
very quickly and that overshadows all negative
thoughts. This feeling is gratitude. When you
are troubled by your burdens, just think of three
things you are grateful for. It might be a ray of
sunshine outside your window, your last pay rise
or just a good conversation. Try to really feel this
gratitude. You will find that you cannot be grateful
and frustrated at the same time.

Joschka Breitner, *Slowing Down in the
Fast Lane: Mindfulness for Managers*

That night I slept fitfully, dreaming of threats and betrayals, torture and violence. When I woke up, it was clear why: on the one hand, I actually had to deal with these issues if I wanted to live to see Monday. But why did my mind keep getting dragged down by negative thoughts? Probably because mindfulness also requires a degree of discipline. My last mindfulness lesson with Breitner had been exactly a week ago. Yesterday had been the first Thursday night I'd spent without any guided exercises in months.

Luckily, Breitner had pointed me to some exercises in his book I could do on my own. I reached for the handbook and read up on one such exercise:

> *There is one feeling that can be generated very quickly and that overshadows all negative thoughts. This feeling is gratitude. When you are troubled by your burdens, just think of three things you are grateful for. It might be a ray of sunshine outside your window, your last pay rise or just a good conversation. Try to really feel this gratitude. You will find that you cannot be grateful and frustrated at the same time.*

So I sat up straight in bed, closed my eyes and tried to think of three things I was grateful for.

I was grateful for my daughter, my health, the full refrigerator, the espresso I was about to have, my professional freedom, Breitner's book, the support from my officers, Emily's preschool spot, the unbroken bond between me and Katharina, my future as a lawyer at my own beautiful law firm, the fact that I'd already fulfilled Katharina's ultimatum and practically Boris's as well . . .

Wow. Off the cuff, that was considerably more than three. In my first mindfulness class, I hadn't been able to limit myself to five stressful things. And now, a week after my last session, positivity was positively bubbling out of me.

I tried to feel gratitude for every single item on my list. It worked: I could almost feel it physically. From my solar plexus, gratitude flowed through me, its warmth melting away the chilling worries I'd felt just moments before. I wanted to spend the entire day feeling this warmth. I wanted to share my gratitude – and I decided to share it with Katharina and Emily.

For dramatic reasons, I probably should've waited to inform Katharina that I had met her demands until the last day of April when her ultimatum expired. But even before my mindfulness journey, I'd never had much truck with drama. I felt that depriving someone of good news just so they would be happier about it later was utterly pointless.

For example, imagine your chain-smoking granddad is turning eighty-five in three days. As he'd been coughing up blood for a week, you took him to the oncologist a few days earlier. Today, the results come in: he only has pneumonia. That's no joke, but also not a death sentence. Of course, you could wait another three days, festively wrap up his cancer-free diagnosis and hand it to him just in time for his birthday – but all you'd actually be gifting him is three horrible days of fear. If you feel like that's worth the dramatic effect, go ahead.

Drama is the opposite of mindfulness.

Because I had just learned that gratitude was good for me, I wanted to share that gratitude with Katharina and inform her that Emily had a preschool spot.

When I called, Katharina suggested meeting at a café in our neighbourhood.

The café was listed as 'child-friendly'. This meant that in every other chair, mums of all ages and descriptions were flapping open their nursing bras while glugging down lactose- and caffeine-free lattes themselves. Buggies in all price ranges happily blocked the bike path outside the café. The women's bathroom had a spacious changing area – at the expense of the men's restroom, which consisted of a single toilet and not even the tiniest changing table. As the mums moaned about their financial constraints, the café's 3.90-euro croissants liberally left crumbs all over their children's designer clothes.

In short, the exact same clientele as Little Fish.

Emily loved it, especially because you were allowed draw on the walls with chalk and then wipe your fingers on the upholstery. Nevertheless, everything looked very neat. One reason for the café's high prices was probably that they needed to save up for frequent paint jobs.

'Since when do you go to cafés like this?' I asked Katharina after we'd found a table from which we could watch Emily draw.

'Since my husband moved out.'

'What does that have to do with it? This doesn't seem like your scene at all.'

'From time to time, I need to feel like there are people I wouldn't want to trade places with, even if their lives never involve underworld bosses or upmarket brothels. At least I don't care whether I can get soy-milk stains out of a Jack Wolfskin jacket at 30 degrees: compared to the champagne problems these yummy mummies tend to whinge on about, our relationship issues are remarkably tangible.'

Other people go to cafés because they like the people there; Katharina went to cafés because she hated the people there. She's just that type of person.

'I have two letters for you,' I said, changing the topic.

I first handed Katharina a letter from Little Fish signed by all three of its founders.

Dear Mrs Diemel,

We would hereby like to formally apologise to you. Last week, we sent you a rejection regarding your daughter's preschool application. That was wrong of us. Your daughter is the most wonderful child in the world. You are the most wonderful woman in the world, and your husband, who is the most wonderful man in the world, also has the most wonderful profession in the world. We apologise for not realising this much sooner. In order to pave the way for a new start, we hereby inform you that on the first of the month we are voluntarily handing over

the management of the Little Fish co-operative preschool.
The new managing director will reach out to offer your
daughter Emily a spot.

Kind regards, to Emily as well,

Katharina looked at me incredulously.

'Is that blood?'

'Where?'

'There, between "most wonderful man" and "most wonderful profession".'

I took a closer look. Since all three chaps had been crying
and stuffing tissues up their freshly broken noses before they
signed, I certainly couldn't rule out any spillage.

'No idea, but if you want I can ask them to print out a
fresh version.'

'No need, I like the letter just fine as is. Do I want to
know how you got them to write it?'

'Through mindfulness.'

'How do you mean?'

'I considered their needs and forgave them. Afterwards,
they were also willing to acknowledge their mistakes and
retract their rejection.'

'And for Emily this means what?'

I gave Katharina the second letter.

Dear Mrs and Mr Diemel,

I am pleased to inform you that there will be a place
available for your daughter Emily at our facility as of
1 August. Emily will undoubtedly prove a great addition to

345

the Little Fish community. Please contact us at your earliest
convenience to make arrangements to sign the contract.
  Kind regards,
  Sasha Ivanov

Katharina looked incredulous again.

'Wait, Sasha Ivanov . . . Isn't that Dragan's driver?'

My stomach started to feel queasy. I took a deep breath. 'Right.'

'And now he runs the preschool?'

'Dragan owed me.'

Katharina stared back and forth at the two letters, and I was scared she was about to slap me about the ears with them. But then, unexpectedly, her eyes grew damp and she embraced me.

'You've done much worse. Thank you.'

Mindfulness can kill people and break noses, but it can melt icebergs too.

32

Jealousy

One of humanity's oldest and fiercest emotions is jealousy. This emotion is associated with anger, hatred, fear and powerlessness. Jealousy usually prevents a person from thinking clearly and rationally – all based on the idea that someone else is responsible.

One way to deal with jealousy is through clear-eyed acceptance. Accept the pain you are feeling as *your* pain. As no one but you is responsible for this pain, no one but you can get rid of it.

Joschka Breitner, *Slowing Down in the Fast Lane: Mindfulness for Managers*

While we were still in the café envisioning what it'd be like once Emily became a preschooler this summer, I got a text from Carla on my non-bugged prepaid phone.

'Hotel Domino, now.'

Katharina's mood instantly snapped back to icy. 'Can't you *ever* put your phone down?'

She knew I'd taken the mindfulness course for our family's sake. I'd protected my times with Emily, even quit my job and secured the hard-won preschool spot.

She didn't know I had to murder Dragan, blackmail my bosses and threaten the preschool's founders to do it. Let alone that this meant putting my own life on the line.

But she could have noticed how at ease I'd felt with her just then, how happy.

And still she thought it appropriate to tear that all down with a cutting remark.

At that moment, it became clear to me that it would be impossible to change my life for her as long as she did not change her own. So I would no longer change my life for her at all: I'd change it for me, and for Emily – which felt more than good enough.

In response to Katharina's helpful remark, I looked at my

watch: eleven o'clock. I looked around the café: I was the only man there. Then I said:

'Let me put it this way: the fact that I am the only man here at eleven in the morning drinking an overpriced espresso with his wife and daughter does have a lot to do with my job and this mobile. After all, all the other dads are at the office, parked in front of a landline and not giving a fuck what preschool their kid gets into.'

The atmosphere in the café seemed to affect Katharina. She looked at the other mums, at the two letters, at me. And then she said something she hadn't said in years: 'Sorry, you're right. Whatever you did to finagle this, thank you.'

We got there in the end.

'If you need to answer that, go ahead.'

She meant well, but she was still overstepping. Katharina was unable to understand that her giving me permission presumed she had the right to forbid me from doing something.

At that moment, however, I didn't care. I had more important things to do. According to Carla's text message, the first step of the plan I'd hatched back in the forest and discussed with the officers the previous night had actually worked.

Carla had asked the girlfriend of Klaus Möller, the cop on Toni's payroll, to meet her at Hotel Domino at 3 p.m. This was based on a mindfully thought-out idea.

During my woodsy brainstorming session, I'd realised I could exploit Möller to get Toni where I wanted him. I'd simply redirect the mole to my own ends.

But how could I use mindfulness to get a corrupt

policeman to obey me? The first thing I needed to do was empathise with the copper's emotional life.

Police officers are civil servants. Civil servants are usually rational thinkers, less guided by their emotions. Manipulating someone who's rational is more difficult than manipulating someone who's irrational. So the first thing I needed to do was get Möller to throw rationality overboard.

Of course, mindfulness is primarily intended to do the opposite: to cope with irrational emotions. What's especially great about mindfulness is that it enables you to peaceably defuse even the most violent, explosive emotional outbursts, but fortunately this is not a one-way street.

Feelings can be defused just like bombs. The fundamental difference between practising mindfulness and disarming a bomb is that being a bomb disposal expert comes with the serious risk of dying on the job. Not so with practising mindfulness: if mindfulness methods cannot solve a problem one day, they might still do so the next.

But if a bomb disposal expert has a bad day, there *is* no next.

Yet the crucial thing is that since a bomb disposal expert knows exactly how a bomb works, they can also re-fuse one.

The same goes for mindfulness: with the knowledge that mindfulness provides about establishing peace of mind, you can also turn a rational person into an irrational bundle of nerves. Simply pull the emotional rug out from under them.

So I was looking for a feeling that would cloud our mole's rational brain, one that would ensure I could do whatever

I wanted with him. In Dragan's name, I had thus enlisted Sasha, Carla, Walter and Stanislav in a beautiful plan.

Möller lived with his strikingly attractive girlfriend, Basia, in a de facto marital union untethered by actual wedlock. Ten years younger than him and originally Polish, Basia saw earning a civil servant salary with pension rights as a status symbol. And for Möller, her attractive appearance was more than just a status symbol. Though they looked entirely mismatched, the two were actually very happy together – perhaps also because Basia took care to avoid places where she might get hit on by other men.

But that didn't mean she wasn't open to compliments, especially from women.

That's why Carla would be the one to approach her on the street. As the legitimate director of a modelling agency looking for new faces, she'd ask Basia to have a coffee with her at Hotel Domino – a respectable-looking establishment that was actually a by-the-hour hotel for Carla's upmarket escorts – so Carla and the housewife could discuss earning some money on the side by model-ling for ads.

Once I had confirmation from Carla that Basia had taken the bait – and permission from Katharina to send off a few texts – Sasha and I conducted a scripted text exchange on the mobiles that Möller was tapping.

Me: 'Do you know where Toni is? Can't reach him.'

Sasha: 'I'm sure he's just busy bonking that copper's wife again.'

Me: 'Who?'

Sasha: 'That young blonde off that porn-stached nobody from homicide.'

Me: 'Möller's missus?'

Sasha: 'Yep.'

Me: 'Her and Toni?!'

Sasha: 'Whenever clueless Möller is on duty. Always at Hotel Domino, suite 812.'

Me: 'Good to know. Thanks.'

Since I now had some experience maintaining my work–life balance, I turned my attention back to my family. I'd not only understood the idea behind delegating, I internalised and practised it in such a way that I could let go quite comfortably of what needed to happen next. Satisfied, I put my phone away.

Katharina told me about her plans to take Emily to her parents on Saturday. We both knew I could come along, but we both knew I wouldn't. We decided to go on a family outing on Sunday instead. I suggested showing Emily the preschool. Though she'd been there for the admissions interview, her daddy hadn't been in charge of it then.

So Sunday would be a family day. If her daddy was still even alive by Sunday – which depended, among other things, on what would happen today.

When you're delegating, open feedback from everyone involved is key. Fortunately, Sasha was able to tell me what happened with as much accuracy as amusement.

For Möller, reading that SMS exchange must have been the tremendously emotional event we'd intended it to be. As I slipped my phone back into my jacket pocket and waited for at least a put-on smile to appear on Katharina's face, Möller had already erased the intercepted text exchange from police records and jumped into his car to race to Hotel Domino, only to find his girlfriend's car in the car park.

Crazed with anger, hatred and fear, he rushed up to the eighth floor and kicked in the door to the suite. From the bedroom, he could hear sexy moans and groans. But the bedroom was behind a massive pair of sliding doors: locked – and not very suitable for kicking in.

What happened next must've been even more exciting live than it looked to me on video afterwards. Of course, Carla had tiny hidden cameras in every room of the hotel. There are no more precious memories than those of adultery, at least from the point of view of who's filming said adultery.

The recording from the suite's living room showed a police officer who had lost his mind rattling a locked bedroom door.

Inside the bedroom, a TV was playing the hotel's own porn channel at maximum volume, Sasha and Stanislav were leaning against the wall that separated the suite's bedroom from the living room, and my two bodyguards were waiting in the bathroom, naked.

Möller was trying to shout over the voices he attributed not to the TV, but to Toni and his girlfriend.

'Toni, open the door right now, you conniving cunt!'

Nothing happened. The groaning continued unabated.

'I've given you everything you asked for and now you want to take my girlfriend too?'

Nothing happened, except for one lustful shriek from behind the door.

'I risked my job for you, now come out and risk your life, you coward!'

Nothing happened, except for a rhythmically increasing double roar.

'If you don't open the door on the count of three, I'll kill you and that bitch right there in bed!'

Nothing happened, except for a drawn-out 'Yeeeeeees!' behind the door.

'One . . . two . . . three . . .'

Furious, Möller fired an entire magazine through the bedroom door. The bullets pierced the empty and already somewhat ramshackle double bed.

When his service pistol's magazine was obviously empty and Möller's blind anger had achieved nothing, Sasha turned off the TV. Now that the bed was safe, Stanislav directed the naked bodyguards to get into it before he finally opened the sliding doors.

Möller was trembling with anger and foaming at the mouth, his white knuckles clamped to an empty gun.

'Surprise!' Sasha called out.

'Smile for the camera,' Stanislav called, pointing out the smoke detector in which the surveillance camera was installed.

'But . . . What . . . Where . . . ?' Möller stammered.

'We were hoping you could enlighten us, Mr Möller,' Sasha replied. 'You have just shot an entire official police magazine through the closed bedroom door of a hotel suite – which you illegally entered, by the way – that was occupied by a couple of complete strangers. But why? Where are your manners?'

Möller was stunned.

'But my Basia . . . and Toni . . . Where did they go?'

'Where Toni is, we don't know. Neither do we much care about that right now,' Sasha informed him.

'As for your Basia, however . . .' Stanislav continued.

'Or as you say, "that bitch",' Sasha added.

'. . . she's here at the hotel,' Stanislav explained. 'She's just meeting the managing director of a casting agency eight floors down. If you'd like, we'd be perfectly happy to send for her. Then she can find out you almost shot two complete strangers out of baseless jealousy.'

'Our video recordings are really top-notch.'

'And in the process, Basia would also learn that you actually believed she'd have an affair with that cunt Toni,' Sasha added. 'And that you'd just as soon have shot "that bitch" too. By the time she's in the lift back down, she'll probably have left you.'

'And even if Basia doesn't care about the recordings, the commissioner certainly will. Once this friendly couple file a complaint against you for attempted murder, he'll *have* to look at the footage.'

'But I . . .' Möller stammered.

'And then you'd probably lose your job *and* your girlfriend too, right?' Sasha added. 'Because without a job, the missus will only see you as half a man.'

'Bit of a shit day for Mr Möller whichever way you look at it, innit?'

In some near-death experiences, a dying person supposedly sees their entire life play out before their eyes like a movie. Thinking about his possible future, Möller could also see a movie play out: a horror movie. Since Möller had just been on quite the emotional roller coaster (*Fuck, my girlfriend is cheating on me! Hurray, my girlfriend isn't cheating on me! Fuck, my girlfriend isn't cheating on me, but she's leaving me anyway! Now I've lost my job too!*), he offered no resistance to the proposal Sasha made him next.

For one last time, Möller would pass Toni some police information, information that was completely false. After that, Möller would never hear from Toni again, nor from the couple in the hotel bed, and he'd never have to see the video of him in the hotel suite ever again.

When all was said and done, he would marry his Basia and retire happily ever after.

Of course, all that stuff about getting married and retiring would never happen, but it painted a beautiful picture. And threats alone are not motivation enough to ensure co-operation; lies work much better.

33

Lies

Lies weigh on your conscience; the truth will set you free. That is what people say, but it is not true. Dealing with the truth is often more difficult than dealing with a lie, and the truth sometimes hurts more than a lie. And since some truths are nobody's business, there is no harm in shielding them with a lie. What matters is the mindset with which you decide to tell the truth or tell a lie.

Joschka Breitner, *Slowing Down in the Fast Lane: Mindfulness for Managers*

As planned, it didn't take long before Sasha and Stanislav had Möller where we wanted him. He was like wax in Sasha's hands: he just needed to be moulded into shape before he would melt away.

'When you're not calling your girlfriend a bitch, what do you call her?' Sasha asked.

'I . . . Basia, my girlfriend's name is Basia,' Möller replied.

'I'm well aware, but some people like to give their wives pet names. Because they're called something completely un-erotic like Hildrun, for example, or they actually smell like a rose. So, what do you call Basia when you're in a romantic mood?'

'Bunny.'

'And what does she call you?'

'How is that relevant?'

'It's not, but since I'm the guy with the silly little video, I get to ask my silly little questions.'

'She calls me . . . Buck.'

Sasha choked down a laugh as he imagined Bucky Möller getting lovey-dovey with his Polish bunny.

'Well, then it's time for some dictation, Bucky boy.'

Sasha put a pen and paper on the small desk by the wall and told Möller to sit down.

'What happens now?'

'From now on, you will no longer be mister "I'll-kill-that-bitch" but mister "I-want-to-spend-the-rest-of-my-life-with-you". That's why you're going to write your little bunny a letter explaining why you'll be away for the weekend.'

'What do mean . . . away?'

Sasha ignored Möller's question. 'Write this down: "Dearest Bunny, I need to go away this weekend on a mission for our love. Don't ask why. Just know that it's about our future. You'll find out everything on Monday. Love, Buck."'

When it came to this part of the plan, I had a bit of a guilty conscience. Morally, it was not OK to force Möller to lie to a girlfriend who had no part in any of this. But since I was already dealing with one policeman and two gangsters, it'd be annoying to also have to deal with an oblivious girlfriend hysterically looking for her missing Bucky. Fortunately, Breitner's handbook assured me that lying is not a bad thing in itself. In this case, it wouldn't even be a bad thing at all.

Lies weigh on your conscience; the truth will set you free. That is what people say, but it is not true. Dealing with the truth is often more difficult than dealing with a lie, and the truth sometimes hurts more than a lie. And since some truths are nobody's business, there is no harm in shielding them with a lie. What matters is the mindset with which you decide to tell the truth or tell a lie.

It would've made no sense if Möller had written: 'Dear

Bunny, I'm a bent cop. I have no idea if we'll ever see each other again. I'll probably be dead soon. Yours, Buck.'

And as Sasha told me afterwards, any mindful means of motivating Möller would've been surplus to requirements.

After Möller had called his Basia a bitch and almost shot her, it was relatively easy for him to lie to her in writing. Especially since two gangsters were threatening to destroy his reputation, and this lie was the only way his girlfriend would never find out. Even without any mindfulness training, lying made things much easier for him.

Möller even wrote out the letter in his most beautiful cursive.

Sasha read through it and gave it to the female bodyguard, now fully clothed again.

The security team left the suite and headed down to the hotel bar. There, the note made its way into Basia's handbag unnoticed, probably to be found an hour later when she opened it to get her house key.

'So,' said Sasha, 'then I think it's about time for you to make your call to Toni.'

'Why should I call Toni?' Möller asked anxiously.

'Just one last call to Toni that will mark the end of your years working together.'

'What should I tell him?'

'Tell him that our nice lawyer, Mr Diemel, is holding a guy called Malte prisoner in the basement of Walter's security company.'

'But . . .' Möller was obviously thinking along, 'how do I know that?'

'Because Mr Diemel texted that to me, of course,' Sasha explained, 'which you then read during your work as an investigating police officer.'

'Or do you need us to fake that text for you as well?' Stanislav added.

'But what *exactly* should I tell him?'

'Alright then, let's just run through it.' Sasha picked up the vase of flowers that was on the table in his left hand.

'This here is Mr Diemel.'

Then he took the remote, which was on the TV, in his right hand.

'And this is me.'

He raised the remote.

'I text Mr Diemel: "The guy in Walter's basement is slowly waking up."'

Now he raised the vase.

'Mr Diemel goes: "Has he said anything yet?" Me: "Nope. Only that his name is Malte. He's still totally groggy. Should I call Toni?" Mr Diemel: "Not yet, I want to talk to the guy first." I'm like: "When?" He's like: "In two hours." Both are like: done.'

Sasha looked at Möller. 'Understood?'

Obviously more comfortable at this basic level of conversation, Möller nodded.

'Then make the fucking call.'

Möller took out his phone and called Toni, who answered right away. Without any follow-up questions, Toni fully bought that the killer he had hired was apparently cowering in Walter's basement and about to spill the beans: within two hours, Malte would tell Diemel – that is, me – everything.

Toni thanked Möller and hung up.

As we had discussed the night before, Stanislav then took Möller under his wing, and Sasha called me to say we were ready to go. Toni was already on his way to Walter's.

Sasha and I were on our way too, so I got to experience what happened next in person.

34

Inner Smile

There are muscles in your body that, when activated, effortlessly facilitate a state of mindful relaxation. These muscles are the ones you use to smile. Please take a moment to smile, just to yourself. Track how your smile moves across your face. Feel how activating the muscles around your mouth automatically releases tension around your neck. Now feel this relaxation ripple through your body as your smile spreads through your entire body.

So smile to yourself as often as you can.

Joschka Breitner, *Slowing Down in the Fast Lane: Mindfulness for Managers*

While Toni, Sasha and I were making our separate ways to Walter's headquarters, Stanislav took Möller in his car to a remote truck stop in a very quiet industrial estate. Having parked behind an HGV with Polish plates, Stanislav asked Möller to handcuff himself to his steering wheel.

Since Möller was a little stubborn and Stanislav a little annoyed, this led to a brief tussle in which Möller broke his left thumb, left index finger and one metacarpal.

Once Möller realised that Stanislav had not only more intact bones but also at least one more gun than him, the policeman finally complied. To his great amazement, the loading doors of the Polish lorry then opened, revealing a large compartment with an SUV in the back. Two of Stanislav's employees attached two ramps to the HGV, pushed Möller and his vehicle in, strapped it in properly and closed the doors again.

Sasha and I arrived at the sunny car park of Walter's company at the same time. Toni's car was already there, right in front of the entrance. We waited another five minutes before walking into Walter's ground-floor message centre – the room where all the data from his patrols, property surveillance and in-house CCTV converged.

Behind a control panel, Walter stood with one of his

operators – a smart, muscly guy with three-day stubble and rimless glasses – and looked at a screen showing the basement interrogation room.

We could see Malte lying apparently unconscious on a sofa and Toni checking to see if the interrogation camera was off. The moron didn't even notice the ceiling cameras through which we were watching him. And he obviously also didn't realise that since there were intercom speakers, the room must be outfitted with microphones too.

'When did he get here?' I asked Walter.

'Arrived ten minutes before you did. Made a beastly fuss about why he hadn't been immediately informed about the "prisoner". I made it clear to him that we didn't have any prisoner, just some bloke our patrol watched as he followed you around for an entire day. I told him that when the patrol spoke to the guy, he pulled out a gun, which was then kicked out of his hand. Unfortunately, our guard couldn't stop her foot before it hit the guy's chin. The guy's been unconscious ever since and would probably have a headache, but he's just coming to.'

'And?' Sasha asked. 'Did Toni swallow that?'

'Absolutely. He instantly starting shouting up a storm. Reminded me, in front of my people, that Dragan had only entrusted *him* with any interrogation. Three times he asked whether the guy had said anything yet, then he rushed downstairs.'

Which is where we were seeing him.

Toni examined Malte, then he slapped him. Nothing happened. The fact that Malte was unconscious was primarily due to the fact that Walter had roofied him. Now Toni took a closer look at Malte's swollen blue chin, which had even burst in one spot.

'How'd you manage that?' I asked with interest. 'He really does look like he got kicked in the chin.'

'He got kicked in the chin,' Walter explained.

'But . . . ?' I looked up in surprise.

'After the roofies had started to work, he was on the floor anyway. He was right there. It was more like . . . a floppy little free kick.'

'Was that really necessary?'

'We could've also sent in a make-up artist, sure. But nothing looks more like a kick in the chin than a kick in the chin. Also, faster and cheaper than a make-up artist. And look at it this way: it's not like the guy felt any of it. He was already knocked out.'

'Right, right. A pragmatic approach, Dragan will appreciate that.'

Everyone in the room was now anxiously waiting to see how Toni would react. We were sure Toni wanted to eliminate Malte as a witness. That was the basis of Dragan's plan – meaning mine. We disagreed, however, on how we thought Toni would take him out. I was of the opinion that Toni would just kill Malte on the spot. Walter was of the opinion that Toni would first torture the guy to find out if he had said anything. And Sasha was betting that Toni would torture Malte to death at once, regardless of whether he'd actually say anything.

Each of us bet 50 euros.

After my positive experiences with intentional centring and overcoming internal resistance, I had no major issues with the fact that someone was about to die. After all, it would be the desired result of my mindful considerations. So I wasn't experiencing any unresolved emotions. I was, however, feeling a certain tension about how exactly Malte would be killed. Though too minor to try to breathe away in front of all these people, the tension was pronounced enough to affect my well-being. I remembered another one of Breitner's relaxation exercises. He called it the 'Inner Smile'.

There are muscles in your body that, when activated, effortlessly facilitate a state of mindful relaxation. These muscles are the ones you use to smile. Please take a moment to smile, just to yourself. Track how your smile moves across your face. Feel how activating the muscles around your mouth automatically releases tension around your neck. Now feel this relaxation ripple through your body as your smile spreads through your entire body.

So smile to yourself as often as you can.

In order to quickly and effectively release the tension I was feeling, I started smiling to myself. And I hadn't started my little exercise a moment too early.

We watched Toni lean over Malte and feel his pulse. He then pulled Malte off the sofa onto the floor. Then he turned away, and for a moment it looked like he was about to leave. But then, out of nowhere, Toni turned back around, swung out his right steel-toe-clad foot and kicked the unconscious man in the head with full force. After that, Malte's head was at such an unnatural angle there was no doubt his neck was broken; the man was dead.

Walter, Sasha and the operator shrank back in shock and looked away in disgust. Due to my 'Inner Smile' exercise, however, I had reached the utmost serenity and was able to follow the events on screen unfazed. When Walter and Sasha saw that I was just smiling in a situation even they found disgusting, they probably drew some conclusions that were fundamentally false. They didn't understand I could only endure the sight *because* I was smiling. Still, the misunderstanding didn't hurt my growing reputation as a leader. I wasn't just the brilliant strategist who could make the police believe Dragan was dead; I even smiled in the face of death. Another element in my favour was the fact that my prediction had been correct: Toni had taken Malte out immediately, without any torture or fuss.

Without a word, Walter and Sasha each gave me 50 euros.

We watched Toni feel Malte's pulse again. He no longer seemed to have any. Toni hoisted Malte back onto the sofa and positioned him exactly as he'd found him. But when he wanted to leave, he found the door was locked.

This was the moment I'd been waiting for. I pressed the intercom button and lowered my vocal register two notches.

'Hello, Toni.'

Toni flinched.

'My, aren't you a jumpy little bunny?'

'Who's there?'

'I wear many faces. Maybe I'm Malte, a little pissed off you just killed me? Or maybe I'm Murat, who you had shot by Malte? Or Dragan, who you wanted to kill too?'

'What is this shite?'

I assumed my normal voice again.

'OK, Toni, let's cut this shite. I'm just the guy whose daughter you happened to threaten because you wanted to see Dragan. Which is why I won't take you to Dragan, but to someone who's much more eager to see you.'

Toni started kicking the steel door with all his might. The door remained utterly unimpressed.

'You lawyer twat, open the door right now or I'll fucking end you.'

'Hello, Toni,' said Walter. 'Now, I never got my A levels or anything . . . so I just thought I'd ask: how exactly are you going to kill Björn with the door shut?'

'I'd also love to know,' added Sasha.

'Get me out of here! That guy is screwing with you. Dragan is dead.'

'OK . . .' Walter said, 'but wait a minute: if Dragan is dead, why did he tell us to send you into this hidden-camera trap?'

'You were filming me?'

'We were,' Sasha contributed. 'Just like we filmed Malte's confession.'

'And let me just say,' I just said, 'Dragan was not amused.'

'Open the door right now, arsehole, I'll end you! I'll break your f—'

I turned off the intercom. I had him exactly where I wanted him. For someone like Toni, who solved every problem by force, it must be awful to be helplessly stuck in a room with a guy who was already dead while no one outside paid him any mind. It would be exceptional agony not to be battled but ignored.

We would leave Toni in that basement's total silence the entire weekend. Along with Malte, who, due to Toni's violent outburst, was no longer much of a conversationalist. On Sunday night, Malte would be disposed of in the waste-to-energy facility per the usual method – Sunday was supposedly the best day for this, Sasha had explained to me. Life really was a never-ending learning journey. Toni, meanwhile, we would take to Boris on Monday. In short, we were on schedule.

When we walked out to the car park, Walter took me aside.

'Listen, Björn. It's none of my business, but . . .' he dithered.

'Just tell me, what's up?'

'Well, it's about Dragan and these newspaper pages.'

Despite the sun still shining overhead, I felt a sudden chill. What the devil had Walter found out now?

'What about them?'

'I don't mean to tell you your business . . .'

'Just say it.'

'Well . . . my people have been following you for a few days now. And it's quite clear that there's only one place you go and pick something up every day.'

'And where is that?'

'McDonald's.'

I was beyond stunned. I had no idea where this was going. 'What are you trying to say?'

'Well, if even my people have gathered that Dragan can only get you his messages at McDonald's, then the police can too. Maybe you should try to find a more subtle strategy . . .'

I stopped short. The fact that I'd been to McDonald's to buy a newspaper every day that week was suddenly yet more proof that Dragan was alive.

I smiled to myself, just because. Because I actually felt like smiling.

35

Pain

There are two types of pain: the pain of a wound and the pain of poking a wound. A wound itself cannot be undone, but if we avoid poking it, the wound will heal much faster.

Joschka Breitner, *Slowing Down in the Fast Lane: Mindfulness for Managers*

That Saturday was very relaxed, at least for me. I started the day with a simple breathing exercise in front of the open window. I sensed the closeness of the tree outside whose toasted bark already seemed to be healing. In my mind's eye, I could see the lake where just a week earlier I had taken my first step on a path that would lead me to a profound inner peace.

I felt the breath and life inside of me.

I felt grateful.

Long before their Monday expiration date, two of the three ultimatums I'd been given were now off the table: Emily had her preschool spot and Toni no longer posed a danger to me, stuck as he was in Walter's basement. I no longer even felt any hatred or resentment towards Toni either. I had come to see him more as a gift. Well, not in the sense of 'What a gift our Toni is to humanity', but more concretely as my gift to Boris. Now he just had to be handed over with appropriate pomp. Boris would be happy to be able to do whatever he wanted with Toni, and I would be happy to be able to share in his joy. Especially since that would finish off the first half of the third ultimatum: Boris would be able to take his revenge on Toni. He'd only want to see Dragan afterwards. But by now I was no longer too worried about that either. With a little luck, that would work out as well.

I wouldn't see Emily today, because she and Katharina were visiting Katharina's parents. I'd been invited too, but I was mindful enough to know that accepting that invitation wouldn't do me any good. I'd had quite an eventful week, what with five deaths and a few fundamental career changes. I didn't want to dilute this experience with two hours of meaningless chit-chat with people who would never understand my life.

Mindfulness had helped me a great deal in terms of my emotional attitude towards Katharina's parents. Before Breitner introduced me to the mindful arts, I'd regularly gone to see my in-laws, even though I hated them.

Now I didn't go to see my in-laws because I loved them.

This change in attitude was doubly positive: on the one hand because I no longer had to go see my in-laws; on the other because I had no guilty conscience whatsoever.

When it came to my in-laws, Breitner had very quickly convinced me what love had to do with them.

'Regardless of what you think of your in-laws, they gave life to your wife,' he'd explained to me in one of our first sessions.

'So? If that was so undeniably great, I wouldn't be sitting here with you right now.'

'Together with your wife, you gave life to Emily.'

'And what does that have to do with my in-laws?'

'You are the lawyer here, you know the but-for test better than I do.'

I rummaged through my first-year training.

'OK, according to this test, a circumstance can be considered the cause of a success if the success would not have occurred "but for" the presence or involvement of that circumstance.'

'Right. Now apply it to Emily and your in-laws.'

'Factually speaking, Emily would not exist without my in-laws.'

'So you should be grateful and love them for their contribution to your daughter's existence.'

'And what should that love look like in practical terms?' I enquired.

'What love looks like? I trust I don't need to explain that to you. Love doesn't look like anything. Love is a feeling. So it has nothing to do with having coffee, forced visits or receiving well-intentioned advice. Forget all that. Love your in-laws and stay at home. Out of your love, give them a few nice hours with their child and their granddaughter without their grumpy son-in-law having to be there too. Instead, give them a loving son-in-law who thinks of them fondly from afar.'

'Sounds quite good.'

Since then, I've stayed home, and the visits have been much more relaxed for all involved.

So this Saturday, I finally had the peace, the quiet and the opportunity to happily take care of the everyday professional duties that had fallen by the wayside during the week, what with all the mindfulness and death threats. I had to start a new law firm, I already had a client, and I had my eye on a wonderful new office. The fact that this space belonged to my client and that he was also dead constituted attendant circumstances that were entirely favourable.

First off, I wrote a general agreement between me and Dragan: I would work for him as a lawyer, charging a monthly retainer fee and additionally a reduced hourly rate based on the retainer, which was still exorbitant. After printing out and signing this agreement on a blank sheet already signed by Dragan, I wrote out a lease agreement between myself and Dragan regarding the office space above the pre-school – the advantage of doing them in this order was that it also enabled me to invoice Dragan for drafting the lease.

I sent a letter to the Law Society informing them of my new address, took out professional indemnity insurance online, opened a bank account for the firm and thus became an independent lawyer.

Newly independent, I then went into town. At a toy shop, I got the last tool I needed to stop Boris from killing me and then took it to Sasha so he could practise with it.

It felt good.

As Stanislav told me that night, Möller's Saturday hadn't started out feeling so good. Around the time I was taking out my professional indemnity insurance online, the Polish HGV that contained both Möller's car and Möller complaining about his broken hand had driven straight across Poland overnight and was about seventy kilometres from the Belarusian border.

As Möller knew neither the first thing about the principles of mindfulness nor what his impending fate might be, this meant he was under a certain existential stress. Instead of simply accepting that he was tied to his car, that he was in pain, and that he neither could nor need do anything about that, his thoughts were spiralling. As he was upset that he had pointlessly resisted his attacker, this only worsened the situation. And since he hadn't the slightest idea what would happen to him, he was imagining the most horrific scenarios. This meant, for example, that he spent the whole journey afraid he was being driven to a scrapyard to be tossed into a garbage compactor right along with his car. When Stanislav finally freed him from the car after a good eighteen hours' travel, Möller realised this concern had been unfounded: the truck was in a car park on the outskirts of a Polish town on the border with Belarus called Sokółka. Basia's home town.

In a mixture of confusion and incipient Stockholm syndrome, Möller told his captor that he'd been afraid he was going to anonymously end up in a garbage compactor. Stanislav later told me it annoyed him that he hadn't come up with the idea himself. It would've saved him the eighteen-hour drive.

Stanislav and his fellow driver had reattached the ramp to the Polish HGV's loading area, and rolled out Möller's car and the SUV.

Once Möller was freed from his cuffs, he rubbed his heavily swollen hand, astounded when he recognised the car park. He knew the area well from his visits to his future in-laws. Their house was right across the street. Maybe Sasha really did just want him to finally get married?

'What are we doing here?' he asked Stanislav.

'Not "we", you. You're going to cross this street, ring your future father-in-law's doorbell and ask for his blessing.'

'But why?'

'Firstly, because you love Basia. Secondly, because married men are less susceptible to doing criminal shit. And thirdly, because we want you to.'

Stanislav handed the bewildered policeman a bottle of whisky for Basia's father and a bouquet of flowers for her mum. Möller was as relieved as he was perplexed: it was all going to be OK. As of that day, he'd no longer be a bent cop. His criminal past was finally behind him. It may have earned him a broken hand, but that was a price he was willing to pay.

Out of sheer relief, Möller didn't notice the SUV turning on the country road a hundred metres away. He also didn't notice it going full throttle the second Stanislav pressed the bouquet into his hand.

On the contrary, Möller was already composing the speech he would give his surely surprised father-in-law. This country road was now the only thing separating him from his new life, just twenty or so steps. As he was about to take his first step, Stanislav held him back, saying:

'There's a car coming up ahead.'

'Nah, it's still a long way away . . .'

'Exactly,' Stanislav said, holding Möller by the collar.

Möller looked incredulously at Stanislav, then at the car. He realised he'd not be asking for Basia's hand, at least not in this life. When the car was three metres away, Stanislav pushed him into the road.

The SUV hit Möller straight on, hurled him onto the tarmac and ran over him. There was no doubt he hadn't survived the accident. The SUV stopped, Stanislav got in and drove to the edge of town, where the HGV was already waiting with its ramp out.

Later that night, the truck, the SUV, Stanislav and his boys were back in Germany. They disposed of the SUV in a garbage compactor, and Stanislav resolved to remember this option when he next needed to eliminate someone.

36

Minimalism

Let only that which is good for you into your life. Any people, objects, thoughts or conversations that burden you, let them pass like clouds overhead. At any time, you should feel free to divest yourself of any burdens, anything that neither serves nor helps you.

This minimalist mindfulness will soon make you realise that you can be enough.

Joschka Breitner, *Slowing Down in the Fast Lane: Mindfulness for Managers*

'His mileage is what's so strange about it,' Peter Egmann said.

We were having a coffee in Little Fish's garden. Our children were merrily romping around the Flipper group's ball pit, while our wives were taking a closer look at the preschool's facilities inside.

Peter had called me on Sunday morning because his wife had a few questions about the preschool. Since Emily, Katharina and I were in Katharina's car on our way to Herderstraße anyway, I invited him and his family over for a tour. Both the mums and kids were enthusiastic about the set-up. Even Katharina had no complaints.

When Peter and I were finally alone in the sunny garden, he told me about Möller.

'You know Möller, don't you?'

I nodded – with mixed feelings.

'He died in a traffic accident yesterday.'

'Oh?' I feigned surprise. 'On the job?'

'No, in Poland.'

'How so?'

'It's all very strange. He wrote a note to his girlfriend that he was going on a "love mission" over the weekend. Then he was run over on her parents' doorstep on the Belarusian

389

border. He had parked in a lot across the street and, from the evidence they gathered, he must've been carrying a bottle of whisky and a bouquet of flowers.'

'Maybe he wanted to propose, what's strange about that?'

'The strange thing is his mileage.'

'His mileage?'

'Möller told everyone he rolled into his annual inspection with exactly 100,000 kilometres on his odometer. He's the kind of guy who's proud of things like that.'

'And?'

'Our colleagues in Poland told us that the odometer in the car they found reads exactly 100,058 kilometres.'

'And?'

'Möller didn't get his car back from the inspection until Thursday afternoon. And it's rather more than 58 kilometres from his garage to the Polish town of Sokółka.'

Good heavens, the police really liked getting granular, didn't they? Wasn't it more important that this traitor cop's odometer had rolled over for the last time?

'And why are you worrying about that? As far as you told me, the odometer didn't cause Möller's death, did it?'

'No, Möller must have been hit by a large speeding car. It was a hit and run. But the thing is . . . the last number Möller dialled was Toni's.'

'Peter, which story are you telling me here? One in which Möller was run over on a Polish street with a bottle of whisky and a bouquet of flowers in his hands, so nervous after a long car ride that he forgot to look first left and then right? Or one in which Möller called Toni, had his car flown to Poland and was then deliberately run over? In front of his wife's parents' house?'

'I just have a feeling, especially since Toni has also been missing since Friday.'

I put my arm on Peter's shoulders.

'Peter, when you're looking at a preschool for your son, you're looking at a preschool for your son. If you want to go looking for a killer who doesn't exist, go looking for a killer who doesn't exist. But do me a favour, please, and don't go looking for a killer who doesn't exist while you're looking at a preschool for your son, OK?'

'What kind of philosophy is *that*?' Peter looked at me in amazement.

'I told you, it's called mindfulness. So, what's more important to you, a killer or a preschool?'

Peter didn't even need to think. 'A preschool! Maybe the odometer was just broken.'

Maybe the odometer was just broken. Maybe Peter was also slowly starting to appreciate the principles of mindfulness. Or maybe he didn't want to endanger his son's preschool spot with further inquiries.

In any case, any investigations into Möller's death were not at all what I wanted or needed to burden myself with.

When the Egmanns had left, I showed Emily and Katharina the empty rest of the building. Now that she was seeing it in the light of day, Katharina was enthusiastic not only about the preschool, but also about my offices above it. The idea that I would be setting my own schedule and working one floor above my daughter was a great thing not only for me, but for her too. Regardless of what would happen to our marriage in the future, this solution would clearly be best for Emily.

'Are you guys hungry too?' I asked at the end of the tour.

'A little, what do you suggest?' Katharina asked.

'How about McDonald's?' I suggested it on the one hand because I wanted to give Emily a treat; on the other hand, it was also obviously convenient for me to pretend to still be communicating with Dragan.

Katharina was about to summon some pedagogical outrage, but Emily was quicker: 'I want Chicken McNuggets, vanilla ice cream and chocolate milk.'

Katharina looked at Emily and laughed. 'OK then, I guess I can't say I've never taken Emily to McDonald's before.'

'Since, as your lawyer, I'm bound by confidentiality, no one outside this office will ever know.'

Katharina gave me a spontaneous hug. 'It's nice to see you so relaxed. I've never seen you like this.'

She was right. A good week after completing my mindfulness course, I was happy to watch all my professional problems gradually vanish into thin air. At our last session, Breitner had given me some rather abstract advice about minimalism.

Let only that which is good for you into your life. Any people, objects, thoughts or conversations that burden you, let them pass like clouds overhead. At any time, you should feel free to divest yourself of any burdens, anything that neither serves nor helps you.

This minimalist mindfulness will soon make you realise that you can be enough.

It was really fulfilling to see this abstract advice take real shape in my life. I had broken away from my client. I had broken away from my firm. I had let go of Möller. By that evening, Malte would go up in smoke at the incinerator and pass as a perfectly filtered cloud overhead. And by the next day, Toni would no longer exist either. I could not have minimised my professional environment any further – at least, not if I wanted to keep a few potential clients around.

After an ample family dinner at McDonald's, Katharina drove me back to my apartment. As she stopped in the parking bay where my company car had exploded, she gave the charred tree an irritated look.

'What happened *there*?'

'A car caught fire, but don't worry: the tree will grow back.'

'Whose car?'

'Definitely not mine.'

Which wasn't even a lie.

That evening, I called Boris.

'Yes?' Boris grumbled curtly.

'It's me, Björn. I was just looking at my calendar and I realised that Monday is almost upon us.'

'Very true, and if you're calling to ask for more time, mister lawyer man, you can start googling what "nyet" means.'

'That's not why I'm calling, Boris, quite the contrary. I'd like to start by thanking you.'

'Are you now? And for what?'

393

'For sticking to your part of our deal and letting us find the traitor in peace.'

Gratitude not only provides relief to yourself, it also relaxes the other person and your entire atmosphere with it.

Boris suddenly sounded much more open. 'It's not common in our line of work for someone to say thank you for sticking to an agreement. But I also gather that you've found the arsehole.'

'Correct.'

'When do I get him?'

'That depends – Golden Delicious or Granny Smith?'

'Sorry, what?'

'Should I stuff a Golden Delicious in his mouth or a Granny Smith? I already have some Golden Delicious.'

'You can stuff a horse apple in his mouth for all I care, long as I can do whatever I want with the bloke.'

'It's all been cleared with Dragan. You'll get the thumb-stamped newspaper, the traitor and a Golden Delicious.'

'And when do I get to see Dragan?'

'Afterwards, we can all go see him together. You with your officers, me with Dragan's. We'll clear up the whole thing at all levels.'

'Sounds good, and where is this supposed to happen?'

'You'll understand I can't tell anyone that beforehand. Dragan's officers don't know where either. Everyone will find out when we meet up. In return, you can determine where we should hand over the traitor.'

'Why don't we meet at this motorway lay-by where all this started?'

'Where Igor got torched?'

'That's the one. When there are no coaches full of kids, nights are usually very quiet there.'

'Tonight or tomorrow night?'

'Tonight, at 3 a.m. Are you coming alone?'

'No, we're doing this officially – all the officers will be there.'

'And the arsehole.'

'One of the officers *is* the arsehole.'

'I figured.'

'You really are clever, Boris.'

'Save your sucking up for later. When we see Dragan, feel free to tell him how much you like me.'

That was exactly what I was planning to do.

37

Death

Everyone thinks that death is so very awful, yet
death is our best friend – 100 per cent reliable,
first of all. Death does not care what you have
accomplished in life. And even better: it does
not care what you have *not* accomplished either.
Death accepts you exactly as you are, so why on
earth would you think life would not do the same?

Joschka Breitner, *Slowing Down in the*
Fast Lane: Mindfulness for Managers

'The apple's not staying put.'

Carla was getting annoyed. Since Toni was understandably unwilling to keep the apple in his mouth, we had to somehow affix it to him. Carla's idea was to clamp the apple's stalk to Toni's nose using a hair clip, then the apple would at least be dangling in front of his mouth. But even though both Toni's hands and feet were cuffed, he could still shake his head so violently the apple would come flying off.

'Do you have any knitting needles in this van?' Walter enquired. 'Then I can just stuff the apple into the son of a bitch's mouth and skewer it through his left cheek with the knitting needle until it comes out the other side. That should hold.'

'Just use that duct tape over there,' Sasha suggested.

Sure enough, a half-empty roll was rumbling around the footwell of the Ford Transit, and Carla and Walter used it to keep the apple in Toni's mouth.

Sitting next to Stanislav in front, I watched the other four in the rear-view mirror.

Toni had fought tooth and nail when we dragged him out of the interrogation room. This despite the fact that he should've been happy to get some fresh air finally, if only for a few minutes before his death. Due to Malte's advanced state of decomposition, the room's stench was overpowering.

Now, Malte and Toni had parted ways. When Toni had been immobilised with a Taser dart, Sasha told Walter's people to take the package containing Malte to the waste-to-energy facility. While still on our way to the lay-by, we received word that Malte had passed through the combustion chamber and out through the facility's emission control system.

When Toni's apple was finally in place, it was 3 a.m. and we were already driving into the completely deserted motorway lay-by where the whole sticky wicket had begun the Saturday before last. Two Mercedes were parked in front of the public toilets, which looked filthy even in the dark. In front of them stood Boris and four of his officers.

Stanislav parked our Transit beside them, and we all got out, except for Toni.

Behind a copse of trees a few metres away stood an abandoned Opel Kadett, a red sticker from the motorways agency declaring the vehicle would soon be removed.

Boris couldn't have chosen a more fitting meeting place. Some police tape fluttered on a forgotten wooden post right where Dragan had burned and beaten Igor to death nine days earlier because the arsehole we were about to hand over had lured both of them into a trap.

But instead of Boris and his officers executing Dragan's officers in retaliation, now everybody was amicably shaking hands.

'Boris,' I said. 'Dragan sends his best regards. He would like to apologise once again for what happened, but he now knows who the culprit was. Dragan also fully recognises you should be the one to hold the traitor accountable – no matter the position he previously held with Dragan.'

I handed Boris a newspaper signed with Dragan's thumb, which said exactly that, as well as a smartphone.

'What am I supposed to do with this phone? Does Dragan want to talk to me? I'm supposed to go see him in a minute! Or is the coward about to cancel?'

'No, there's a confession video on it.'

Boris looked at Malte's tortured testimony.

'So it was Toni. I knew it. Why isn't the man making these allegations here himself?'

'Because we watched Toni kill him in an attempt to prevent exactly that from happening. That constituted enough of an admission of guilt to clear any doubts we may have had, so that's why we're here handing over Toni in person.'

Sasha opened our van and pulled out a fiercely squirming Toni. Two of Boris's officers immediately took possession of him.

Boris looked impressed.

'Dragan kills my number two and hands me his. That seems fair. Now, how did you get that apple to stay in place? Is that duct tape?'

'Yes,' said Clara. 'A hair clip didn't hold.'

'And sadly we didn't have a knitting needle on hand,' Walter added.

'Is there any more of that tape?' Boris asked.

'Sure.' I gave Sasha a sign and he tossed over the roll.

Boris caught it and passed it to his people, who were just

pulling down Toni's pants. No one paid any more attention to Sasha, who slipped out of sight behind the trees and
opened the boot of the Opel Kadett.

'Good stuff, duct tape,' Boris raved. 'It completely solves
the pesky question of how to attach the hand grenades to
the traitor's balls.'

'You're really going to . . .?' I heard myself say.

'Never let it be said I don't keep my promises.'

'A very honourable attitude,' I said with the greatest respect
as I watched Toni get a pair of grenades stuck to his scrotum.

'How are you going to manage the safety pins? I mean,
someone still has to pull them out, right?' The technical
logistics really interested me.

Boris pointed at two reels of kite string, each of which
had one end tied to a grenade pin. In the meantime, Toni
had been tied upside down to a St Andrew's cross that
Boris's people must've gotten from a brothel.

'What about all the shrapnel and splatter? Won't it make
a mess when this guy blasts all over this place? I mean – your
beautiful cars . . .' No one paid my objections any heed.

Boris's officers just lifted up the cross and carried it
behind the toilets. There were now eight square metres of
filthy concrete between us and the sure-to-be-bloody mess.

'The bloke really does think of everything,' Carla noted
with approval.

In fact, Boris's cool approach to Toni's execution was the
polar opposite of the emotionally charged violence with
which Dragan had dispatched Igor to the afterlife on the
very same spot. Still, the result wouldn't be much different,

neither for the imminent victim nor for the inevitable crime-scene cleaners.

When the officers came back, they handed Boris the coiled ends of kite string.

'Don't you want to say anything to him, a few last words?' I suggested. 'Something theatrical?'

But Boris just gave both strings a jerk.

'Why would I?'

'I just thought, because we went to all that trouble with the apple and—'

My sentence was cut short by two simultaneous explosions behind the restrooms. Bits of Toni and the cross went flying far and wide, everywhere that wasn't shielded by the toilets.

As the double bangs faded away, an irregular whirr suddenly became audible. I looked up. Boris followed my gaze. A drone came tumbling down to us, shattering right between Boris and me. It had a camera and an antenna.

'What the fuck is that?' Boris demanded.

'That's . . . a drone. Someone must've been filming us.' I tried to analyse the situation with a maximum of surprise in my voice.

The drone was actually the same model as the one I'd taken down with a stick in the forest – except I had stuck a small sticker on this one that said 'Police'. And the sticker did its job.

'That's a cop drone,' Boris cursed.

'Some fucker must've ratted us out,' I said.

Boris was already trampling the drone and its camera.

'*No one* films me during an execution!'

I held Boris back. 'It won't do anything. Do you see that antenna? The drone pilot will have already stored the footage on some computer.'

'What does that mean? Are we fucked? We're not just going to wait around until we're arrested, we're leaving. All of us, right fucking now!'

Boris's people frantically ran to their cars. My officers had also already jumped into the van. I tried to live up to my new leadership role.

'Wait! If we all panic and leave, we won't be able to get our stories straight. If this drone filmed everything, then . . .' – I turned to Boris in a convincing panic – 'Then the police know you're responsible for this murder and we are compromised too. What's important is getting you out of the line of fire while the rest of us coordinate what we're going to say.'

'How do you suggest we do that?'

'First, you need to go into hiding. The rest we can do over the phone.'

'Go into hiding where?'

I pretended to think for a moment. Then a brilliant idea came to me.

'I'll drive you straight to Dragan from here. His hiding place is safe, plus you two are in the same boat now anyway. But we have to hurry. It's about to be teeming with cops here.'

Boris looked at me. Anxious at first, then considering it, before finally something clicked. A satisfied grin appeared on the man's face.

'You, sir, you're a genius. That's what we'll do. Guys – you're all leaving. Björn will drive me to Dragan. I'll be in touch. Vladi! Give the lawyer the car keys.'

Vladimir, one of Boris's officers, tossed me the key to one of the Mercedes. All the others were divided between the other Mercedes and the Ford Transit. Boris and I were heading to the car when Sasha appeared next to me.

'Great flying!' I whispered to him.

'Thanks, I've been practising.'

'Pick up what's left of the drone and make sure it disappears.'

'Of course, just like we discussed.'

Sasha walked over to the toilets. The Ford Transit and the other Mercedes left the lay-by with squealing tyres. Boris was about to get into the passenger seat when I put a hand on his shoulder.

'Sorry, Boris. From now on, you mustn't be seen by anyone. You need to disappear completely.'

'Where do I go?' Boris asked, suddenly frantic.

I opened the boot.

'It's not comfortable, but it's safe.'

Boris climbed in.

'And I'll see Dragan soon?'

'You'll see Dragan soon.'

At peace with myself, I closed the boot lid with love and without judgement. Mindfully, even.

Acknowledgements

This is my first novel. Any generous reader will notice that (despite all the funny business) mindfulness really is important to me. A mindful attitude to life makes many things easier. It's not a panacea, however, even if we're now always just an easy Google search away from a mindfulness exercise to address any conceivable problem. I am grateful for all this inspiring advice. This novel thrived on its abundance.

On my way to finishing this book, I have been inspired by encounters with countless people. Each was a necessary building block. I want to thank every single one of these people, and a few of them here by name.

When I first felt the need to put the vague idea I had for this book into actual words, I was sitting in my favourite pub on my favourite island. I'd like to thank the waitress who lent me her pen and order pad. These six pieces of paper, densely covered in writing, are now framed on my wall. And this book begins exactly as I first drafted it.

Marco, that same evening your café became my theatre, you my first audience. You listened to me and gave me *Der Mob* by Dagobert Lindlau for research. In addition, one of your patrons unsuspectingly inspired me to turn them into one of the book's supporting characters. Thank you.

Marcel, thank you for so lovingly taking me in and supporting me at your agency.

Anvar, you took wonderful care of me and my work. If books were baptised, you'd be the godfather.

I would like to thank Oskar Rauch, the editor at Heyne Verlag who believed in this novel from the start. I'd also like to thank Joscha Faralisch, who maintained that level of faith during Oscar's paternity leave.

I would like to thank Heiko Arntz for his detailed and stimulating edits. It was great fun to go over my work so intensively.

And thank *you* for reading this book to the very last page.